# DIAMOND

—

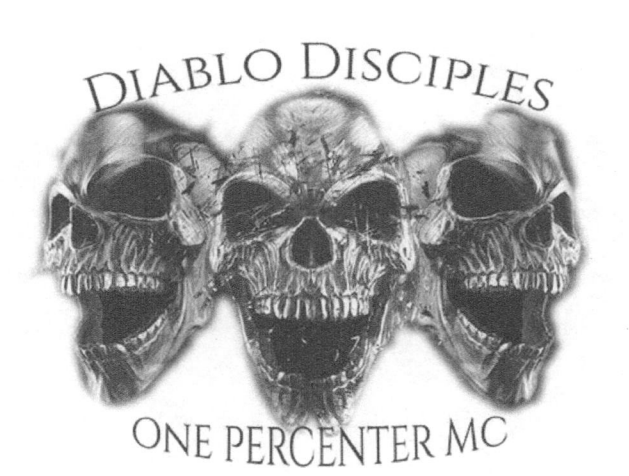

### DIABLO DISCIPLES
### ONE PERCENTER MC

By V. THEIA

This is a work of fiction. Names, characters, places, and events are the products of the author's imagination or are used fictitiously. Any resemblance to persons, living or dead, is coincidental.

Names and characters are the author's property and may not be duplicated. Using actual companies and/or product names is for literary effect only. All other trademarks and copyrights are the property of their respective owners.

## Diamond

Cover photo: Depositphotos.com
Cover Design: V. Theia. ©2024
Published by V. Theia 2024
All Rights Reserved

## DEDICATION

For the readers who want a big protective bear in the streets and a dirty talker in the sheets.

## Joelle

If Joelle hadn't been three floors up, afraid of breaking every bone, also able to shimmy down walls and not be a plus-size woman, she would have considered jumping out of the window.

Alas, all those things were very valid, so here she was, standing in front of the mirrored wall, primping for yet another party she was reluctant to attend.

The start of the holiday season was the worst.

There was a polite knock on her bedroom door, and without turning around, she called out, "I'm on my way, Kenneth."

The house butler was as delightful as they come, but he was as prompt as the Easter Bunny and detested any deviation from the meticulously scrutinized itinerary.

Joelle didn't know why she had to attend, let alone rush to get there. No one at the party cared if she came or not. She didn't fit in and didn't want to. People thought she was odd.

Those among the elite were invited to their suburban mansion in the heart of Utah to schmooze and gain favor with her father, Judge Snow. Her father was a celebrity in these parts, an untouchable man.

It was always business connections first.

That had been the family motto for as long as Joelle could remember.

It was vital for them to uphold their social standing. But it was a total mystery to Joelle why it mattered. She never cared about impressing anyone and wouldn't start now.

The Snows were nothing if they weren't impressing someone or making others pea green with envy.

No wonder Joelle had been in therapy since she was twelve years old. Living under the Snow umbrella was hectic as fuck.

But every woman had a cross to bear.

And her life wasn't terrible.

She had more than enough money, thanks to her grandfather's inheritance.

Like in past generations, he hadn't put a stupid stipulation on his will that Joelle must be suitably married before she received the money. He'd included a note in his will and told her he loved her so much and to live under the rainbow.

She smiled at her reflection. The patchwork maxi dress with the V-neck and long sleeves would hit the right note with her grandfather if he were still around. It was decorated in every color.

Joelle liked colors.

No, that was weak. She *loved* colors.

They made her happy.

Not everyone understood Joelle.

But that was okay. She'd accepted it.

And you know what? She was twenty-eight years old and a college graduate, and she still didn't understand fractions, so everyone had their quirks.

There was another knock as she finished with her long hair. Without waiting to be announced, her mother walked in.

Sandrine Snow was impeccable from her wavy gray hair, festive red two-piece suit, down to her kitten heels. Her makeup was light and natural. Joelle liked to joke with her mother that she was divaesque like the Kardashians because she, too, had a Glam Squad that came to their home most days to dress her mother in the style she was accustomed to.

Not one soul on earth had ever seen Sandrine Snow going to the market in sweats and greasy hair. Joelle suspected her mom would spontaneously combust if she got near stretch knit jersey fabric.

Joelle never met sweatpants she didn't love. She had a shelf in her walk-in closet dedicated to sweatpants in all colors.

"I'm not late." Yet. She announced before her mother could say anything. Call it pre-emptive before the gentle scolding.

"Sweetheart, I know you're not late." Her mother clicked her tongue, but her eyes said so much, and Joelle didn't have to wait long once her mother had finished with the once-over of her appearance. "Oh, Joelle. I thought we discussed you having natural hair for the party. I miss your blonde hair. Your grandmother gave you the nicest color; all you do is hide it under all these dyes."

"*You* discussed it. I ate cookies and dyed it blue while watching vampires fighting over a teen girl."

No one would know by Sandrine Snow's demure personality that she was the backbone of the Snow family. She never yelled, but you sure felt her disappointment with the raising of a perfectly threaded eyebrow.

Joelle had long since stopped trying to impress anyone.

All it got her was taking medication for depression, even before she'd hit puberty. Following years of therapy and now without medication, she lived life on her terms as a former people pleaser.

She loved her mother. Entirely, flaws and all. Even if her mother questioned her dress sense and everything else about Joelle's life choices almost daily.

"Mom, you're an absolute babe. You'll have a few men wishing they could get you under the mistletoe tonight." Turning around, she smiled and hugged her mom despite her initial huff. She always smelled like lavender, which Joelle found comforting.

Lavender is purple. In color therapy, also known as chromotherapy, purple means balance and spirituality, and that embodied her mother.

It would be black if she had to assign a color to her father.

Black meant secrets, magic, and elegance.

"Well, will I do for this thing, or should I stay up here with my books and TV shows?" *Please choose the latter.* Joelle would do anything not to play a society daughter for hours. The job represented the utmost level of monotony.

Living in the west wing of her family home at her age was already a problem. There were sixty-five rooms and fifteen bathrooms in total. She hardly ever ran into anyone, but it's unbelievable that they used emotional persuasion for her to stay at home all these years just to make themselves look like a close-knit family.

"Yes." Her mother replied, almost like the word might burn her tongue off. Joelle suppressed a grin and threaded her bangles and charms onto her wrist.

"Oh, Joelle, please, no. Can you leave all that costume jewelry off for tonight?"

Joelle almost gave in, but she had boundaries in place for a reason, so she only tilted her chin up.

"Mom, you take me as I am or not at all."

"Oh, fine." She huffed sweetly. "I don't know where you get this rebellious streak from."

"You only need to look in the mirror, mother darling. I didn't fall far from your wild tree."

"I never." She gasped, nearly clutching her antique pearls, and Joelle giggled, threading an arm through her mother's daintier arm.

On the first floor, servers were dressed immaculately in festive red and white.

Hosting top-notch parties was Sandrine's specialty. They were the talk of the town. No doubt there were journalists coming tonight, and the party would be splashed on Page Six tomorrow. She only hoped to avoid the spotlight. It was bad enough she'd have to hold a smile for hours. Joelle anxiously rolled the bangles around her wrist. Her silver rings glinted under the hundreds of white Christmas lights.

"Sweetheart, find your father. I need to check with Serge about the appetizers."

"Okay, mom, break a leg." Isn't that what you said for a successful party? If only she could break her leg to get out of this thing.

Joelle's silver heels clicked on the shiny floor as she went to her father's private office.

No one entered Judge Snow's domain without knocking, so she raised her clenched hand to rat-a-tat on the door when she heard raised voices coming from inside.

Her instinct was to stop and eavesdrop, so she inched closer to the partially open door and listened.

"I need your best men on this, Tucker. And I don't need to remind you of discretion."

"I'm not in the business of advertising who I work with, Snow. You know this already. You're not a first-time customer."

Joelle was surprised when the Judge didn't react angrily to the disrespectful comment.

"How long for?" Came from a rough-speaking voice.

"Until the threat is neutralized. My son may give you problems, but he refuses to have security details. So you'll need to be discreet while guarding him. Sandrine has agreed to whatever is needed, and she understands its importance. Joelle will be... difficult."

Joelle's spine straightened as she heard her name.

It wasn't a surprise her father thought she was difficult. Since she didn't conform to her father's ideal picture, everything she did disappointed him. Though she would have accepted that character assessment, his words still hit somewhere soft and vulnerable.

And yet she still loved him.

She knew he cared, but didn't know how to be a typical father. He maintained a distance, as if he were merely an outsider looking in on his family.

Who the hell was he talking to in there?

And why was he putting security on everyone?

There was only one way to find out.

She tapped on the door, every bracelet jangling like symbols, and pushed it open.

She was taken aback to see two men, plus her father.

Joelle approached her father in the spacious office with a Snowworthy fake smile. However, she'd momentarily peeked at the two strangers. Now, she was more curious than ever to know why the formidable, law-abiding man of the bench was in a conference with two Diablo Disciples MC men.

"Sorry to interrupt, father, but mom sent me to get you. The party is about to start." Just as he was about to talk, likely to give her a gentle scolding for interrupting, she quickly glanced at the bikers, all decked out in ripped jeans, heavy boots, and leather jackets. These two were definitely sketchy.

You couldn't live in Utah and not have heard of them.

They were infamous for all the wrong reasons and often featured on the news.

Her father made his distaste for those club men clear, arguing that they were bad for Utah's economy and respectability. This then made Joelle wonder why her law-abiding parent would offer them a job, not to mention an invitation into their home.

"Hello, I'm Joelle." She held out her hand, and the man with the shoulder-length hair twitched his mouth but reached for it, shaking gently. "Axel."

"And you are?" she asked the stoic, behemoth blond man. His eyes were like two ice blue crystals, pinning her like he thought she'd stolen the last Italian struffoli.

He didn't shake her hand, and he didn't answer.

Okay then.

"Are you gentlemen coming to the party? It's going to be wonderful." Every Snow knew how to lie.

She felt like a monkey in the zoo the way they both kept staring.

Hadn't they seen a chubby girl in a fabulous Zimmermann dress before? She guessed not. What a sheltered life those bikers must be living.

"Joelle, tell your mother I'll be along shortly."

"I sure will. Try not to be late. Santa Claus is dropping in, and you don't want to miss him."

The long-haired biker smirked. The stoic Viking didn't move a muscle, but his ice-pick eyes hadn't left Joelle, and she knew it wasn't because her burgundy lipstick was smudged.

"Close the door on your way out, Joelle."

She wiggled her fingers at the two strangers, and as she walked out, she addressed the head of the household. "Of course, father. This is me not being *difficult*."

She heard one biker chuckle, but couldn't identify them as she was already closing the door and walking away.

She was baffled more than anything else.

Because she'd had bodyguards in her youth, she was familiar with the dangers that often came with her father's job, particularly from the criminal underworld. There was a constant presence of death threats against him. This had a ripple effect on his family, leading them to hire bodyguards, especially when traveling abroad occasionally.

Why was he using the Diablo Disciples if they needed to beef up security?

The date was December 1st. The month Joelle disliked the most and knowing she'd have to deal with a muscular biker's presence was about to irritate her, especially when there was merriment to avoid.

Getting through this party was mission one.

She planned to tell her father she was too old for a babysitter. The police were there to handle any problems that arose.

Dangerous bikers might intrigue her as much as the next woman with working eyes and shakeable ovaries. She recognized desirable men; she wasn't blind, but Joelle didn't have time to be followed by one of them.

Instead of turning into the party hall, she headed back upstairs.

Now that this new dilemma was weighing on her mind, she wouldn't settle until she slipped on another bracelet. A green one, she decided, to ease stress and bring upon calmness.

The night was less Ho! Ho! Ho! And more, oh, no, no.

Diamond

If it looked like a duck. And walked like a duck. It was probably a viper snake.

The guy who owned the mansion was a man of many masks, definitely leaning toward being a viper, that was for damn sure, and Diamond wouldn't trust him as far as he could piss.

"How the other half live, huh, Prez?" he muttered, raising his head to take in the three-story mansion. It had to be worth over twenty million, if not more. The pair had ridden fifteen miles outside of their hometown of Laketon to Babington, Utah, where all the posh knobs and dickheads lived in their pretentious and high-brow estates with electronic gates and housemaids.

They'd been given instructions to use the back entrance. Of fucking course. The prick Judge wouldn't allow bikers through the main door. He looked down on the Diablos like they were trash, even though he begged for this meeting.

Diamond was already in a pissy mood without being summoned by the jackass and his ego.

The level of corruption in that guy was unmatched.

But that wasn't why Diamond didn't like him.

Some of his closest buddies would be called criminals. It didn't make them bad guys.

But he couldn't stand people thinking they were better than anyone else just because they drank with their pinkies in the air and rubbed shoulders with dignitaries.

The last time he checked, everyone still took a shit in the same way.

Diamond rarely saw Snow, but when he did, the old fart acted superior. Though, every time, he'd needed *the Diablos*.

Cranking his neck from side to side, Diamond switched off the engine and climbed off his Harley Davidson Breakout.

His favorite baby girl.

She never gave him any trouble, was never a brat, and didn't fuck other guys while he was out working to keep her in the princess lifestyle she thought she deserved.

No, his baby girl was loyal as fuck and treated him well. He patted her brushed gold and matte black bodywork as he hooked the helmet around the handlebars and straightened his spine.

Axel, the president of his MC, was climbing down from his bike. Diamond had a seat on Axel's council as head of security. But when he went to unknown places like today, Diamond was his bodyguard. Not that Diamond expected trouble. Judge Snow wouldn't do shit on his home turf, and from the number of catering vans that were parked outside, the guy was putting on a party tonight.

"What do you think he wants?" Diamond asked.

"I doubt it's about a Christmas bonus." Smirked Axel. "But it's something big. He's hit up my phone more than once while I was out of town with Scarlett."

"Bet he didn't like being kept waiting."

"Who the fuck cares? I don't jump when he clicks his fingers."

Throughout his long tenure on the bench, the community highly regarded Judge Snow as a pillar of justice, removing criminals from society. Undoubtedly, he was surrounded by sycophants, too afraid to disagree. But the Diablos weren't involved in that crap.

On their first face-to-face, he rolled up to the club's HQ in a fancy Mercedes, with a chauffeur behind the wheel.

He'd desperately needed a problem taken care of *unlawfully*. An old case was about to blow up. If the guy serving a twenty-year sentence had shown that Judge Snow took a bribe to convict him, it would have messed up all his other cases. He got the Diablos on board because they could do things that traditional methods couldn't. He'd asked for their help more than once since then.

Unbeknownst to him, he was now at their beck and call to make things vanish. The Judge had no other option since he willingly climbed into bed with them.

"Who has butlers these days?" The guy in his sixties wearing a pinstripe suit showed them into an office.

Diamond was blue-collar and proud of it. So were his parents and two brothers. His father and brothers owned a large car dealership. He'd come from working stock, learning you got nothing from life that you didn't put into it first.

He wasn't hurting for money, far from it. The Diablos filled his pockets nicely, but this rich shit he'd walked into, like fucking Narnia, was making his skin itch.

"You don't want staff to run around after you, D?"

"Fuck no, we have the probies for that," he answered, and Axel chuckled. The door opened, and the elitist snob came strolling in. He shook Axel's hand and only offered Diamond a nod.

"Thanks for coming, Tucker. I'll get right to the point. My wife is hosting a party soon, and I must be there."

No offer of a coffee and finger sandwiches, then? Charming manners. Diamond kept his face neutral as he parked himself on a dainty as fuck couch on the back wall. He weighed two-seventy, all muscle, and was six-foot-five. It probably wasn't made with someone his size in mind, and the little couch creaked as he settled. No doubt it was one of those swooning couches posh knobs had back in the day for all the fainting they did because they were oh-so-delicate.

Axel took the chair in front of Snow's desk.

"I have a rather diplomatic situation. I'm paying for your silence."

"You ain't paying for anything until I know why you wanted to meet," Said Axel. The Diablos weren't hurting for money, far from it.

They were so far in the black nowadays that no one had to worry. That meant they wouldn't take any job thrown their way.

The club was more than a business.

It was a found family.

It was acceptance and loyalty.

Diamond was hoping Axel wouldn't agree to whatever this was. Snow rubbed him the wrong way, and being inside his gold-encrusted house made him antsy. He needed to be around the smell of motor oil and the stank of sweat inside a gym. Honest smells, not the scent of old money in his nostrils.

"There's a situation."

"So you said. You wanna spit it out, Snow? We don't have all night."

He looked pissed at being rushed, and Diamond smiled to himself. It must stick in his craw to ask the Diablos for help so much. A man of power had to come crawling to the local bikers with his begging hat on.

"I need security for my family for the next few months."

"Did your bodyguard service quit?" asked Axel, crossing a leg over his knee. "I'm betting they'd be cheaper."

"I don't want cheap." Snow snapped and then composed himself. His hair was as white as his namesake. "I want someone who can do the job right and protect my family."

"From who?"

"A situation has gotten out of hand."

"Snow," Axel stated, "you can call it a situation as many times as you like, but we're still gonna need to know what we're working with here."

The older guy's jaw worked with an annoyed tick.

Diamond didn't have to chime in. He operated a stable of security professionals. Some of them weren't patched brothers, and during training, he emphasized the job required more than physical prowess and fighting skills. It involved staying silent and paying close attention to every detail. Body language spoke a lot louder than a gun ever would. People always gave their intentions away long before reaching for a weapon. It was the twitch of an eyebrow, a prolonged inhale.

Diamond noticed everything.

And it had saved his life countless times.

Snow was so annoyed. But he was also scared of something. Or someone.

"Let me help you out. Is a lunatic out of jail and gunning for you?" Axel said. "Are you being blackmailed by a hooker after you snorted coke off her tits?"

Bingo. Diamond saw the reaction going through Snow's eyes.

"I love my family very much."

"You're preaching to the wrong choir, Snow."

"A woman I was meeting with casually, unbeknownst to me, has connections to the Irish mob, and she's threatening to tell the media. That I can deal with, but now she has warned the Irish will take my family out one by one."

"Why not pay her off?"

"Do you think I haven't? Several fucking times." He snapped.

Axel flipped his eyes toward Diamond. Silently asking him what he wanted to do. The security for hire was Diamond's brainchild, and he'd grown it into the strong stable it was today. Snow might have invited Axel to the meeting, but it was Diamond's decision.

He might not like the guy and what he represented, but he enjoyed having fuck-stains like him in their favor. He gave Axel a subtle nod.

"Right then. To protect your family around the clock will cost you, Snow."

"I don't care what it costs. Just keep my family safe until I deal with this. And I reiterate, no one will hear about it, Tucker." He meant it as an *or else* threat, like he thought he held power in the room.

Snow spent the next few minutes giving them details of his family. There was his wife, who would agree to anything hubby dearest told her to. He had a nineteen-year-old son, who, from the sounds of it, was an entitled twat who would give Diamond and his team some trouble by not complying with orders.

Then there was his only daughter. A twenty-eight-year-old Prima donna. "Joelle will be difficult."

Great, Diamond mentally rolled his eyes into the back of his skull. He got to spend however many days and weeks babysitting a spoiled diva princess who wouldn't listen, either.

Then the door opened, and a woman with the bluest hair he'd ever seen walked in. It was wavy and long and went down the middle of her back, swishing with her ample hips.

This must be the spoiled princess as she smiled saccharinely at Snow, apologizing for interrupting when Diamond got the impression the princess had meant to interrupt.

If Joelle Snow turned out to be a privileged, silver-spoon-in-her-mouth diva, she sure was a beauty. That wouldn't be a problem, even if Diamond were in the market for rolling around in his sheets with a soft, mouth-watering body.

He wasn't.

But his point was he didn't fuck clients. Most of his clients were men, anyway. And he didn't swing that way.

But yeah, Joelle was a looker with her soft, round hips and belly encased in a tight dress, that had been dipped in the whole color palette.

When she turned to leave, she locked eyes with him, maybe testing to see if he'd say anything since he ignored her fake greeting. Diamond only stared, and as she went to close the door, she addressed her father. "Of course, Father, this is me not being difficult."

Diamond's hunch was correct. The brat had been listening with her ear at the door. Naughty.

Thank fuck brats weren't his flavor either, or miss skittles and her ample curves might have interested him. And that would have fucked up the entire job. Diamond couldn't think of anything worse than being around someone daily, wanting them, and keeping his professional hands off them.

Since his ex-girlfriend had screwed him over, he'd sworn off women until he could tolerate one that wouldn't make him want to put his head through a wall of insanity. She hadn't broken his heart, but a wounded pride was hard to live with.

"Right," Axel said, replying to Snow. Diamond looked away from the door, realizing he'd been staring at where the blue-haired rainbow had left moments ago. "I'll let Diamond take over. He's your point of contact, Snow." Axel stood. "I'm gonna wait outside." He'd already pocketed the cash payment.

Snow looked harassed when he was left alone with Diamond. He rose from the too-small couch and stood in front of the desk.

He knew his stature intimidated people. It proved to be a useful tool.

"Let's get this over with," sighed Snow in a bored manner. "I don't have all day."

"Neither do I," Diamond told him. "So, I'll tell you in words you'll understand, Snow. You've paid Axel, that means you've paid my club. You've paid *me*. I'm in charge from this point on. You don't question my methods, you don't micromanage, and you sure as hell don't give me orders. Are we clear on that?" he pasted on a tight smile. "Good. Let me tell you what'll happen from here."

## Diamond

With his first day coming up tomorrow, tonight he was looking forward to a relaxing evening of beer, steak, and hockey on TV.

Diamond had already met with his guys and set up who'd be watching the Snows. He'd put Mike and Kem with the son. Davey and Larson had the unlucky job of shadowing the senior Snows. And Titan was on Joelle Snow duty.

This was one of the cushier jobs, no doubt about it. Babysitting rich folks who only knew how to shop and go to the country club was going to be a cakewalk for his men.

Their usual jobs got a lot grimier, and more often than not, fists were thrown. Titan had only just recovered from broken ribs.

Diamond had considered babysitting the daughter for a hot second, but he didn't want to be around a pretty face all day long and have to listen to her bratty whines about how unfair her life was.

"My main man, D. How's it going?" Reno came to a halt in front of him. The guy was all smiles these days. Back when he first met the terrible twins, as he used to call Reno and Ruin, and sometimes still did, if he wanted to wind Ruin up, Reno always looked like he carried a bucket of stress on his shoulders.

He had a soft family to go home to today, and his twin brother was settled, too.

"Not too bad. Thought you'd gone home for the night?"

"I had, but Chelly left her dragon here earlier, and she can't sleep without it." He was such a dad, Diamond grinned. Michele was technically Reno's step-kid, but she felt like family to all of them. Bright as a button, that kid. She called Diamond Uncle River. Besides his family, she was the only female to use his given name.

"You're a good dad, Reno."

The younger guy, by about ten years, cracked a smile. Diamond was coming up fast on forty, just another ten months.

He flashed a grin. "I won't be tomorrow when I toss my girl out the door when her dad picks her up."

Diamond smirked. He knew that look. "Gonna romance your woman?"

"I won't be leaving the fucking bedroom all weekend, my brother."

They laughed, and Reno went to find his kid's stuffy toy so she could sleep.

Diamond would head home soon. He spent most of his time at the clubhouse. It had everything he needed. Good company, beers when he wanted one, food all day long, and he was a true-blue-foodie, so his stomach was constantly happy. The gym was just a few feet away in the basement, and he loved working out, sometimes twice a day. Plus, as a perk of being on Axel's council, he had an assigned bedroom to crash in.

Diamond had never needed much in life.

Some might call him basic. He only made practical purchases, such as his bike, truck, and home. He wasn't inhaling coke worth thousands of dollars or losing big at craps tables.

He embraced a simple lifestyle and saved a substantial sum for his retirement.

Bikers lived complicated lives.

Diamond intended for his later years to be smooth sailing, so he earned the cash now and planned for those relaxing times fishing on a lake somewhere.

Halfway through the game, he felt a presence hovering at the side of him. Cocking his head, he saw it was Charli. He couldn't say how long the woman had been a club sweet bottom, but it was a while.

"Hey Charli, you're here late. Everything okay?"

He didn't want company, especially the female variety. Diamond wanted to enjoy his beer and the game alone, but she sat on the couch next to him.

"I was changing the bed sheets on the third floor and putting on a load of laundry. Those hangarounds got car oil all over them, and god knows what else," She puffed out air, blowing up her bangs.

He knew little about the sweet bottoms. Did they have kids, families, or homes of their own? Truer still, he wasn't all that interested to know. It was a shame that one woman had soured him against the entire sex.

"Why are you here? Are you looking for some special company?" she asked, smiling with a flirty glint.

"Relaxing with the game." He said with his gaze on the mounted TV.

"So no, then?" she half chuckled. "The girls have been talking..."

The girls meant the sweet bottoms because as much as there wasn't a lot of hate between the sweet bottoms and the old ladies, they were not sitting around gossiping together. If anyone, it would be Scarlett, the First Lady, who had more to do with them.

"That sounds dangerous," he remarked, and she laughed again.

"You don't mess with any of us, Diamond."

He cocked his head to the side, arching an eyebrow. "Is that what you talk about? Who I'm fucking or not fucking?"

"Well. Yeah, sometimes," she wasn't embarrassed, and he wouldn't have expected her to be. Sex wasn't a taboo or shamed subject around the clubhouse. "I mean, any of us would spend time with you if you were interested. Since you split with Gloria, you don't bother with any of us. We all thought you had a lucky escape there, by the way. Do you have a new girlfriend?"

Diamond stared at the woman with her knee pressed against his. "You thought I had a lucky escape?"

"Babe, yeah. She was *awful*." She stressed the last word, and Diamond felt a twitch of a smile. "You only brought her around a few times. That was very telling, by the way. Usually, the guys who fall hard always want to bring their women here to hang out. It annoys some girls, especially Sonya, but not me. I enjoy seeing you guys happy, you know? But anyway, Gloria didn't fit in at all and didn't try to. She looked down on everyone. When you weren't near, she'd bitch about everything. The food, the noises from the bikes and garage, the distance to get here. You could tell she didn't like the old ladies, too. Oh, and how dirty the place was." Again, Charli pulled a face, "Bitch, please, I know this place is clean because I'm one bitch who cleans it. You could eat your breakfast, lunch, and pussy off this floor."

Diamond knew Gloria didn't like the clubhouse, so he rarely brought her with him, but it wasn't the primary reason. He realized it wasn't right between them when she moved in. It was only months later he found out about her cheating escapades.

"We didn't even think you looked that happy, but now you don't mess with any of us, so we reckon you must still be holding a torch for her."

That's where Charli was wrong.

"Charli, let me ask you something. Do you want to fuck one of us every day? You're in the mood to fuck every day?"

The woman blinked and hooked her lip between her teeth. "Well, maybe?"

"It wasn't a trick question, babe." He half-smiled.

"Sometimes, I'd like to hang out and watch a movie, you know? But that's not what this place is about. Unless a guy wants to make you his old lady, we get sex or nothing. And I like sex, and you guys are good at it." She threw him an impish smile.

Fair enough. Diamond could respect her answer.

"So you know, you're not gonna be kicked out of the clubhouse if you don't want to fuck someone."

"Yeah, I know that."

"Do you, though?"

She looked away.

"Scarlett pays you for the cleaning, doesn't she?"

"Yeah, it's all on the books. I even pay taxes! But I thought... well, some of us thought..."

"Thought what?"

"We wouldn't be needed around here, and we'd get kicked out if we didn't fuck those who wanted to fuck. I like sex, Diamond. That's not what I'm saying. None of us girls are forced."

"No, I get what you're saying."

"Party nights are so fun. And sometimes, when I hear Axel and Scarlett in his locked office..." She didn't have to elaborate, everyone had heard the prez and his old lady getting it on. "It kinda turns me on, and then I need sex with someone. Oh, shit." She gasped, "Please don't tell Scarlett or Axel I said that! They'll kick me out for sure!"

"I won't say anything." That would be funny, though. Axel wouldn't give a shit. He didn't care who heard him romancing his old lady. Scarlett would blush as red as her hair.

"So, I guess that's why you don't fuck around at the parties anymore. You're not in the mood? Or don't the girls do it for you anymore?"

Diamond couldn't even remember the last sweet bottom he'd looked at, let alone touched. He knew he'd slept with Charli at least once, but that must be at least three years back. Long before Gloria came along and distracted him into thinking he wanted something serious. He used to party hard years ago, but nothing in recent times.

He didn't share his thoughts. "It's late, babe. You should get to bed."

She climbed to her feet. "I think the fun-loving Diamond is in there somewhere. Don't let that sour-faced bitch ruin you for the right girl. And until she comes along, you can always knock on my door, handsome." She winked and sauntered off.

Once upon a time, Diamond would have considered it and probably tossed the woman over his shoulder and took her somewhere quiet to waste a few hours.

But he didn't even feel a flicker of interest.

He didn't want to blame one woman for the destruction of his dick, but it correlated to the same time Gloria did him dirty and made him lose trust in everything.

After kicking his legs out in front of him and hooking up his nearly empty beer bottle, he settled in to watch the end of the game before riding home.

The thought of meeting with the Snow family the next day didn't fill him with enthusiasm.

If he had to choose between dealing with rich people and their quirks or having a conversation with Gloria, well, he'd have to take some time. That's all he was saying.

## Joelle

"What do you mean I can't go anywhere without the security? Isn't that a little overkill?"

Her father's answer was a resounding sigh.

"Nothing is overkill to keep this family safe. And just this once, Joelle, could you not argue with something I've asked you? I know you think you're a free-age feminist thinker, but not everything is an argument."

"Says the Judge who only believes in his opinion." She muttered, but he snapped his eyes up. "And I'm not a free-age feminist. I like asking pertinent questions when things are going to interrupt my life."

"Dear," her mother said. Of course, she'd jump in and take up her husband's mantle. Nothing new there. "It's not for very long, and it is important. The security company has assured us they won't get in the way and will be as discreet as possible."

"That's all you had to say. I'm not being difficult." She threw the word at her father, "but it's nice to be kept in the loop."

"Count me out." Her brother, Reeves, stated. Standing up from the breakfast table, he grabbed his keys and phone.

Naturally, her father didn't say boo to him. Of course not. Reeves had male anatomy, so the same rules didn't apply to him. God, if it weren't such a disgusting habit, she'd spit on the floor with how mad she was feeling.

"You know, you wouldn't need to have these conversations that irritate you if I lived alone like I've wanted to do for the past five years."

Her parents believed she was disorganized and lacked direction in her life.

She had three freaking degrees. Unlike her wealthy mother and aunts, who married for money and social status, she didn't live a life of charity board meetings. How was it her fault they'd never allowed her the freedom to explore her options?

When asked to prolong her stay at home, she avoided conflict to keep the family harmonious. Despite the challenges caused by her father's job, the police had always handled them before. She didn't get why it had to change her life. Yeah, okay, there'd been several kidnapping threats over the years. But those people had been caught, and she'd never honestly thought someone would kidnap her just because she was Judge Snow's daughter.

Joelle was about to lose it. But she couldn't let the family down, so she shut her mouth. Trying to reason with her parents was pointless. She'd say yes and then do whatever the heck she wanted.

Feeling better, she grabbed a triangle of toast. She was slathering a thick layer of strawberry preserve when Kenneth entered the family dining room to announce there were guests.

At seven in the morning?

Joelle sent her father a glance, but he didn't appear surprised. Then, the room was filled by three men, all standing on ceremony. Oh, the bodyguards, goodie. But they were not like any bodyguards she'd ever seen.

Weren't suits mandatory for anyone who stepped into their house? She swallowed her chuckle, along with a bite of toast.

It was then she recognized the tallest of the three. It was the Viking-esque guy from yesterday. And because she wasn't being rushed out of her father's office this time, she could look at him for as long as she liked. While she took bites of her toast, she compiled his appearance.

Her last steady boyfriend, if it could be called that, was five foot seven. The Viking was way bigger, easily a foot taller than her. He stood like a fortress, covered by muscles and olive skin and decorated in tattoos. Yesterday, the leather jacket was black. Today, it was brushed brown and suited his complexion. He wore it with well-worn denim and thick-soled boots with twin buckles on each boot. He was imposing, but immediately, the color gray came to mind for him. Gray was for calm and peace.

Usually, her father was the dominating figure in every room. But he shrank in the biker's presence.

Joelle continued to crunch through her toast, but the food dried in her mouth when those icy blue eyes came at her. She realized this man didn't want to be here. The animosity rolled off his broad shoulders like mist.

What had she done to earn the biker's ire? Her father, she could understand. He was split down the middle. You either revered him or hated him.

"This is Diamond and his staff. He'll be in charge of your security from now on." Her father announced.

Diamond? What kind of name was that? But she could see why as she tilted her head back to look at him better, with his tight jawline that seemed sculpted on his face and those full lips.

Women were reluctant to share something shiny and precious, like diamonds. Joelle held in her immediate giggle and reached for a second triangle of toast, knifing on more sweet preserves.

"My men aren't here to give you a hard time. Your safety is what's important." He stated. His voice was not booming. Speaking quietly, there was an air of authority, making everyone take notice. His men were statues behind him. She caught the eye of one, but he didn't smile. Okay then, that's how it was going to be. Unfriendly shadows.

"But that doesn't mean we'll put up with bullshit. Just putting it out there so we know where we all stand." He mentioned. Once more, his eyes were directed toward her as though he believed Joelle required a cautionary signal.

What had been shared about her if she was the focus of the lecture? Reeves would be better off hearing it because he had a problem following most rules.

"Shouldn't Reeves be hearing this?" she threw her baby brother under the bus.

The Viking biker raised an eyebrow, but then lowered it. "Your brother is already under surveillance. He'll be told the same if it's needed."

Bleurgh. Same old misogynistic bullcrap. One rule for men, another altogether more burdensome rule for women.

"Joelle. I need you to follow whatever Diamond says."

"Sure thing, Father." She crunched, her chin defiantly tipped up before she sipped coffee from a delicate cup. And since she was playing nice, she offered, "I'll be home all day on the grounds, so there will be no need for a guard."

"I'll decide what's needed." The biker replied, glacially cold, a gravel edge of warning to his voice.

Joelle only smiled. "Whatever you say. Would you gentlemen like to sit and have breakfast? There's plenty."

"Oh, sweetheart, there's no need for that. They're here to do a job. Kenneth can always fix them a plate in the kitchen." Her mother said, and Joelle nearly choked on her toast. Yes, she'd forgotten the class divide. God forbid her mother let a man eat at her Milan marble table. And no way would she let the lower classes drink from her crystal glasses.

"We're fine," Diamond answered. And then shifted his gaze to her somewhat silent father. "A word outside."

When it was only her and her mother, she said. "Some shady shit is going on, Mom. I can feel it in my kneecaps."

"Oh, Joelle. You have the worst imagination, dear."

Yeah, and she'd bet her life on being right.

However, she had to face having a bodyguard who seemed to despise her family.

The next few days would be interesting.

It might just be what she needed to get out of the holiday doldrums.

Feeling a tad perkier, she stabbed the pink grapefruit on her plate.

## Diamond

It was only five days into December, and Diamond felt a headache coming on as he prepared to answer yet another call from one of his men about the fucking Snows.

It was like dealing with toddlers who couldn't follow basic directions.

Rubbing his temple, he grabbed the bottle of pain pills in the desk drawer and tossed three into his mouth, followed by a chaser of cold coffee.

His men were good. Better than good, they were competent, and he rarely had to micromanage them once they were on a task. But this was the third time he was getting a progress report from them in less than a week, and none of those reports said, "There is nothing to report." It was always a wall of what shit was happening over there.

Diamond read the messages again and then pressed the contact number.

"Boss."

"What's going on, Kem?"

"The younger Snow must know about us because he's running us a merry-fucking-dance."

"Bring him to me."

"To the clubhouse?"

"Yeah. I'll clear it with the gate."

"On it, boss."

Less than an hour later, the blacked-out Escalade arrived with the passenger prick glaring through the windshield. It wasn't Diamond's usual approach to a job, but he was figuring these fucking Snows weren't his usual type of clients, and he'd have to adapt to their prissy ways. He reached the car and swung the door open.

"Get out."

"I don't even know you. This is fucking kidnapping." Reeves Snow snapped. A determined glint in the young boy's eyes.

"I won't tell you again. If you want to know what's going on, get out."

He got out but held his shoulders back like he expected a fight.

"I know who you guys are. What this place is."

"Good for you. Follow me."

Diamond turned on his heels and walked back into the club, holding the door open for Reeves Snow to follow. He led him over to the bar where Scarlett was restocking the bottles.

"Scar, do you mind giving us some space?"

"I'm due for a coffee break, anyway." She took off, and Diamond pinned the boy with a *don't fuck with me* stare.

"Your father hired my company to guard his family."

"I know that. But I told him I didn't need one. Then I spotted your guys yesterday."

Huh. That never happened. The younger guy had a keen eye.

"Hate to tell you this, but you're protected whether you approve, so it's up to you if we make this easy or hard for you."

Reeves Snow squinted. His jaw went tight. "That sounds like a threat to me."

Diamond smiled. "Take it any way you want, as long as you accept this is happening."

He stayed silent a good while, processing. Then he asked. "How long is this going to last for?"

Diamond shrugged. "Only your father knows that."

"Fucking hell. Me and Joelle are always getting dragged into his shit. So, your guys will follow me wherever I go?"

"Yes. Every time you step out of the house."

He sighed. But looked resigned to it. "Fucking great. So when I take one of my girls out on a date, do I have to rock up with bodyguards? I'll look like a pussy who can't take care of her."

"My guys are discreet. They won't get in your way. Just don't ditch them. This isn't the Fast and the Furious. They will catch you. And then I gotta get involved. And I won't be happy if I have to micromanage your whiny ass."

The reality seemed to sink in, and Reeves stared into space. The clubhouse was reasonably quiet, and everyone was at their jobs, but a few sweet bottoms walked by toward the kitchen, and Reeves Snow sat up straight, his eyes following their short-wearing asses.

"Whoa. Who are they?"

Diamond smirked. "They'd eat your preppy ass for breakfast and spit out the bones."

Reeves smiled. "Shit, what a way to go. So..." he started, "you're a biker?"

"Yeah."

"Do you do dangerous stuff?"

"Shall I break your legs to find out?" Diamond arched his eyebrow.

"That's a mind your own business, yeah?"

"Now you're getting it."

"You know my dad is a Judge?"

"Yes."

"Does he work with your MC often? Is that even allowed?"

"That's something you're gonna have to ask him. If this Q&A is over, my guys will take you home."

Reeves frowned. "But what about those gorgeous women? I thought you could introduce me."

"How old are you?"

"I'm nearly twenty."

"Come back in five years. You might be ready to handle them."

When he looked pleased with that info, he smirked and nodded. "I'll do that."

Standing outside by the Escalade, Kem was waiting to take Reeves back to their mansion.

"Hey." Reeves paused, looking toward Diamond. "If you're guarding us, will you take extra care of my sister?"

Diamond frowned.

"She's cool for a sister. But she trusts people too easily, which sometimes gets her feelings hurt. My parents can take care of themselves, but Joelle is special. We've always kinda stuck together."

He didn't say more before he climbed into the back seat and slammed the door shut.

Diamond didn't know how to decipher what he was asking; he was probably just a worried kid brother for his big sister. But he knew one thing: he needed this Snow job off his plate.

"Who was the blazer-wearing kid?" Devil asked, sidling up to Diamond. No matter the time of day, the guy always had food in his hand.

"He's Judge Snow's son. He's been giving my guys the runaround."

"I hear the daughter's a wild one," Devil remarked, sinking his teeth into the baguette.

Instantly, flickering images of the blue-haired woman came to his mind. "I wouldn't know."

"Fucking rich people, man." Grumbled Devil and walked off.

Yeah, fucking rich people.

Diamond was mistaken about how the rest of the day would go. After doing another gig, he was halfway back to the clubhouse, intent on working out, when he received a message.

The other Snow sibling was now being a pain in the neck.

He sighed and restarted the bike, heading toward the Snow mansion. Once there, he took the back entrance.

"The master isn't at home." The butler informed.

The fucking master. Diamond rolled his eyes.

"It's Joelle I'm looking for."

The butler's face changed into a smile. "Oh, yes. She's in her wing. I'll let Miss Snow know..."

"No need. I have the layout of the house. And permission to be here from the Judge."

"Yes, of course, sir. Can I fetch you refreshments?"

"Nah, I'm good."

The house was like a maze, but luckily, Diamond had a passable memory, and in case of an ambush, he'd memorized every inch of their property. He trekked up the never-ending staircase, getting his workout, anyway. The wide hallway leading to Joelle Snow's suite was thickly carpeted, and his footsteps were silent. Outside of the door, he knocked and waited.

It opened comically fast, and she showed little surprise to see him.

"Kenneth warned me you were on the way up. You took longer than I do, and those stairs are a killer on my small legs."

Like magnets pulled his eyes, they dropped to her legs, covered only in bicycle shorts. They were multi-colored swirls, almost hallucinogenic. Realizing what he was doing, Diamond snapped his gaze back up.

"We need to have words."

Her golden eyebrows shot up. "We do? I don't see what I'd have to say to a bodyguard."

"I'm not a bodyguard."

She leaned in the doorway. "What are you then? A heavy? A goon? A thug?"

"You've been watching too many B-roll movies, Miss Snow. Invite me in."

"Oh, that sounded very vampireish," she grinned. "You can come in only if you drop the Miss Snow. It makes me sound like a maiden from the Little Women era." She swung the door wider and walked off, expecting him to follow.

He didn't have a clue what she'd just said, but Diamond stepped over the threshold. Surprise made his footsteps halt. He thought he'd be walking into a bedroom. But it was even bigger than a hotel suite, more like an entire apartment within a mansion. It was bigger than his two-bedroom place at the Dyson Gates apartment complex. It didn't matter that he owned all ten apartments and rented them out. This suite would eat his place and spit out the crumbs.

It smelled of vanilla and something warmer, and Diamond inhaled because it was a pleasant fragrance.

"Take a seat. I've put on a pot of coffee. I hope you like the good stuff. It's not a pod or instant." With an open-plan living area, their gated house offered expansive views of open land through its windows. The living room had an oversized L-shaped cream couch with about fifty scatter cushions in every color. Just like a paint palette, the rug was a chaotic explosion of color. He belatedly thought he should've taken his boots off. He bet the princess wouldn't like dirty shoes in her house.

"Sit," she repeated from the kitchen, filling two cups.

Diamond sat on one end of the couch, eyeing the TV, which paused on two kissing people.

"I was watching The Vampire Diaries. That's why your *invite me in* line made me chuckle. Have you seen it? It's so good. It's a constant love triangle between this young girl and two vampire brothers. I've seen it so many times. It's a comfort show. I always thought Elena chose the wrong brother." She babbled, uncaring if Diamond wanted the useless information.

He'd learn in the next hour that Joelle Snow was a talker.

She talked so damn much that he almost forgot why he was there, wondering if she'd ever stop to take a breath so he could say something.

## Joelle

Okay. So she had a crush on the bodyguard.

It was no big deal.

It must happen to every woman he was around because his silent, stoic act was an absolute panty-melter.

Unlike some other girls, Joelle didn't hold back from openly admiring his handsome face as she rambled on. He'd hardly even touched the coffee, whereas she'd already had two and considered a third because coffee was life's happy juice, as any sane person knew.

On her deathbed, instead of confessing to her sins, Joelle would ask for one last coffee.

She had no clue what she was talking about, but she just kept babbling to avoid the awkward silence while her hormones woke up and drooled over the hot guy in front of her.

The sheer muscle-bulging size of him was mouthwatering. She bet he worked out a lot and lifted weights to give him arms the size of tree trunks. Shoulders that wide definitely didn't come naturally, she thought, admiringly.

He wouldn't go for a girl like her. Joelle was soft all over, carrying extra pounds she was okay with, and she was, with no room for misinterpretation, allergic to exercise. Okay, fine, she wasn't genuinely allergic. That would have been neat and a perfect excuse. She enjoyed a stroll in the park. And occasionally, she attended a dance class with her friends Molly and Sadie. Beyond that, Joelle disliked the idea of getting fit. So, she felt safe knowing she could admire his face without rejection at the end.

Smiling, she sipped her coffee.

"So, what brings you to my door?"

"Have you finally finished?"

Joelle blinked and lowered the cup to her lap. "I guess so. Unless you want to know all about this other show I'm watching at bedtime? It's not as addictive."

"Fuck no." He frowned, and she thought he looked adorable. Like a big hostile bear. "My men tell me you're giving them issues."

Her eyebrows hit her blue hairline. "Your men are snitches. Running to their daddy because I asked one little teensy favor."

She saw his lips twitching, and Joelle felt her chest aerate, knowing she'd made him react.

"I already had to talk with your brother today. I don't wanna have to keep coming back here to sort you both out."

"First, you talked to Reeves? You better have been nice to him. He's not like our father. And second, neither of us needs sorting out, as you eloquently put it. We're people, Diamond. And people need understanding. We're not pot plants you can move from room to room and not expect them to have an opinion. I have many opinions."

"No shit, Sherlock."

"Joelle, not Sherlock." She grinned and tucked her legs underneath her on the couch. If she was going to get a lecture from the serious bodyguard, she needed to be comfortable.

"What was the problem today?"

"I simply asked Titan if he'd mind waiting at the house while I went to a quick appointment. He got all growly about it and refused, which was unreasonable. I even tried to bribe him with macarons, but he was steadfast. I'm sure the chef has the right baked goods to make him crack."

The biker's head dropped over his clasped hands, and Joelle couldn't decipher his muttering, but it wasn't very complimentary from the tone. When his head lifted, his eyes pierced her down to the marrow, and her needy nipples became hard pebbles.

"Have you ever followed the rules?"

Joelle snickered. "If only you knew."

There was little choice in the Snow family but to follow every rule laid out for you. From kindergarten through college, Joelle had been the good girl who didn't cause waves or argue the point. Everything ever written about her had been rumors and lies. She never denied those lies because they made her sound wild and exciting. Something she was not.

That didn't mean she didn't get up to stuff.

She was just clever enough never to get caught.

It was easier than trying to rebel.

"What was the appointment?" his gravelly, assertive tone broke into her musing, and Joelle lifted her eyes. Finding Diamond watching her was unsettlingly good.

"Excuse me?"

"This important reason you tried to ditch Titan for."

"Oh, yes, that. It's private and not something I want to discuss with a virtual stranger, but I stress it was important, and I've had to rearrange the appointment for Friday."

Another gusty sigh. It sounded like the bodyguard needed a deep-tissue, stress reliever massage asap, or the top of his skull might burst open with all that frustration he was carrying.

"I hate to break it to you, Bluebell, but privacy doesn't matter a lick of shit right now. We can't protect you around your schedule when it's convenient."

Bluebell.

He'd given her a nickname, and it was adorable!

Joelle flashed Diamond a smile and decided she would try to be more amenable with him and his staff. She would *try*.

This sucked, though.

Usually, in December, she liked to hunker down alone as much as possible to get through the holiday season. Between the parties and gatherings, that is. And there were so many on her calendar it nearly brought Joelle out in an anti-social rash.

"Kidnappers don't take into consideration that you might need privacy so that you can go for a waxing or your nails painted."

Joelle blinked at his assumption.

But she focused on the more pressing matter. Her tongue dried when she asked, "Is it that serious?" She'd hate being held for ransom. She wagered they wouldn't allow her to watch Schitt's Creek before bed.

Diamond's eyes focused, his jaw relaxed, and he unclasped his hands, leaving them dangling between his manly spread legs. He was just so masculine and appealing to the eye.

He didn't answer. Which, as anyone knows, was an answer in itself.

"My father isn't forthcoming with explaining himself. He's of the generation that feels like they don't need to, especially not to a female. It's *follow my orders and don't ask stupid questions, Joelle*." Joelle inhaled and let it out slowly. She wouldn't spiral with overthinking. It wasn't like masked rebels were about to burst through the windows. The house had been standing for over eight decades, built by her grandfather, and could withstand attacks. The house would eventually pass down to Reeves as the next male heir.

She didn't care about the house. It was way too big. She would be content living in a three-bedroom townhouse if the opportunity arose. The thought of having a home that belonged to her was blissful.

Without breaking his eye line, she said. "I'll make an assumption and guess his latest affair hasn't gone away as quietly as the others usually do."

She saw by the flare in his eyes that she was right. The ball of air in her lungs came out in a frustrated sigh.

"Did you know my parents have an open relationship? I'm unsure how well you know my family or what you were told. It's a family tradition. How funny is that?" though she stretched her lips, she wasn't smiling with happiness. She'd been ten when she found out, and when she'd asked her mom why, Sandrine had only said, "This is what the Snow men do."

It wasn't something she'd ever tolerate.

"And though my father has these discreet affairs, ask me how often my mother has done the same. The answer is zero. She loves him, you see. My grandfather and generations before him did the same, and it will be expected of Reeves." She watched while Diamond reached for the coffee and took a long sip. "So, you might understand now why it's difficult to follow these instructions when it's not my doing and always because of someone else's selfishness. Do you know the sordid details of this latest dalliance?"

It looked like she wouldn't get answers from the tight-lipped biker, adding more frustration to her brain, but he said, "I know some. But knowing the reason isn't important. My job is to keep you and your family safe."

"This woman is dangerous, then?"

"You need to ask your father that."

"But I'm asking you." Joelle nearly lost her cool, but speaking from experience, there was little point in doing that. And she added when he remained silent. "I'd have a better outcome if I asked you to dress in my finest ball gown."

Diamond's lips twitched this time, and something loosened in Joelle's tight shoulder blades.

"I get the situation is fucked up."

"So fucked up." She agreed.

"Why would your mom stay if she's not taking advantage of an open marriage, too?"

"Love. Why else?" she answered. "Women do a lot of dumb stuff under the umbrella of love. Crazily, my father adores my mother. But why does he need to sleep around?" Joelle lifted her hand. "Don't answer that. I'm oversharing again. This isn't common knowledge, so I'd appreciate it if you didn't spread it around. This whole thing is vexing that another person's decisions affect my life."

His stare was penetrating. "You live under their roof, Bluebell. They pay the bills and everything else you're accustomed to."

Joelle's head snapped back, almost like a physical slap.

The criticizing expression was evident on his face.

He'd formed a twisted opinion about her with no proof. He had been doing it ever since he entered the house.

He saw the mansion and everything within the walls and condemned her for being a pampered doll living off Daddy's riches. He probably thought she didn't have a brain rattling around in her head, too.

She unfurled herself from the couch and rose to her feet, collecting both coffee cups and traced her steps to the kitchen area. When she turned back to Diamond, he, too, was on his feet. Standing like a skyscraper in black leather and sexy boots.

"For someone who's paid to care for others, you make a lot of snap conclusions, Diamond. You ought to be careful because you'll say something you can't take back one day." She smiled tightly and walked toward the door. "I'll see you out. And I'll let Titan know when I'm leaving the house in the future. You won't be contacted about me again."

Sometimes, crushes died as fast as they appeared.

It would have been nice to have this one for a week, but oh, well. Easy come, easy go.

Diamond might have the most handsome face she'd seen in a long time, but he sure had a cold outlook on people.

She didn't part with a pleasant greeting, as manners dictated; she waited for him to exit and then closed the door behind him.

Pressing her back against the wood, she inhaled the last remnants of his cologne. It was earthy like musk, exactly what a man should smell like.

If she were another type of woman, she'd march to her father's downtown office and tell him to sort his shit out once and for all before they all got dragged down with him.

But that wasn't who Joelle was.

Instead, she set up the easel in her studio, slipped a smock over her clothing to protect them, and with a few swipes of a brush, she painted a perfectly sculpted jawline, dusted in fine facial hair from memory. She used all the colors to soothe her inner turmoil.

Hours passed within a blink, and she was aching as she stepped back from the canvas.

A face stared back at her, and Joelle caught her breath to see the biker captured perfectly on white paper.

His face was an abstract of colors, but the only part she used the correct color for, was his piercing, ice-blue eyes.

The portrait stared from the easel, and Joelle stared back.

It had been months since she'd picked up a paintbrush. Her muse had dried up, and though she could paint anything from memory, Joelle hadn't felt the urge to.

But one encounter with a critical biker caused her mind to overflow with creativity again.

Because she didn't want him staring at her, she took the canvas down and turned it toward the wall, ignoring him.

There was a metaphor in that somewhere.

## Diamond

While sitting on a bench in a local park, Diamond answered his vibrating phone, seeing it was Tomb calling.

"What's up?" he asked.

"Are you coming in today, Diamond? Could do with a hand in the garage. Reno called in sick. He caught something from his kid and has been spewing all night. I'm backed up with three cars in the bays."

"Yeah, I've been seeing to maintenance over at the Dyson. I'm on my way now."

It was true, but the maintenance checks were quick because the manager he hired for his apartment community was excellent at her job.

For the past two hours, he'd been playing stalker.

It was fucking ridiculous because he could take over from Titan at any time without explanation. However, he remained seated across the street from where Titan had taken Joelle Snow a while back. It was Friday, and she finally made it to the mysterious appointment she had rescheduled.

The man protecting Joelle was someone he trusted. Titan never needed someone breathing down his neck, so Diamond acted stupid without cause.

He saw her leave the Escalade, carrying a tote bag, wearing pink leggings and a long white coat with fur on the hood. She climbed the porch steps to the brownstone house and has been in there ever since.

Was it a boyfriend's place?

There was nothing in the info from Judge Snow to say his daughter was working, so it couldn't be job-related. She was likely grabbing lunch with a friend. Didn't all the fancy girls do that? Just wasting time on nonsense.

He'd picked up on her facial expression the other day and knew he'd hurt her with his assumptions. There'd been a flicker of fire in her eyes like she'd been ready to rip him a new asshole, but then it fizzled out, almost as if Joelle had reined herself in. She'd told him what she thought of him by showing him to the door in that rich person's haughty way.

Chuckling, he walked down the stairs that day, appreciating her controlled behavior.

There'd been no more issues with the Snow family.

He waited ten more minutes, but Joelle didn't emerge from the building, so he tossed the empty takeout cup into the trash can and headed to his parked bike. Returning to the MC compound, he worked alongside Tomb for the rest of the day, fixing engines and bodywork.

With his back aching and his belly chewing on itself, he needed a hot shower and something to eat when the garage shut and the last customers had collected their vehicles.

"Fuck, I could eat a whole cow," Complained Tomb, washing up next to Diamond in the double sinks. "You wanna come home with me for burgers, D? Nina is working late, and I'm not picking her up until nine."

"It beats cooking something when I get home, thanks. I'll follow you."

"You don't wanna ride backpack with me?" the asshole joked with a massive grin on his weathered face. Diamond flicked him with the wet towel. "Not even if you begged me. I'll grab a six-pack of beers on the way."

"Good man."

They broke off, and each went their way. Diamond changed out of his work overalls and left them in the garage. Before switching on the engine, he straddled his bike seat and checked in with the secured group chat with his guys.

Everyone had checked in and said their clients were back home and the following shifts would take over soon.

Though Diamond was interested in seeing all the reports, his eyes shifted down the list and automatically searched for a particular one.

**TITAN**: Snow #4 is secure.

That meant she was at home.

He considered texting back and asking where she'd gone earlier, but refrained. Knowing if she was visiting a booty call wasn't his job, even if the growl in his throat begged to differ.

Just as he switched on the engine, he heard another bike approaching and turned his head to see Axel and his old lady coming through the opened gates. Diamond waited, and Axel parked in his president's parking spot. Scarlett jumped off, handing the half-bucket helmet to Axel.

"Hey, Diamond! We're going to have a Christmas movie marathon in the movie room. Do you want to join us?"

Axel glared at his wife. "No, he doesn't."

Diamond chuckled. The rude translation was Axel didn't want company because he had plans of the dirty kind with his old lady he didn't want an audience for.

"Hey, you be nice." With a blushed grin, she chastised and bopped a finger on Axel's chin. "I'm freezing. I'm heading in, and I'll get set up."

Diamond noticed the prez watched his woman going the whole way inside before he turned around.

"Spoiling your woman tonight, Prez?"

He sighed, but didn't look too harassed. "We have a perfect TV at home where it's warm, and the roads aren't slick as fuck, but she insists the screen is better here at the club."

"You built her the movie room, Axel..." Diamond reminded him. "And installed all those candy and popcorn machines."

"Yeah, yeah." He admitted with a smirk.

By the time Scarlett had come to them, she'd lived a whole life of missing out on ordinary shit people took for granted. She'd hardly known anything about pop culture, so Axel had been indulging his woman with movies, TV shows, music, and traveling.

"I better get inside before she's filled a bucket with enough candy she'll be bouncing until New Year's Eve."

"Enjoy Jack Frost and all the Ho! Ho! Ho!"

Axel waved over his shoulder, striding inside to spoil his woman. Even if he did it grumbling, no one took it seriously. He'd rip the Eiffel Tower out by the roots if Scarlett mentioned she wanted it for bathroom decor.

Diamond rode off to have burgers and beers with his buddy.

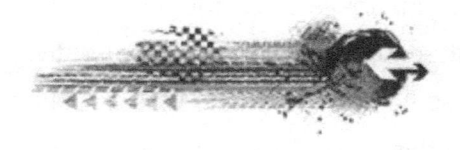

## Joelle

"Ahhh, wine and cake. There's nothing better than this." Molly sprawled out lengthways on Joelle's couch. Fuzzy socks were on her feet, a glass of Moscato d'Asti was in her hand, and a platter of sliced vanilla cake, liberally frosted, sitting on the coffee table.

Joelle's other friend, Sadie, was at ease, sitting cross-legged on the floor with Joelle.

"Sex is better." Remarked Joelle, her smiling lips touched the rim of the glass. Both girls looked over and nodded.

"That's a given. But right now, nothing is better. The baby is home in bed, and my gorgeous hunk of a husband is in his gaming room, probably having an epic battle with a twelve-year-old from Boston. And I'm sipping wine." Said Sadie, toasting to the air. "Cheers to no longer breastfeeding, and Mama can drink again."

"Cheers to your free tits." Molly toasted. "Although, the way Dan looks at them, they won't be free for long." She snickered.

"Be nice," Joelle said. "Dan's a cop. He deserves her tits for the service he gives to this country."

The wine couldn't even be blamed for their joking since they were on their first glass. It was an impromptu get-together. They'd become so few, as was life when people had adult responsibilities. Her friends were happily married, and now Sadie was the mom of a beautiful fifteen-month-old girl, Joelle's goddaughter.

Getting together now happened infrequently. Mostly, they talked over the phone, so having them over was a real treat.

"Did you bake this cake?" Molly asked, pushing a pillow-soft piece into her mouth and moaning at how delicately sweet it tasted.

"Did it break your teeth? Then, no, I didn't bake the cake. I did, however, request it. So it's like I baked it."

Molly laughed. "I should have known that. You burn everything."

"Remember, she nearly burned down your first apartment, Mols? When Joelle thought she could make toast under the broiler."

"That was years ago," she protested at their laughter. "I've excelled in toast making since then. I even do bagels sometimes if I'm feeling fancy."

Sadie flashed her a smile. "You're going to make someone a beautiful wife someday."

"Is that what you do for Dan? Make him toast?"

"Nah, she gets on her knees and asks to see his baton. Oh, Officer, I didn't mean to break the law." Mocked a laughing Molly.

Sadie didn't deny it, which made the three of them laugh even more.

The rest of the evening continued in a similar fashion.

They shared several bottles of wine. They gossiped about everyone they didn't like, including Molly's witch of a mother-in-law, and finished the cake platter. When Joelle walked them down to the front door, where a town car was taking them home, she was ready to soak in the tub and then fall into bed.

Making her way to the bathroom, she switched on the faucet for hot water and dropped in a scented bath bomb.

As it filled up, the lighting became warm, and her music started playing. She sighed, satisfied, and sank into the comfortable water until it reached her chin.

Dozing, sometime later, the music on her phone dipped out as a text pinged through, and then the music kicked in again. Joelle sat up and grabbed the phone from the stool by the bath. If Reeves was texting after midnight for a ride home again, she'd break her brother's neck.

But when she opened it, she saw there was a string of texts from a number that wasn't in her contacts, but it was a local area code.

**UNKNOWN**: Are you alone?
**UNKNOWN**: I know you're there.
**UNKNOWN**: I see you, pretty.
**UNKNOWN**: Sweet dreams.

"Ugh, what a creep." She muttered, pulling a face. Even having an unlisted number, the weirdos crawled out of the woodwork. Joelle didn't know who it was, but she wasn't about to acknowledge them. If she did, they'd keep harassing her.

Joelle's thoughts turned toward a particular biker once she was curled up warm in bed. However, she soon banished him out of her mind, deciding to watch an episode of her vampire show.

She no longer had any interest in that guy.

Fictional men were more reliable.

Good riddance to her short-lived crush.

## Joelle

The second week of December started with snowfall.

It snowed incessantly for days.

Joelle sighed in disgust as she saw acres of snow-covered ground through the living room window.

She hated the stuff with a passion. It's no surprise her mood dropped. It was a day that needed more color.

All summer long, people complained and prayed for colder weather. Well, she hoped those people were happily frozen now. Who would exchange serotonin-boosting sunshine for the dreary wetness? Nothing made her sadder than the winter months.

Turning from the window, she padded through to her walk-in closet, choosing the brightest sweater she had. A blended mix of red and silver. After slipping into a pair of jeans, she laced up her knee-length, off-white ski boots with the fur around the trim.

The only thing she tolerated about the yucky season was the gorgeous fashion. Teamed with the light gray woolen trench coat, going outside soon would be bearable.

It was one of those days when she had to eat breakfast with everyone in the family dining room. Her parents were already there and halfway through their food. Her father looked over his copy of the Financial Times. He grunted hello and returned to the news. Her mother was the first to speak.

"Good morning, sweetheart. Where are you off to today?"

After kissing her mom's cheek, Joelle collected a plate and helped herself buffet-style from the side table. She chose poached eggs and a much-needed coffee.

"I have a few errands I need to run in town and a last couple of gifts for Reeves to pick up."

Joelle didn't have kids of her own yet or even a pet, so Reeves was who she spoiled rotten. He may no longer believe in Santa Claus, but would have everything on his wish list under their tree. Or near enough. She wouldn't buy him a Maserati, no matter how much he begged.

As usual, conversation around the breakfast table was sparse. She didn't know why her father insisted they eat together. He left, soon after, for the office, and her mother was organizing an extended family dinner this weekend, so she'd be busy most of the day.

Knowing she'd have to be shadowed by Titan, as she had several times last week already, Joelle expected to see him standing in the entryway.

The bodyguard couldn't be considered friendly, with only a few monosyllabic grunts. But she came up short when it wasn't Titan looming by the front door.

"What are you doing here?" she asked Diamond, whose eyes had zeroed in on her the second she stepped into the foyer. "If you're looking for my father, he's already left for work."

"I already saw him, and it's not him I'm here for."

Realization landed heavily in Joelle's chest.

This was the last thing she needed today, to have him crowding behind her.

"Where's Titan?"

His jaw was set tight. "It's his day off."

"I didn't know round-the-clock security got days off," she remarked, buttoning up the coat.

Like he was born avoiding questions, he asked one of his own. "Where are we going?"

Joelle tried not to notice how good he looked today. His blond hair, clipped short around his head, appeared slightly damp, as though he'd only had a shower recently. And his leather jacket was all dinged up and sexy, fitting him perfectly.

If there was a handbook on how to appear masculine without trying, she bet Diamond's face was on the cover.

Now, she was mentally trying to decide if she could cancel what she had to do today and wait for Titan to return from his day off.

Knowing Diamond was trailing behind her didn't fill Joelle with seasonal happiness.

"I have errands to run in town."

"Okay, we can take my truck."

Her eyes widened. He didn't show up on his bike? Ah, of course not. It would be risky for two-wheeled vehicles to navigate the snowy roads.

"I'm not going with you."

"Joelle," he sighed, his eyes so intense, like she exasperated him.

She snapped to attention. "Only friends and people I like use my name. You can address me as Miss Snow."

His lips tightened. "You're still pissy after what I said the other day."

She didn't dignify him with a response; instead, she pulled open the door and left him standing there. Out in the snow, she navigated to her parked car, depressing the locking mechanism.

He was behind her.

She heard his heavy footfalls on the crunching snow.

"Get over it, Joelle."

"Miss Snow." She corrected over her shoulder. "I don't know you and don't want to get to know you, either. Titan is nice. He at least stays quiet."

"Titan has a woman." He grated, and that's when Joelle whirled around to glare at him.

Of all the nerve.

"You think I'm chasing your employee just because I admire how he keeps his opinions to himself?" She huffed, steam coming out of her lips. Joelle pushed a strand of blue hair away from her eyes and glared up at the behemoth man with a low opinion of her, which she couldn't fathom. Maybe he was a born woman hater, or she just brought it out in him.

Lucky her.

"And even if I was chasing him around the furniture and locking him in the pantry to enjoy stolen kisses, it's none of your business."

There was a fire in his eyes. It flashed like lightning, and Joelle shivered. It must be because of the snow. Not because a hot guy was angry.

"Try not to crowd me if you insist on following me. I have a reputation in this town, and I don't need you sullying it."

She was talking nonsense and being disobedient. However, people would be shocked to see her gallivanting with a known biker.

She said nothing else to him for the rest of the morning.

But she was aware of Diamond driving behind her in his big F150 truck. And every time she stepped out of her car, he was mere feet behind her, shadowing her steps.

She remained silent while gathering Reeves' presents. But he was there to unburden her with the packages and to place them in the trunk.

Nor did she tell him why she stopped at the animal sanctuary and the local children's society to drop off her donations. She didn't speak to Diamond when she parked outside a library with two enormous boxes of donated books. When she'd attempted to lift them out, he was there, taking over, carrying both boxes of heavy books at once like they weighed nothing. Though sighing, she let him help, but nearly bit off her tongue to stop herself from thanking him.

She was a spoiled rich diva, wasn't she? According to him. Divas didn't show their gratitude.

After talking to the manager for a while, it was heavily snowing when she came out of the library. With his eyes fixed on her, she couldn't help but be fully aware of the ominous shadow by the doorway.

"Damn," she muttered as she squinted against the bleak whiteness.

Determined not to give him any excuse to call her privileged or pampered, she ordinarily would have called Kenneth to pick her up. Driving in the snow was a nightmare come true, but she climbed behind the wheel, not glancing at Diamond. She'd have him out of her hair in just a short while. She could endure a snowstorm until then.

But she nearly came out of her skin when he knocked on the window. She whirred it down.

"You're not driving in this, Joelle. I'll take you home in my truck." He said.

Joelle wasn't a stubborn woman. She knew her strengths and was well acquainted with her weaknesses; she could admit she was wrong and was always quick to apologize when she meant it. But looking up at that stern jaw and seeing the blueness of Diamond's eyes against the snow made every stubborn bone in her body roar awake.

It was on her tongue to tell him she didn't need his biker help. This diva could get herself home through a snowstorm without winter tires and with less visibility than a house fly had. The words were right there, but he got there first.

"Don't be a stubborn ass, Joelle. I'm taking you home. Get out of the car."

He really was showering her with sweet names, wasn't he?

"I can't just leave my car here."

"It's a private parking lot. It'll be fine for now. I'll have it picked up. Keys." He demanded, and she handed it over for some strange reason. To a virtual stranger slash pain in her ass.

The snow was whipping around them, though it was only a couple of feet from his truck. Joelle felt like she'd trekked through Antarctica, protected from the brunt of it by Diamond's body so close to hers.

"I need Reeves' gifts," she said as he opened the passenger door.

"I'll get them. Get in."

With his truck elevated about fifty feet, he had to help her up, holding onto her waist. Joelle's skin sizzled at the touch through three layers of clothing, keeping her chin up high and her breezy attitude in place as she watched a dark blur through the swirling snowflakes retrieve the packages from her trunk. The interior was neat, not even an empty takeout box, and it smelled like Diamond's cologne. Once he climbed in, the inner cab grew even smaller by his proximity, and she sat with her spine ramrod straight and her eyes forward. Without warning, Diamond stretched across her and buckled her in.

He drove carefully with skill. It must have taken three times as long to reach the house, and she was relieved when she could climb down from the truck.

"Thanks," she mumbled, though she hadn't wanted to thank the bodyguard for anything. Despite her attempt to assist by retrieving the packages from the backseat, he insisted on getting them all, resulting in another muttered thank you.

Kenneth was waiting at the door, smiling at the pair of them. She was taken aback when Diamond followed her inside.

Even so, she told Kenneth. "Can you arrange a hot drink and something to eat for Diamond? Thanks, Kenneth."

"It'll be my pleasure."

She didn't wait around for Diamond's refusal. He could eat or not, not her problem. But her traitorous eyes looked back once she was on the first-floor landing and found his head tipped up, watching her.

It wasn't exactly animosity. It was something else.

If it were another man, she'd swear it was attraction, but there was no sign of it from him in their limited interactions.

Yeah, she was holding a petty grudge; his snap criticism hurt her feelings, and she couldn't let it go.

Thank god Titan would be back tomorrow.

Without giving Diamond a wave, she headed up to her section of the house.

What the hell?

Where was Titan?

She'd been stuck at home for two days while it snowed, the kind of snow to trap people in the wilderness.

She was sure she'd see the quieter bodyguard when she went downstairs, but there Diamond stood, waiting by the door.

"Isn't Titan coming?"

A twitch in his jaw nearly made her laugh.

He really didn't like her mentioning his employee.

"He's been reassigned."

She blinked. "Reassigned, why? Because I was difficult? Did he tell you I was *difficult*?" Oh, and to think she would've gifted Titan a box of sugar cookies for Christmas because he hadn't been a demanding, bossy jerk like the man standing before her.

"If he did, he's lying. I'm a freaking angel. A paragon of delight to guard. I hardly gave him any work at all."

Diamond's lips twitched, and she felt a softening in her chest as his eyes lit up with amusement. She was glad someone was amused.

"His woman is close to giving birth, and he wanted to be nearer home."

"Oh." The wind went out of her sails. "Then who else have you got?"

She didn't mean it in the way it came out, but Diamond interpreted it negatively with how the smile dropped off his face.

She just meant she didn't want to be a bother to *him*.

"It's me or no one." He rasped.

"It's fine. I can do what I need to do online. I'll stay home."

As she started to climb the stairs again, she heard his stormy sigh. When she glanced behind her, Diamond had his hands resting on his hips, staring at her.

It was his fault if he was frustrated. He could have sent someone else to secure her.

No, it was her father's fault for not making this stupid mess disappear. Between her father and a biker, they were causing her all kinds of infuriation.

The following two mornings, Joelle discovered Diamond waiting in the foyer, looking like he was chewing on rocks, oh-so-thrilled to be on Joelle Snow duty.

She frowned and tossed her coat over the newel post.

"I changed my mind," she told him.

His eyes flared.

The day after that, she tried to sneak out before he usually arrived at eight a.m. She thought she was being sly and tittered as she skipped down the stairs before seven. Only to nearly take a header down the rest of them when she saw him at the bottom.

Before she could headbutt the marble staircase, a sturdy pair of arms grabbed her and put her right on her feet. She hadn't even seen Diamond moving, but there he was, playing Superman.

"Going somewhere?" he husked, looking her dead in the eye. That look dared her to say she was hoping to go out alone.

"I didn't know you were here. Don't you usually come at eight?"

"I get here at six thirty." He smirked. "Your cook feeds me before you come down."

"Oh," she murmured, realizing she still held onto Diamond's forearms. She stepped back or tried to, but the stairs nearly made her tumble backward.

If not for the hero breaking her fall. Again.

"Careful, Bluebell."

"Yeah, thanks." She muttered, walking down the stairs this time without doing a forward head roll. Her legs usually worked just fine when he wasn't around.

"I guess I don't need to go anywhere today." She informed. But it was a lie. She'd be considered a shut-in if she stayed home much longer.

"Goddammit, this has gone far enough." He snapped, and Joelle's eyes went as round as a beach ball hearing his raised tone. Her shock continued when Diamond took hold of the top of her arm and all but marched her into the adjourning reception parlor her mother used for greeting guests. It had vintage furniture, a cozy fire, and thick curtains from Paris, and it was decked out for the holidays with a tree and twinkling lights.

Before she could admonish him for the manhandling, however good it had felt, she whirled around and found Diamond standing in her personal space.

He topped her by a foot or more, so she had to tip her head back to glare at him right in the eyes. He had a severe expression, and his jaw muscles were ticking.

"You need to get over it."

"Get over what?"

"Babe..."

Joelle's stomach whooshed. That gravel voice could cause forest fires. "I'm not your babe."

Diamond's eyebrow winged up. "But you don't mind being called Bluebell?"

Huh? He had her there. "Bluebell is cute and personal to me. Babe is generic and could be for every woman. And I ask again, get over what?"

"You didn't like how I spoke to you last week. You're holding onto your hurt feelings. You gotta move on. I'm here for the long haul."

Oh, goody. She rolled her eyes, even as excitement tightened her throat. How would it feel to see this roughened biker every day? Stalking through her house with his incredible boots, broad shoulders, and swaggering walk. Diamond and his staff had brightened the place up. They descended on the kitchen like they'd never known food before. The cook was having a great time feeding them.

"Are you always this smart-mouthed?" he asked, almost softly.

"Not until recently." And that was the truth. "You rubbed me wrong, judging me. It was rude."

"Babe," he grinned then, and his entire face changed, morphing into a god of a man. Joelle had to swallow and move her feet, taking her away from him so she could inhale without smelling his evocative fragrance. "Can you say you didn't judge me when you walked into your father's office that day?"

"Only because you were glaring at me like I'd just lifted my leg on your granny!" she huffed, and he burst out laughing.

"That was the first analogy you came up with?"

"Well, yeah. It was the worst thing I could think of. And besides, my assessment was more of a shock. Not every day do you see an esteemed justice taking a private meeting with..." She hesitated to finish because she didn't want to say the wrong thing and make him angry again.

"Go on..." his eyebrows were high on his forehead now, and Joelle met Diamond stare for stare.

Fine. She wouldn't back down.

"Meeting with bikers known not to be law-abiding citizens."

"Diplomatic, Bluebell." He chuckled, leaning his ass on her mother's antique fainting couch. "You gonna move on now and stop acting like a brat so we can leave this fucking house before the scent of pine gives me a brain aneurysm?"

She couldn't help but burst into a fit of giggles at the imagery of him dramatically fainting.

"I never knew bikers could be dramatic."

"You never met Splice then." He muttered.

"Ohh, who is that?" her ears perked. She had to admit that ever since Diamond and his employees had been around the house, she'd become increasingly fascinated by bikers and their culture.

His smile dropped.

Good heavens, what had she said now?

"You won't get to meet him, so he doesn't matter." He said through his teeth. Warningly.

"You're being rude again. Are you even aware you're doing it? Is it medical? Do you have a note from your specialist?"

His lips split wide again, giving his face a softer edge. "You're funny."

Joelle rolled her eyes but smiled. "Sure, I should be in a circus."

It could have been the heat from the fireplace, but Joelle suddenly felt a sizzle over her skin. Lifting her eyes, there was a jolt in her limbs, finding Diamond staring at her.

No, not staring.

Checking her out.

Running his eyes up and down her body. Unbridled. Unfiltered. His eyes had been painted in red hotness, and the attraction bounced between them.

And then it was gone in a blink, shutters came down over his vision.

The calm and collected biker was back in the room.

But boy, had that gaze left her feeling shaken to the core.

She hadn't imagined it this time.

Joelle knew what she was working with. She saw her body more than anyone else did. There was a time when she resented her inability to be as skinny as other women. She'd never be a size two. Her framework wouldn't allow for it.

With a lot of time, aging, and being gentle with herself, she'd learned to appreciate her body. She felt confident about her looks and had been praised for her beauty. Her confidence stemmed from the way her curves flawlessly fit into every pair of pants. Her curves and voluptuous figure exemplified femininity. Even though her belly was soft and jiggly, Joelle never hesitated to wear a bikini during her summer vacations. She refused to resent her body or delay happiness until she was perfect, knowing life was too short.

She'd rather live today and enjoy every second before it was over.

Maybe it was her confidence that made her attractive. She didn't know, but her skin was still sizzling under Diamond's admiring stare.

She cleared her throat. "I guess if you're not busy, we can leave. I have a few things I need to drop off at a local art store." She was selling a few pieces of her work. It had been over a year since she'd offered any of her older paintings. The store owner was a friend and art collector and often begged Joelle to give him more because the last shipment sold out in days.

She'd lost her confidence in her talent until recently, when she'd been doing much more painting. She wouldn't delve into why, but she side-eyed the biker as she heard him push off from the couch and follow her. It might have something to do with him.

Artists needed pretty muses around them, and the handsome biker became hers.

"Thank fuck." He said. Getting into step with her. He grabbed her coat over the newel post and held it out. Surprised, Joelle turned around and slid her arms in. "We'll take my truck. It's still icy."

"This isn't your normal duties, is it?" she asked.

"Nope."

She grinned. "I thought so. You're bored out of your mind guarding my family, aren't you?"

He only cocked his eyebrow.

"It's okay. I don't run to my father to report the bodyguard's behavior."

"Not a bodyguard, babe."

"Bluebell." She corrected him and then cursed. "Shit, I mean, Miss Snow."

Diamond only chuckled and held the door open for her to walk through first.

"Whatever you say, babe. Let's get the hell out of here."

With a tiny pep in her booted step, Joelle led the way over to Diamond's parked truck, waiting patiently for him to help her inside again.

The eagerness wasn't anything to do with wanting him to touch her, even for a second. No, nothing to do with that at all.

But she was still shivering from the contact once inside the cab as she watched him rounding the hood to climb in.

## Diamond

D iamond felt naked.

He couldn't remember the last time he wore a suit. Maybe for his prom forever ago. And he'd only dressed up that night because his then-girlfriend was going to sleep with him.

Checking the silver watch on his wrist, he turned when the Judge's office door opened, and the man walked in.

"Good. You're here."

Snow kept Diamond waiting at the house for an hour before they could talk. The asshole didn't give a damn about wasting someone else's time.

"It's an invitation-only event tonight, but as you suspect, people can get around that. I want you and your men to be extra vigilant. With absolutely no weapons drawn, but if anything were to happen, I need you to neutralize the situation as discreetly as possible. I don't want my wife embarrassed."

"You might have thought about that before you let your dick wander around with a psycho bitch." Answered Diamond, uncaring if he was overstepping his station.

The Judge's head snapped up, and he glared, tightness thinning out his lips. "That's none of your damn business. Just do your job."

Diamond had already scouted out the location they were going to. His men would be on the Judge, and his Mrs. Reeves was staying home. Diamond would take Joelle. Every thought of seeing her again made his gut flex. She hadn't been out in a few days, so he'd spent most of his on-duty hours sitting in the foyer, bored out of his mind, and picturing what she was doing upstairs in her apartment suite. The time he spent thinking about that woman was becoming obscene.

It was like an obsession amplified to the extreme.

Only his immovable willpower stopped him from kicking down doors so he could sniff the curve of her neck and hold those fantastic curves again.

"Have you figured out a way to make this shitshow go away yet?"

The Judge sighed, seating himself behind the desk in his tailored tuxedo. "Not yet."

"Money isn't working?"

Diamond didn't give a shit that he was in a mess. He'd spoken a few times to Sandrine, and he liked her.

Diamond was a man of action. He'd never let shit touch his family, and not through selfish means like Snow was doing.

"If money would solve it, do you think I would have engaged you?" he spoke curtly, and Diamond half grinned at the show of temper.

"Bet it's sticking in your craw, isn't it, Judge, that you had to come crawling to the Diablos? You're so used to your power being able to fix anything."

Someone knocked on the door, and Joelle walked in.

Diamond's breath caught, and he couldn't tear his eyes away.

Jesus Christ. He'd never seen a woman like her.

Beautiful was a meek word to describe what he was looking at, but he couldn't find anything else rattling around in his empty head.

She was dressed in a shiny silver dress with long sleeves. It was a modest dress above her knees and tapered around her hips. He thought it might be the first block of color he'd seen her wearing until he skated his gaze down her creamy bare legs to see the high stilettos in a metallic rainbow.

Her hair was wavy, flirting around her shoulders, bouncing as she moved her head. She had the deepest red lipstick and silver glitter makeup on her eyelids.

Their eyes met, and it felt like Diamond was sucked into a vortex, unable to look away from her bemused face as she smiled.

"Good evening, Diamond." She said, sounding unaffected by whatever shit had grabbed him by the throat and was choking the air out of him.

If he sprang a boner right now, he'd shoot himself in the fucking head.

He'd known for a few days he was attracted to the quirky diva. But he'd been able to ignore it. Even with being constantly surrounded by attractive women, he remained unfazed by them.

But Joelle Snow had somehow gotten underneath his skin.

After her little tantrum the other day when he'd had to all but tackle her into his truck so she didn't drive in the storm and get herself killed, he hadn't been able to stop thinking about her. It was as if putting his hands innocently on her waist to boost her up had triggered something in him.

She was fucking lush all over.

So soft, and his hands, even now, itched inside his pants pockets to get on her again, to see if she was soft and warm all over.

Turning to leave, she smiled at him again, told him she'd be in the foyer, and left Diamond with her father.

He let out an exhale.

A woman shouldn't be that hot.

It should be fucking illegal how Joelle monopolized his thoughts.

"Larson and Davey are outside when you're ready to go," He informed and turned to leave. Only to hear. "Don't even fucking think about it."

Diamond stopped and cocked an eyebrow at the old man. "Come again?"

"I saw how you looked at my daughter." Rising to his feet, he seemed prepared to strangle Diamond.

"Any man would look at a pretty girl, Judge. You're an expert at that."

"I'm warning you now. It goes no further than just looking. Do you hear me?"

Diamond's mouth twitched with a grin. He shouldn't be getting a kick out of rattling the silver-haired goat.

Sure, he'd roamed his eyes over her because she was stunning in her silver dress and wavy hair. It made a man think about messing her up by smudging her lipstick, but it was as far as Diamond would go.

"I have perfect hearing, Judge. But the thing is, I don't respond well to warnings. Enjoy your evening." He walked out smiling.

Joelle was buttoning up a white wool coat with fur trim as he approached the foyer. She turned and smiled.

"I nearly didn't recognize you." She was taking in his suit with a slow peruse, and he could tell she liked what she saw. And that just made it even harder for him to resist temptation. "Was this my parent's idea?"

"Yes." He answered, and she tinkled a laugh.

"You should have told them you're more comfortable in the leather jacket and boots." He could have sworn she mumbled how the jacket and his biker boots were hotter, but she'd already turned and headed for the door. He took longer strides and got there before her, pulling it open. He rode in the town car up front with the driver, Joelle, in the back. But each time he checked on her in the rearview mirror, she was staring back at him with her oh-so-fucking-sultry come-to-bed eyes.

Diamond swallowed the extended inhale.

It was going to be one hell of a long night.

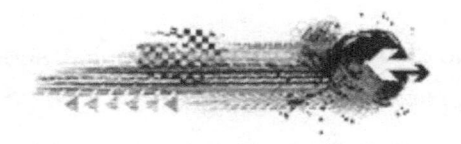

## Joelle

This night was a nightmare!

Joelle was sick of smiling, passing around holiday greetings, and asking about someone's spoiled kids.

The annual Marmaduke holiday party was the season's highlight, so she was told repeatedly. To Joelle's observation, these things were used as bragging rights. Her mom loved these parties. She shined like a star. And her dad was never short of a conversation.

Joelle hated them with a passion.

She'd rather be at an art exhibition or home painting her toenails.

It wasn't only the party that bothered her.

Whenever her eyes sought Diamond, checking where he was discreetly stationed, he watched her from underneath hooded eyelids. And each time she caught him watching her, she got a thrilled buzz between her thighs, making her heart palpitations even more potent.

The sight of him in his navy blue suit, with the top buttons of his white shirt undone, left her speechless and breathless. If not for her father in his office, she might have done something appalling and thrown herself onto the desk and begged Diamond to make her pussy aches go away.

It was unbelievable how strong the chemistry was between her and a rugged, uncensored, foul-mouthed, attractive biker.

While she slipped away to grab a drink from a server, she took her phone from the silver clutch purse to send a quick message to her friends.

As she was about to slip away the phone, it vibrated in her hand.

**UNKNOWN**: Hey, pretty.
**UNKNOWN**: I see you.
**UNKNOWN**: Silver is your color.
**UNKNOWN**: You'll wear it for me soon.


That last text officially crept Joelle out, and the base of her spine turned cold.

The atmosphere at the Marmaduke party was electric, with the lively chatter and laughter of three hundred people filling the air. It would be impossible to know if someone was pranking her. She scanned the crowd but didn't spot anyone with a phone.

Throughout the week, she had received similar messages from the unknown number. She attributed it to a foolish teenager attempting to frighten a stranger. Yet, this person commented on Joelle's outfit. That made it personal to her.

Who was it?

And why were they trying to mess with her?

For tonight, she ignored the messages. It certainly wasn't the right time for sleuthing or hysterics. She'd had her orders from her mother to act like the dutiful Snow daughter.

"Joelle!" she heard. "I wondered if I'd see you tonight."

A sigh hung in the air as Joelle weighed her options: champagne or confrontation with her ex. Their breakup happened more than a year ago. Instead, like manners dictated, she pasted on her best smile, hoping it looked genuine.

She didn't want to go to the Marmaduke's party because of their eldest son. Their relationship, lasting three months, felt like an eternity.

He reached for her hand, bringing it to his lips to kiss. Joelle recoiled inwardly, remembering how bad that mouth was... at... everything.

"You look incredible, Jo."

Ugh, she hated how he abbreviated her name. How difficult was it to include four more letters?

"How have you been, Trent?"

On the outside, she thought he was good-looking. She was initially flattered by his attention, but any woman would find it off-putting if a man was so unskilled in bed that it made her lose interest in sex. She certainly didn't feel any flicker of residual attraction now as she took her hand back.

"I'm great." He launched into a conversation about his successful career.

It was obvious after two minutes of his monologue that he was trying to impress her.

No amount of peacock feathering would make her date him again.

She was never swayed by money, regardless of her financial situation.

She wanted more than wealth from a partner.

"I thought you'd call after we split up. You're all I've thought about." He simpered. "My number's never changed."

Ah, so Trent couldn't be the phantom texter.

"I'm sure you're inundated with offers, Trent." She extended kindly. However, a man who couldn't make a woman come and thought the clitoris was a myth shouldn't be given compassion.

She chose tact over honesty, sparing him the truth about his abilities. It was fortunate she only has a few memories of that, not years of awful sex. She blamed the breakup on their different goals. Weeks later, he continued to pursue her with flowers and pleas.

He moved closer and gave her a wink. "Why don't we get out of here? No one will miss us. My parents are talking to your father. You know, they always expected us to get married one day."

Joelle didn't need a sip of champagne to nearly choke.

Then a presence loomed over her left shoulder, and Trent's face blanched.

"Joelle." She heard in that husky, spine-shaking tone and knew she'd been rescued.

It didn't matter the level of attraction she felt toward Diamond then. He was now her hero for saving her from a conversation worse than boredom.

But the way he stared at Trent, she felt a definite throb in places that shouldn't be throbbing this close to many Christmas trees.

Diamond had muscles for days. Even wearing a tailored jacket, he was bulging all over, and her mouth watered as Trent appeared intimidated by Diamond's presence.

"Oh, hi." She turned to him. "I said I'd only be a minute, didn't I?" she lied, keeping her smile in place. "This is Trent." She introduced and appreciated Diamond's stoic expression, which revealed nothing about his lack of understanding. Instinctively, she moved closer to her bodyguard and touched his arm. He broke his stare and glanced down at her.

Clueless, Trent couldn't take the hint, and he opened his mouth.

"Jo and I go way back. And you are?" he stuck his hand out, and Diamond looked at it like Trent was offering him shit dipped in glitter, and Diamond was deathly allergic to glitter.

She held the giggle at bay.

He didn't shake Trent's hand, filling her with excitement she hadn't felt in a long time. These parties were always overstuffed with ass-kissers and braggarts. Both of which bored her silly.

Diamond couldn't be shoved into either category, even if she tried. He was probably the realest person in the room.

And she liked that very much.

"River Durand."

*What*?

It was unbelievable that Diamond had the hottest name ever, and he went by *Diamond*.

"Durand?" Trent said, eyeing him. "Durand?" he repeated. "I don't think I know your family."

"You wouldn't," interjected Joelle, gripping Diamond's arm like her fingers had fused to the jacket material. "River is new money. Anyway, we have people we need to see before we leave. Nice seeing you, Trent. Happy Holidays."

"Call me soon, Jo," she heard behind her as she let Diamond lead her away.

Holding her waist, he guided her into a hallway bustling with staff.

"Where are we going?" she asked, half-amused. She didn't care as long as she could escape the party for a bit.

They halted, and Diamond leaned down to her ear. "Stay here a minute. I'll be back." She watched him striding through the crowd toward one of his men, who was hovering near her father.

Because she needed to use the bathroom anyway, she did that and came out a minute later.

A woman in a black Coco Chanel dress and corkscrew ginger hair stepped in her way. Joelle smiled in a friendly way and attempted to walk around her, but the woman stepped directly in her path. Smirking.

"I've wanted to meet you, Joelle." She said, the sounds of Ireland in her melodic voice.

"Oh?" Joelle politely smiled. "Do I know you?"

"Not yet." The woman's lips curled at the corner. "But your father does."

And Joelle knew then.

This was the woman he'd had an affair with.

The entire reason she needed security.

And the smirking woman was right here, in the same place as her mother.

## Joelle

For a home wrecker, the woman looked ordinary.

Beautiful, but nothing about her spoke of danger that would warrant security.

"What do you want?" she asked in a bitter tone.

The Irish woman smiled like she'd expected the hostility.

"Just to introduce myself."

"Don't take this the wrong way or do, but I have no interest in meeting you."

"You know who I am?" She nearly beamed with delight. Something was off about her eyes. She seemed to take pleasure in making Joelle uncomfortable with a gleam of pure spite. "I'm Shannon."

"Good for you, Shannon. Now it's time you leave."

"No, I don't think I will. I'm here by invite, after all."

"I doubt that."

"Oh, believe it, Joelle." She smiled, sipping on her champagne. "Vivianne and I are in similar circles." Trent's mother. The host of the party.

Shannon wasn't an interloper, Joelle realized. She was someone who belonged, and that made her more nervous. A stack of questions piled into her head. The main one was where her father met this woman.

"If you embarrass my mother, I'll make you pay," Warned Joelle. "You stay away from her."

"There's only one person I want to punish, and it's not your mammy. She should cut your father's cock off and bake it into a pie."

"You knew he was married." Joelle hissed quietly, seething yet trying to remain calm. However, all she saw in her mind was dragging this woman out by her hair before she could horrify her mother. "You're not innocent in this. But now that it's over, you won't leave."

"Is that what he told you?" she clicked her tongue. "He's so naughty."

Joelle didn't respond because she locked eyes with Diamond, and he understood the situation when she read his lips. "*Fuck*." And then he gracefully charged through the crowd toward her. Davey, she noticed, spirited her parents away.

Noticing this, Shannon took a final sip of champagne and set it down.

"It was such a pleasure to meet you, Joelle. I think we could be friends." And she slipped into the crowd.

Un-fucking-believable.

When Diamond reached her, she was so angry that she grabbed his arm for support without thinking. Needing an anchor for all of her anger.

"That was her." She hissed. "She's here, Diamond, with my mother!"

"We took your parents into another room. Come with me." An arm moved around her lower back and forced her down the long hallway, weaving them between the hard-working servers.

"How dare she come here! And talking to me like she knew me."

The one she was angry with was her father.

"Keep it together a second longer, Joelle." Warned Diamond, his hand squeezing her hip.

He found somewhere and hurried her into the room, no bigger than a walk-in closet.

"That woman needs to go." She gritted through her teeth. Woman. She was barely that. It made her feel sick that her father could have an affair with a woman younger than his daughter.

"It's already taken care of." He told her. "She's being shown out of here as we speak."

Her temper was still right on the surface.

The woman's announcement of the affair would have devastated her mother.

Diamond, with a piercing stare, warned, "You're not going out there unless you calm down." A smirk appeared on his face. "You look like you want to murder someone. It's not very festive, Joelle."

"Fuck Christmas. Fuck this whole situation.

"I'm furious that she's at the same party as my mother. And then talking in a condescending way to me!" She turned around and kicked the cabinet, hurting her foot, but it was worth it. "Why did you drag me away?" she swirled around to glare at Diamond. "I could have taken her." She not only outweighed the harlot, but Joelle had a lot of anger that would fuel a girl-fight.

"My priority is to you," he said gruffly.

And though Diamond meant that professionally, Joelle's belly swirled with heat at the implication that she would ever be a priority romantically to someone.

Despite his rough edges and blunt tongue, he was a devastatingly handsome man. If he put the same intensity into a relationship as he did his job, he would make some woman an exemplary partner.

And now she felt a slither of anger for a selfish reason.

She was spending too much time around him.

She was a job to Diamond, nothing more.

Switching her mind back to a safer topic, she knew she'd have to talk to her father. If nothing else, this embarrassment must have woken him up to what he was doing and the trouble his actions caused his family.

"Is it possible for us to intercept her?" She pushed off the unit, intent on pulling open the door.

A brawny arm caught Joelle around the waist, bringing her back into his space. "No, that isn't happening."

She blinked. "You can't tell me no."

"Just did, babe. You're not getting near the woman again. She shouldn't have been able to get that close to you in the first fucking place."

"She needs to know this has to stop; following my father here is crazy. To what end? She was dripping with rubies. If that woman is hurting for money, I'm a virgin."

She saw his Adam's apple bob with a swallow.

"There's shit you don't know about her. You stay away from her, Joelle. I mean it. She won't have the chance to get near you again because I'll be there. But if it happens, you walk away, do you understand?"

"What does that mean?" She thought it was more than just a broken heart. Despite her father's discretion, Joelle had an uncanny ability to spot things others overlooked. She overheard stuff she wasn't meant to hear. The situation was unsettling, especially the decision to hire bikers for protection. Why not call the police? Why not use official bodyguards?

Because bikers would do things an official lawman couldn't?

"It means be careful."

He was avoiding telling her, and that made her mad, too.

"You've been around us enough now to see this isn't right. And you keep something serious from me? That woman was feet away from my mother, Diamond. She could have said anything to her, done anything to her."

"No, she couldn't. We had eyes on her."

"Not when she approached me, you didn't," she accused tightly. Diamond's expression grew even more severe.

"This fucking party," he hissed quietly through his teeth, again dragging a hand over his hair, and she realized he did it when he was frustrated. "People got in my way. I couldn't get to you without mowing them down."

Now, they were throwing glares back and forth in a silent battle of wills.

Joelle opened her mouth to speak, but he pressed a finger on her lips.

With a serious expression, he advanced until he loomed like a centurion, leaving the room devoid of air as she strained her neck to look up at him.

The surrounding space grew syrup-thick with conflict. It snapped and coiled. Her chest rose and fell rapidly with forced inhales.

"Bluebell, shut it," he groaned, suddenly gripping the hair at her nape to control her head and prevent her from moving. Her neck tipped back, and then thick, perfect lips slammed down on hers before she knew what was happening.

On some level, Joelle knew it was a tactic to derail her rushing thoughts or to transfer the anger onto him through the medium of mouths.

But all Joelle felt was a kiss that melted her into a puddle. It rushed heat to all her erogenous zones until she was a woman made up of electricity and screaming desire.

Joelle groaned and fisted Diamond's shirt. His body was so warm her fingers ached to feel his skin directly on hers. If he planned for a brief lip collision before withdrawing, he would need to pry her off because she leaned in and opened her mouth. That's when she felt him grunt, turning his head slightly to the side. Diamond must have changed his mind as his lips started moving on hers, kissing her with abandonment.

Whatever flickering attraction had been between them, it ignited in that tiny room and set fire to every bit of surface around them as she clung to Diamond and went along with how he plundered her mouth in wicked, delicious ways. Flicking his tongue over hers, she mewled for more until he gave her more, and the pleasure washed over her.

Never had a kiss felt so right and so *addictive*.

Perfect kisses didn't happen. Not to her.

But this was utter perfection from the get-go, and she moaned into his mouth, swallowing his grunt as she pressed closer. Then she felt his hands on her outer thighs, gripping her tightly before his hands stroked up her sides and took hold of her head.

Heat exploded in her core. She felt more turned on from only a kiss than she had tumbling around in bed with someone.

His control was wholly exciting.

No one had ever just taken a kiss from Joelle before.

They'd always asked permission. Bland politeness, nothing like Diamond, just taking her mouth in his rough way.

He only touched her in a single spot on her bare nape, and Joelle felt ready to rip his clothes off. It was like his fingers had zapped her with static energy, engulfing her in hormonal flames.

The pressure from his hands in her hair and being devoured like she was Diamond's last meal had Joelle practically grinding against him. Their height difference was apparent until she was suddenly hoisted into the air and deposited onto the cabinet. He hadn't even detangled their mouths to do it.

Joelle would be impressed if not for the distracting tongue in her mouth.

Shards of pleasure zipped through her.

Diamond's kiss ensnared her focus and demanded her devotion and submission. And with a moan, she wanted to give him everything.

His free hand moved from her throat, then down the front of her dress. She instinctively widened her legs, and the material pushed up her thighs, totally exposing herself. If he were to look down, he'd see her cotton panties for sure.

Joelle brought Diamond closer by his shirt, and he stepped into the space her open legs had made. He bent over her, using his hand to angle her head back so he could feast and steal her air.

He was devouring her like she was his favorite dessert.

Had a kiss ever felt this wild? This freeing?

She felt weakened by desire, yet empowered by his passion.

Suddenly, the crush she'd been suppressing for days hit her like a ton of bricks.

Within seconds, Diamond had ended their kiss long before she was ready to relinquish his gorgeous mouth, leaving her dizzy from his rapid release.

Whereas he looked calm as he stared into her eyes, she felt reckless and ready to have sex with him right here.

He maintained his grasp on her nape, and without the distraction of his kisses, she felt increasingly self-conscious under his watchful eyes.

"You're not gonna call that guy, Joelle. He's a fucking tool." He rasped, still too close to her mouth, that her brain hadn't recovered yet, and her body had developed a new craving for a biker who could kiss like it was his vocation.

What did he say?

Oh. It took her a moment to catch up. Was he talking about Trent?

He rose to his height then and scrubbed a hand through his blond hair. The silver chain around his thick neck was especially bright against his tanned skin, and Joelle's mouth watered.

She had to get it together and not stare at the guy like a lovesick fool just because they'd kissed.

A kiss he'd used to redirect her anger.

Which had worked.

"You don't know Trent." Though his eyes flared, he didn't issue her any forbidden rules like she'd wished he would.

"I'm not following you around on dates."

"You'd have to. That's in the job description." She needled. When Diamond dropped his gaze, his eyes heating, she remembered her legs were still open at the knees, and she quickly snapped them shut and slid down to the ground. Joelle swiftly turned, her gaze fixed on the mirror, assessing the damage to her face.

She looked thoroughly kissed.

Her rosy cheeks, fading lipstick, and bruised, swollen lips told a story. She looked over to find his eyes narrowed, fixed on her like a hawk. In that moment, his savagery intensified. She boldly used her thumb to remove her lipstick from his lower lip.

"You have me all over your mouth."

His answering grunt went directly to her pussy.

Even if he hadn't meant it or wanted to do it, Joelle couldn't help but admit that it had been the most unforgettable kiss of her life.

After making herself presentable as best as she could, she faced him.

"I'm ready to go home."

Diamond only nodded and opened the door.

"I should find Trent to tell him goodbye."

"No," he growled behind her, and Joelle's spirits lifted slightly as she walked out before him, swaying her hips in hopes his eyes were fixed on her ass.

She waited until he got in step with her, feeling protected and every bit as womanly as his hand brushed against her waist. Every woman in the place was checking out Diamond.

The social climbers were jealous of Joelle being the woman Diamond was with, making her smile bright and festive.

She spoke without glancing at him, allowing him to guide her with a hand on her lower back. "I like your name, River. And you kiss pretty nice for a biker, too."

She heard him growl, low and warning.

It made her smile even more noticeable.

## Diamond

What was that song about kissing a girl and liking it?

It probably didn't have the same connotation as Diamond was thinking, but fuck him if Joelle's taste wasn't still all over his mouth two days after the party.

The taste of her had been incredible. He couldn't get it out of his head, or forget the feel of her mouth moving underneath his and how she moaned for more.

And he couldn't stop thinking about her, though he knew he shouldn't.

If he had gone there, it would have made all his past poor decisions seem like small potatoes.

Diamond didn't mind making the occasional wrong decision. It was par for the course. You never knew they were the wrong decisions until you came out the other side. But getting involved with Joelle Snow was a mistake he'd knowingly walk into.

The attraction was one thing.

Utter fucking fascination was another.

The first he could ignore.

The second had a tight grip on his dick and wouldn't let go.

Parking his baby girl around the back of the mansion, he lifted a hand when the gardener waved at him. He'd been here too fucking often if the staff recognized him. The back door was always open, so he walked in through the mudroom and into the kitchen, where the staff were busy.

It was his longest security job. They usually only lasted one night, maybe two. It was a major headache. He didn't feel like it was worth his time to guard people like Judge Snow, and two nights ago, he was ready to quit and advise the guy to hire bodyguards who specialized in working with celebrities and would happily take his money to follow him around.

Then, the redheaded woman showed up and got in Joelle's face. From across the room, he saw the demented sneer and taunting smirk. The fucking crowd got in his way, and he'd felt almost feral to get to Joelle.

As he'd been escorting her away to calm her down, his guy was in Diamond's ear over the comms, telling him when he'd escorted the redheaded woman outside, only for five men to pile out of a car. The loony bitch had brought the Irish mob with her.

His blood had run cold because those fuckers had no off switch. Shooting the place up wouldn't have mattered to them, even with all the security and surveillance. The Irish were feral yet motivated by family loyalty.

If the woman had spun a scorned tale about her failed relationship with the Judge, the Irish most likely had put a vendetta against all the Snows.

Any thought of ditching the job fled Diamond's mind.

He didn't give a shit about Snow, but knowing Joelle was in the mix of that danger, he couldn't walk away now. Just the threat of the Irish mafia using her as part of a revenge attack left him unhinged.

Diamond trekked through the mansion and was about to knock on the Judge's office door when he stopped because someone was having a heated discussion. He rested a shoulder on the wall and waited to see what he could hear.

If he hadn't already recognized her voice, the jolt of electricity through his sternum would have told him who was behind that door.

And from the sounds of it, Joelle was angry as fuck.

"Joelle. This is none of your business." Her father told her.

"Not my business?" her voice went comically higher, and Diamond's lips twitched. After the other night, when he'd witnessed her almost going berserk, if not for him redirecting her anger, he knew the woman had a temper underneath the rainbow colors. "You made it all our businesses when you cheated on my mother."

"You'll watch your mouth."

"I'll watch nothing. I'm sick of keeping my mouth shut, keeping the peace, and always saying the right thing while you do whatever you want. And then expect us to fall in line. That's not how a family works, father."

Diamond only ever heard her call him father. Never dad. The affection in this family was scarce. He'd seen warmer ice cubes.

"She got in my face. *Your woman.* She's been waiting to meet me. How nice, huh? Maybe we could invite her for Christmas dinner."

"Don't be facetious, Joelle. Your antics aren't amusing."

"Yes, because I'm rolling around on the floor laughing." She snapped, and Diamond's lips twitched again. Little mouthy brat. "How long is this going to go on for? I don't want bodyguards."

He straightened, and his eyes narrowed.

"Has that biker been inappropriate?"

Was having his tongue halfway down her throat and groping her all over while he stood within the apex of her thighs, feeling how hot she was against his hard dick, considered inappropriate?

"No, of course, he hasn't." Aw, Bluebell was such a little liar. Diamond smiled again. Maybe she wasn't so blue blood after all. They'd made out like crazy in a wash closet, so he knew she had a naughty streak.

A bad girl wannabe he couldn't grapple with, even if she made water pool in his mouth when he thought about touching all her tempting soft curves again.

"You will tell me immediately if that man does or says anything to upset you."

A growl of irritation festered in Diamond's throat, listening to the holier-than-thou prick malign him even though he begged for Diamond's help, because he knew he was the best damn thug in this town.

"Oh, for god's sake, do you hear yourself?" huffed Joelle. "You're the one who's screwed up here, Father. Don't redirect the focus onto someone you invited into our home to clean up *your* mess. Diamond is more the gentleman than you ever could be right now. I'm so angry with you."

"Joelle." Was that hurt in the Judge's voice? Diamond would have laid good money on the guy being a cyborg.

The argument went back and forth. The Judge was unsympathetic, disregarding her feelings and ordering her to be quiet.

"I'm moving out in the New Year." She announced.

"Don't start this again."

"I'm almost thirty. I can no longer play the role of the obedient daughter, living at home to maintain the ideal American image for the voters."

"Your mother will be devastated if you leave."

"I'm sure she'll be horrified if I tell her about the Irish woman approaching me."

*Good for you, Bluebell.* Diamond sent his silent praise.

"You know what is sickening?" asked Joelle. "For thirty years, you've put your career ahead of everyone. You were the DA, now a Judge. Next is the supreme court of justice. Everything is still being put before your family. Including your selfishness by screwing around and not caring where that muck lands. It's on us, Father, if you're not that self-aware." Diamond heard how her voice cracked with emotion. He pushed off the wall again and felt his instincts to protect her roar.

"Joelle! You will not make these foolish decisions while you're emotional. We'll discuss it again when you've calmed down."

The door wrenched open, and Joelle fled the office, slamming it behind her, only to nearly run right into Diamond's chest. He caught her by the top of her arms.

"Oh," she gasped, looking up at him with her large eyes filled with un-spilled tears. He wanted to protect her, not just because of his job, but because he was a man holding a beautiful, upset woman. "Sorry." She said.

And then she burst into tears, flinging herself into Diamond's arms.

He was so stunned that his arms latched around her, instinctively cradling her to his chest.

Diamond had to remember that Joelle was upset, and he shouldn't enjoy how well she fit against him. He would be an even bigger jerk than her father.

He steered her away from the office before Snow came out, and Diamond was forced to punch the asshole in the face for hurting his daughter's feelings.

At least twenty rooms lined both sides of the long hallway. He tried the third door, which opened into a bathroom that looked big enough to hold a football team. He closed them in and turned the lock while still holding Joelle close, skating his hand down her back in a soothing motion.

His heart surged into his throat when she only clung tighter. Her arms were wrapped around his waist, and her face hid in his shirt.

"Baby," he started, cradling the back of her head. "You've got one minute to cry it all out, or I'm gonna have to go back there and kick his teeth in for making you cry this hard."

He meant every word.

It wouldn't take much of an excuse to hit the Judge. Diamond would forget the exorbitant amount Snow was paying the club, and he'd put the man through a fucking wall, and he'd enjoy doing it.

Joelle's head whipped up, and Diamond's first thought was no one should look that cute while tears gushed down their red blotchy cheeks.

She was adorable in a way he'd never found a woman before.

"You'd do that?" she hiccupped.

"Just give me the word."

Unable to help himself, he reached to brush the tears from underneath her eyes. A woman as bright as her should never cry with sadness.

"Thanks, I needed that." She stepped out of his arms and grabbed a tissue from a box on the bathroom counter.

What was with them and bathrooms lately? Was Diamond tapping into a new fetish?

She wet the towel and dabbed it on her face, cleaning up the mascara underneath her eyes.

"That sounded like some argument you were having."

"You heard?" she frowned, embarrassed. "He's been dodging me for two days. It all just came tumbling out. Nothing will change." She shrugged.

"But you got it off your chest, Bluebell. That's what counts."

"Yeah," she brightened, "I feel better for it."

Diamond leaned on the counter, watching her while she kept dabbing at her face, though he reckoned she was already perfect. He was in no rush to move.

"Were you serious about moving out?"

"You listened to the whole thing, huh?" she half-smiled, glancing at him. "Yes, I meant it. But I've meant it every year I've said it. I can't keep putting off my life because my father needs a picture-perfect lie to showcase to the world. We've never been that. All I am is Judge Snow's daughter. I want to be Joelle."

"Who is Joelle?" he asked, and she frowned again, facing him.

"I guess I'll find out." Diamond couldn't take his eyes off her. She seemed so bummed out, and he just wanted to fix things. Unsure why he felt compelled. He hated seeing her so sad. Nobody should have to sacrifice their own life for someone else's shitty ambition.

Not long later, he drove her to the brownstone house he had stalked, only to realize it was her therapist, not her boyfriend. She appeared happier when she came out. So, naturally, he had to stop and buy her an ice cream cone. Fuck if he knew why, but he liked when she smiled. His chest burned as he watched the tip of her tongue flick around the melting ice cream.

Off duty that night, he kicked it back in the clubhouse. Reno came out of the kitchen with his two hands laden with cupcakes.

"Oh, man, did you bake?" he shouted across to Diamond, who nodded in return. "This is the shit. I'm taking some home for my girls."

He used to bake in secret at home, but when he started baking in the clubhouse, they ribbed him good-naturedly. Yet they still fell on his baked creations like hungry vultures.

He couldn't settle tonight, so he pulled out all his pans and made the lemon squares Scarlett enjoyed, followed by a triple batch of cupcakes.

Baking helped him relax.

It focused his mind for a few hours. And tonight, it had been inundated with racy thoughts about a certain blue-haired bohemian.

Once at home, he relaxed on the couch with a beer he hadn't touched yet.

Throughout the morning, he couldn't shake the memory of Joelle running into his arms for solace despite his recent behavior towards her.

He'd made some wrong assumptions based on his dislike of her father and all the bullshit rich ego he brought with him.

He'd been a standoffish jerk with Joelle because the attraction had hit him square in the solar plexus, and he knew he couldn't act on it.

Now he had a hard dick most days when he knew he was going to be around her.

It made little sense.

Wealthy socialites were the last women he'd ever go for.

But he couldn't remember an attraction this strong before.

He needed to get it out of his system so he could think straight again, and not have every thought filthier than the last about kidnapping Joelle and swallowing all of her pleasured cries.

Diamond contemplated jerking off. But he had to see Joelle tomorrow, and that would make him the biggest creeper if he pumped his come into his hand, knowing it was because of her. He had already leveled up by stalking Joelle while his men were watching over her.

He sighed, drank half the bottle, and was about to go to bed when his phone rang.

"Hello?"

"Diamond?"

"Bluebell? What's wrong?" he shot forward in his seat. Any tiredness he'd been feeling vanished.

She sighed. "I got your number from my father's office. I'm sorry to call you so late. Did I wake you?"

"What's wrong, Bluebell?" he asked again.

She was silent for a moment. "Nothing. I was just lonely."

It was like her voice reached down the phone line and crushed his heart, and made his dick pulse in his sweatpants. His reaction was visceral, aligning his thoughts and pumping blood through his veins faster.

Kidnap her.

Own her.

Bathe in her screams.

His thoughts vined out of control, growing weeds of possessive destruction.

"Would you talk to me for a while?"

The vulnerable sweetness in her voice affected Diamond like a hot caress.

He couldn't have the woman for many reasons.

There was a power dynamic in overseeing her safety.

They were also from different social worlds.

But he couldn't—wouldn't—turn her away. And he didn't want to dig into the reasons for that.

"Sure, Bluebell." He answered, scraping a hand through his hair. "Talk to me."

## Diamond

Despite wanting to talk, Joelle remained silent.

Diamond sensed something was bothering Joelle, making him antsy about fixing whatever it was.

*She'd have no problems if you kidnapped her.* His vicious thoughts whispered. He'd care for her in all the ways he'd never craved. There was a constant thirst to be near her.

He enjoyed listening to her voice. She always had much to say, more than any other woman he'd ever known, but he'd never minded the rambling. He found out all kinds of info that way. For example, he knew she enjoyed sunnier days rather than the snow. She detested snow. He also knew her favorite meal was mac and cheese made with bacon bits and real gruyere, no fake cheese. And her passion in life was painting.

Within the short time he'd known Joelle Snow, he discovered her forgetfulness, clumsiness, and dry, sarcastic sense of humor. She would often appear lonely and lost in her thoughts. Diamond had accumulated plenty of poignant details about her. Still, he couldn't figure out the reason behind her silence when she was usually the woman who filled the space with endless words.

"Bluebell, you're not saying a lot." He coaxed and heard her sigh.

"Sorry. I don't know what to say now that I've called you. I shouldn't have. I wanted to hear a voice."

Instead of talking to the people in her house, she'd contacted her surly bodyguard. Why did that break his fucking heart open?

"You wanted to hear my voice." He said what she wasn't saying.

After a second, Joelle answered. "Yeah, I guess I wanted that."

"Did you talk to your father after I dropped you off at home?"

"Do you mind if we don't talk about him, Diamond? He makes me mad, and I'm trying to let this red wine mellow me out."

"You're drinking?"

"Just a tiny bit. What were you doing before I called?"

"I was about to head to bed."

"Darn." She cursed. "Sorry. I'll let you go."

"Stop apologizing. I wouldn't talk to you if I didn't want to."

"Okay," she said after a second. A smile in her voice. And he liked the sound of that much better than her being sad over a prick father.

"Hey, Diamond?"

"Yeah?"

"Does anyone call you River?"

He half smiled. Bet she'd been curious about his name ever since he gave it to the simpering twat at the party. Diamond had felt the first twinge of jealousy as he'd watched her from a distance while the guy all but lapped up her beauty with his drooling tongue hanging out. The snap decision to interrupt their conversation wasn't something he regretted.

"Not really. My parents when I see 'em. Or Axel, if I fuck up."

He heard her chuckling, and then there was a rustling sound as if she were beneath sheets.

*Fuck.* Diamond hoped Joelle wasn't in her bed. He could have done without that picture in his mind.

"I can't see you fucking up. You seem competent in everything you do."

It was a nice compliment, but he was far from perfect. He screwed up like most men.

There was another shuffle, unmistakably the sound of sheets. *Fuck his weakness.* He wiped his face and grabbed the beer, downing it to cool off.

"Joelle, are you in bed?" he had to know.

"I am." And then. "Diamond..."

Just the way she said his name, he sensed what was coming next because the lower half of his body went stiff until he had to use the heel of his palm to grind against his erection. She'd only said his name in that smoke-filled way, and his body conjured filthy, wrong ideas.

He silently begged her not to say whatever was on her mind.

According to the old ladies, he didn't pick up on female flirting cues, but his body only heard his name out of Joelle's lips, and the signals were blaring in his balls.

"If I asked you what you're wearing, would you tell me?"

She fucking went there, didn't she? Diamond swallowed a groan around the pulsation of lust in his throat and lower in his gut.

Joelle hadn't called for a regular conversation. The naughty girl wanted to talk about sex.

Diamond was not a strong-willed man.

Why would some higher being test him right now? He'd grappled with his principles for days.

He wanted her, that much was clear. In a terrible way, and he was tempted to say *fuck it* and have her.

"You're playing a dangerous game, Bluebell." Even to his ears, his voice sounded like he'd been inhaling pure sex.

Her laugh was soft, teasing, and husky, and it went right down to his already too-hard dick. She had a voice made to moan during sex. Their kiss had scorched him to the bones and made him think about fucking her on every surface he could find, treating her rough and sweet until she was a sopping mess. Now he had to contend with knowing she was in bed and horny as fuck *for him*.

"I don't mind games, especially if we both win."

"Is that what you want? For us both to win?"

"Am I being honest?" She sounded vulnerable, like she couldn't decide whether to speak her mind or brush it off.

"Babe, never tell me lies." He issued gruffly. Fuck his rogue tongue. He had to bail on this conversation before things got out of hand, but he clung to his phone and didn't attempt to hang up on her.

Not when he could hear her little puffs of air, imagining how heavier her breathing would get if he were between her thighs, lapping her until she sobbed his name.

By god, he'd make her scream the whole place down if he got his mouth between her pale thighs.

Diamond felt beads of sweat on his forehead, and he held his breath, waiting for her reply.

"I'd ask you to keep talking, just say any words in your deep voice so I... so I can." She paused for a second time, and everything in Diamond's oversized body came alive. His nerve endings buzzed on her frequency, picking up what she wasn't vocalizing. His skin got so hot he thought he might have caught five cases of the flu. And the arousal, *the fucking arousal*, never felt this strong before as he shifted his hips in the air just for the slightest relief from his shaft.

This woman was killing him in the sweetest way possible.

"So you can what, Bluebell? Say it. Don't stop now."

Yeah, he wasn't backing this train into the station. He couldn't even if he tried to. Her voice and vulnerability had grabbed hold of Diamond by the balls, by the throat, by the very fiber of his desire, and she wouldn't let go.

When all he heard was her light panting, there was no way he was letting her shut down now. She'd opened this door, and Diamond was willing to kick it in to get the answer.

"So I can get off to your sexy voice."

Diamond chuckled. Hot white lust swirled in his gut. The all-consuming lust that didn't come along often, the kind that made a man insane if he tried to ignore it.

He'd been turned on for days, ignoring it until he snapped at everyone. Even his men had noticed. It was Joelle's fault. She walked around in those sexy outfits and drove him wild. She glanced his way, and he wanted to put his hands all over her. She existed, and he got hard.

He could easily go to the clubhouse in minutes and be balls deep in a warm, welcoming body. But the thought of getting that empty climax didn't fill him with excitement as it once would have. Even though being attracted to Joelle Snow pissed him off, he hadn't detached himself from the situation. If anything, he'd put himself in her path even more because that pulsing desire was a drug, and he craved it even more.

"Please, don't make fun of me."

"I wouldn't do that," he rasped. And between one breath and the next, Diamond made one of his poor decisions again. Shooting forward in his seat, he almost hunched over his phone like a desperate man. "I want you to do something for me."

"What's that?" she was all breathy.

Was she already touching herself?

*Fuck*. Those lucky fingers. Images stacked up behind Diamond's closed eyelids. How Joelle would brazenly widen her legs to get to the wetness between, frantically fingering her swollen clit, chasing those electric zaps of pleasure, making them grow until she couldn't stand it and would have to push two fingers into her tight little cunt for relief.

Joelle was so tightly wound that Diamond had no problem picturing her as a livewire when she came. She'd let go with abundance.

"Diamond." She broke into his filthy thoughts. "What did you want me to do? Is it to hang up and stop embarrassing you?"

He chuckled again. "No, nothing like that. First, I want you to tell me what color you're wearing."

"Red." She answered instantly.

"A nightgown?"

"Erm. No. Only panties."

She was talking to him on the phone, curled up in her vanilla-smelling bed, wearing only panties.

RIP his dick.

"Red," he repeated. "That's nice." It was passionate. And it suited her.

"You never told me what you're wearing."

"Gray sweatpants."

"Shut the front fucking door. No, you are not!" she shrieked in his ear, and Diamond winced. His hearing would not recover.

"Babe, I wouldn't lie about what I'm wearing."

"Oh my god, slut gray sweats." She moaned, low, sultry, and a blatant invitation to sin with her. "You made it worse, Diamond."

"What did I make worse?"

"The ache. It won't go away."

Her words hit him hard because it was a sweet sexual pain, and all she wanted was for him to make it better.

"This is what I want you to do. Are you listening, Joelle?"

"Yes." She breathed, and he could tell from that one exhaled word that Joelle was already touching herself. He'd give anything to see her legs spread and both hands between them, one holding her soaked lips open while the other one strummed the pleasure of where it hurt the most.

"You're going to make that fire you're feeling into a fucking inferno." He considered turning the phone call into a video chat to see the bloom of color on the prime points of her cheeks, but thought she'd prefer the anonymity of this instead. "You'll slip a hand into your sinful red panties for me, Joelle."

She gasped, and it touched him all over.

"You're doing that already, babe, aren't you?"

"Maybe..."

"No lies, Bluebell."

"I was only touching the crotch of my underwear because I'm aching there."

Fucking hell. Diamond tasted blood, and he realized he was biting the inside of his cheek.

"Well, now get inside those sinning red panties, Joelle, and feel how nice it is, how slippery wet you can make yourself."

"*Oh, god.*" She moaned right into his ear like she was sprawled on the couch with him. He'd fucking devour her if she were. He wouldn't leave a drop behind. If she was wet now, it would be nothing to what his tongue would do to Joelle.

"That's right, you tease all that ache to the surface. Do you feel it building until you can't stand it?"

"Yeah," she panted now. "I can, *Diamond*."

She sharply exhaled through several minutes, and he listened like the dirtiest pervert, talking her through it until he had to grip the edge of the couch with his free hand every time she whimpered his name in that pleading way, which got him harder than a spike.

"Here's what's next, babe. You're messy wet now, aren't you?"

"Very. Yes."

He could picture it. The dirty pig he was, he wanted snapshots of her, exactly how she was in her current, horny state. He wanted to see her glistening with her come and his. He'd frost her from top to bottom.

"That's so fucking hot, babe. You're slicked up and ready. But don't come."

"What?" she shrieked. "You must be crazy."

Diamond chuckled at her disobedience. She was like a kid chasing the ice cream truck, but he wasn't letting her have that treat yet. He wanted her to wait, to scream her way through needing it until she thought she might burn alive.

"Gentle your fingers, Joelle. I know you're all hot and swollen with your tight cunt so empty, needing to be filled with something so thick it will hurt at first."

"Oh, don't say that." her little whimpers were straight-up heroin in his blood, and Diamond gulped the sounds like he might die if he didn't.

He could barely catch a breath, and he'd wanted to stroke off for the past half hour, resisting only because she wasn't here to take it into her mouth, on her gorgeous tits, or jetted inside of her pussy.

He saw the irony of knowing what he shouldn't be doing but doing it anyway and wanting it more than his next heartbeat.

"It's time to slow those fingers, Bluebell."

Her pleading whimper was sweet agony. "But I was right there."

He couldn't stop her if she came, but he wanted to control her orgasms, to see how she'd beg for them.

"And you'll get it, I promise."

Her sex sounds went through him like fire. "Do you mean it?"

Why was that hot as fuck?

He'd dabbled with orgasm control in the past, but nothing at a distance. Joelle could easily hang up and come her brains out, but she listened to him when he told her to make it teeter on the edge for as long as she could stand it.

"Trust me," he rasped into the phone. "Now, keep playing and back off when you feel it getting too close, babe. Can you do that for me? I want you so wet your fingers slide around your tight little clit. And if you put anything inside you, it's only fingers, right? No toys."

"I didn't know you were cruel." She whined so hot he had to swallow his groan.

"Joelle, are you listening, baby?"

"Yes. I'm listening, but it's hard."

He heeled over his cock. Tell him about it.

"I'm hanging up now, but you'll get to come the next time you hear me."

"No, you can't go now!"

Her hunger grabbed him by the throat. She sounded so desperate, so fucking starved for it.

"Didn't I say to trust me?"

She gave him confirmation.

Diamond didn't know if he could trust himself.

Not with Joelle.

She was like the out-of-reach candy.

The forbidden fruit.

She exceeded his league by miles.

The untouchable tiara-wearing princess.

But he wasn't considering the logical reasons as he hung up on her. He then jackknifed off the couch, grabbed his keys, and shoved his feet into his workout sneakers. The snowfall meant he had to take the Ford 150, but he made good time to the Snow mansion with the empty roads between their places.

If the butler thought it was weird how Diamond was at their house well after midnight, wearing only his workout clothes, his face didn't show it. "Left my wallet upstairs." He lied.

"Of course, Sir. Come right in. Is there anything I can do for you?"

"Nope."

Nothing would have deterred Diamond at that moment.

And that's what made him feel so damn dangerous.

His one-track mind took him through the house maze, following the path he'd walked for days now, up the long staircase to the wing where a woman was waiting for his call but was about to get something more personal.

He just hoped Joelle was ready.

## Joelle

She was mortified he'd abruptly ended their call.

It would be next to impossible to face Diamond tomorrow. She'd have to come up with an excuse why she didn't need a security detail. Maybe an out-of-town trip to the moon. It was so awkward confessing to a guy she was horny and wanted phone sex, but then have that guy tap out before it got good.

There ought to be a law that said a man couldn't get a woman all wet and worked up and then drop her right before the finish. If Joelle weren't so sexually frustrated, she would have called Diamond and — The bedroom door came open so fast that Joelle muffled a scream behind her hand. She hadn't even heard someone walking into her suite. It could have easily been a murderer!

Instead, it was a hot-eyed biker whose stride hadn't faltered as he closed the distance between them.

Instantly, white-hot arousal pounded through Joelle. Feeling his magnetism always swept the air out of her at first, before it settled into a lovely wave of desire. But on the heels of that came her mortification. Thank goodness she still didn't have a hand between her legs, but she was almost naked, and she quickly covered her breasts with her hands.

"Don't do that. You're fucking spectacular," he growled, and for some inexplicable reason, she dropped both hands on her lap, letting him look his fill.

Several things she took in all at once.

How imposing Diamond was. He was an exceptionally appealing figure with his tattoos, olive skin, and daunting dimensions.

And he hadn't been lying.

The gray sweatpants were prominent on his legs, hugging low on his waist, and *dear god*, no one could miss the colossal baseball thick pole poking out of his groin.

She instantly slaked her tongue over her dry lips as Diamond's eyes flared, watching her like a hungry lion.

"Did you come?" he rasped. Making her face flame bright pink.

"You hung up on me," she accused, for lack of something else to say.

"*Did you come?*"

"No," she answered. "I stopped, no longer in the mood."

"I told you I'd make you come the next time you heard my voice."

Diamond's eyes were so low-lidded that they were practically closed. The sex appeal oozed out of him like steam, and Joelle was having a hard time keeping her lungs working.

The man was too much.

Extremely tempting.

His presence made her head swim and her pussy in a constant state of spasm.

"I thought you'd changed your mind."

He stepped forward to the end of her bed, making Joelle's neck arch to look him in the eye.

"No. I wanted to see you in person. Touch yourself, Joelle."

She inhaled as though it was coming as a surprise what Diamond was asking, as though she hadn't been masturbating for the last however long to the sound of his dirty talking on the phone. But the phone had given her some anonymity. This was in person, and her skin burned with every hot-blooded emotion.

"Joelle. Touch yourself for me," he grated hoarsely. The look in his eye was arousal itself. "The entire ride over here, I've been hard, wanting it. Needing to see it happen. You smell amazing." He inhaled hard enough to inflate his chest. "And you look so fucking sexy, all flushed and aching for the orgasm. You need it, don't you?"

She breathed the answer.

No nagging thoughts in her mind warned her that this was a regret in the making.

The pulsing desire was too strong to ignore.

So Joelle situated herself more comfortably, inching her legs apart, bracing her feet on the soft cushioned ottoman at the bottom of the bed. As she crept a hand over her belly, he hissed, and though the move wasn't intimate, she knew he liked what he saw.

He liked her curvier body. And that flooded her with endorphins.

She may not have had a stash of feminine tricks, but she could sense when a man was attracted to her, and it radiated from Diamond's entire frame. Which, in turn, climbed her lust until she was humming low from the back of her throat and smiling shyly as she inched closer to the crotch of her damp panties.

"*Fuck.*" He hissed. Grabbing himself.

Jeez. Diamond had no problem showing her the shape of his cock as he outlined himself and made her eyelids lower with yearning.

He was monstrous. More significant than she'd had before, and she sucked on her lower lip as she thought about how he'd feel in her mouth. She was dying to see it outside of the sluttiest gray sweatpants.

"*Joelle*, you're taking too long. *Touch yourself.*" He rasped, moving closer until his knee touched her foot; he was practically up close with her downstairs business. Thank god she'd taken an everything shower earlier and was freshly plucked, woman-scaped, and moisturized. Usually, winter called for the all-over bear-theme. No leg shaving and no de-bushing herself. What was the point if she wasn't sleeping with someone? But since Diamond came into her life, she'd been trimming the goodies, *just in case*.

It was brilliant forward-thinking on her part, especially since the hot biker was standing over her now with sex in his eyes.

"Why are you rushing me?"

He sprang forward, and because he pressed both hands on the edge of the bed, his nose almost brushed hers. Joelle was so dazzled by his eyes.

"Because this is all we have, Joelle. This moment right now, and I wanna get to it. It's all I've thought about. The thought of you stroking it out while I watch you, while I instruct you, is fucking plaguing my mind."

God, he was right.

This was all they could have.

How would dating a biker work? There were so many obstacles and differences in their way. Her not-so-tolerant father would have plenty to say about it since he'd already cautioned her about Diamond.

"Do you want this?"

"Yes," she answered instantly. "I called you, remember?"

"Fuck, yeah, you did. Blew my mind." He said, and he reached down to widen her legs to the width he wanted, leaving Joelle wide open to his eyes.

He expressed his approval with a flared expression, a licked tongue over his lips, and a dirty groan.

"Now let me blow yours, Joelle."

"*Please*." was all she could say around the barrage of lust taking down her internal network.

Diamond stroked over her bare leg, teasing fingertips to her inner thigh, making her shudder, but his travels didn't stop there. He went over her belly and up between her breasts. He palmed each one, tweaking her nipples until they were so hard and puckered it felt like a physical, delicious pain.

"You're going to come for me repeatedly, baby."

Oh, that sounded like heaven.

"Now, get your hand into those panties before I blow right here."

Joelle chuckled. She felt powerful for making him sound so unhinged. So, following his instructions, her fingers disappeared past the lacy red material, and started touching herself. She was already so primed that she jolted, moaning from her throat.

"Diamond." She whispered. His lips drove down on hers, and all thoughts fled the building.

"Open your lips for me, Joelle. Invite me in."

It sounded so sexual, so sordid that when she took a fast inhale, Diamond rushed into her mouth and brought his sinful tongue with him. She moaned at the delicious contact and joined a war she didn't know she was craving until the sexiest man alive was kissing the hell out of her while she rubbed her clit.

"Are you going to make me wait again?"

It wasn't the answer she wanted when he laughed lightly against her mouth and told her, "It'll be so sweet, Bluebell."

She needed it *now*. She relished the sensation of Diamond's teeth against her lower lip as she exhaled. "I'll come without you telling me to."

"Go on then." He dared, and his eyes darkened, turning her on even more.

Why did she want to listen to him? Why did she crave his permission?

She could come if she wanted to. She didn't need him to tell her when she could orgasm.

But that's what she did.

When Diamond rested his knee on the ottoman and leaned in, his gaze dropped between their bodies, watching her frantically ply pressure to where she ached the most. He talked the whole time.

"You feel how wet you are?"

"Mmhm," she bit her lip.

The moment was palpable. All sexual. Private and theirs. If only for right now.

"It's only going to get better."

"It would be better if you let me come."

His laugh was rusty and went right between her legs.

Time after time, as Joelle got to the edge, Diamond told her to back off.

By the fourth denial, she was drenched in sweat and hurling curses at him and his ancestors.

"This isn't what I signed up for, River Durant." She puffed out air.

"Tell me you aren't shaking all over, Bluebell." He said, dropping to his knees on the carpet before her. "You can't, can you? Sweet, trembling girl."

His confidence shot a zing of pleasure through her, and she couldn't look away as he helped peel the underwear down her legs. Leaving Joelle utterly nude while he was still clothed.

He hissed at the sight of her, and she felt like a helium balloon, like she could float to the ceiling with the lustful way he was staring between her legs.

"It's not fair you're still dressed."

"It's better this way."

She frowned. "Why?"

"If I get naked, my dick will be in you in three seconds, baby. And we can't do that."

She liked those kinds of numbers. In three seconds, he could make her ache disappear.

She whined this time, and he smiled so attractively, but the sound morphed into a moan when Diamond ran his thumb along her slit and brought it to his mouth.

"One fuck wouldn't be enough, Joelle. You know it, I know it. I can make you come so many fucking times, though. You ready?"

"I've been ready for ages." She snapped, and he dared to laugh again.

It was so intimate having a man touching her between the legs, but it felt right because it was Diamond, and she didn't feel an ounce of embarrassment as he continued to make her crazy, working her clit into a state of euphoria.

"Can you at least take your shirt off? This feels like you're my gym teacher."

His eyes shot up. But his fingers kept going.

"You did this with your gym teacher?"

The laugh ripped out of her. But then he whipped the shirt off, and her mouth gaped open. He was perfection itself. Artists must have designed that body. It was insane, with the valleys and dips of muscles along each inch of his torso. And so much ink she was spoiled for choice where she looked first.

Joelle didn't anticipate Diamond's mouth on her pussy.

He attacked with expertise, his lips around her clit, and two long fingers pushed into her dripping entrance without ceremony. It was so unexpected that Joelle screamed and had to slap a hand over her parted lips.

The orgasm tore through her with abandon. It was the biggest, wildest orgasm of her life. Wave after hot wave licked Joelle all over as Diamond's wicked mouth and hand fucked her right over the finish line until her vision blinked in and out.

His lips glistened like she'd painted him with gloss when he lifted his head and smiled, looking so sex drunk and turned on.

This was the moment she'd look back on one day. The way love walloped her in the middle of her belly.

But her heart was beating so hard she couldn't think about the feelings drowning her, so she reached out, knocked the hair from his forehead, and ran her thumb over his wet lips. "Messy boy."

He attacked her again.

Full-on animal attack, pushing her back on the bed, his mouth went wild on hers, kissing with enough force she felt the heat rise off his skin. She tasted her tartness in his mouth and chased it like a drug. That was a surprise; she'd never thought she'd enjoy the taste of her arousal, but when it was on the tongue of a sex god, yeah, she wanted more and fought around his tongue to slake it all.

"That's one." He declared.

"Wait. What? We're keeping count?"

"You think I traveled all this way, with this hard dick, just to see you come once and then fuck off?" his smirk was hell on earth, and she'd sell the Snow estate to continue seeing it on that face.

"Well."

"You've never been corrupted by a biker before, Bluebell, and it shows. Now, get back into position. You'll do that again, and I'll talk you through it."

"You better not make me wait again." She scowled, and he laughed.

He was going to deny her orgasm again.

She had a better idea.

Okay, nothing was a better idea than coming again. She felt so unfettered, like her body wasn't even hers anymore because she wanted *more*. She wanted to glut herself on Diamond if all they had was now.

But she ran her fingers over the ridges of his stomach and watched him tremble. His nostrils flared.

"I'll do that again if you join me." She dropped her eyes to the bulge. It was impossible to ignore. He must be hurting so badly.

And Joelle craved to see Diamond coming undone.

"*Joelle*." He warned. He was kneeling on the ottoman, and he grabbed her thighs, keeping her right on the edge, giving him a full view of her wetness.

"Please. You can make me ache by waiting until you tell me I can come. But I want to see you do it, too. Give me that." She pleaded, vulnerable.

He looked to the ceiling like he could see the heavens and muttered to himself, but when his blond head dropped and he stared at her, nothing but unabridged lust was staring back.

Oh yeah, she was going to get it. *Yay.*

"You're gonna kill some lucky motherfucker one day who gets to come home every day to see you like this," He rasped so low she shivered. "Keep those killer legs open. They close even an inch, and I'll make it hurt so fucking good you'll beg for death."

Why was that hot? She must be mad.

"Do I get to see you coming?"

"Open your mouth." He issued and didn't wait for her to do a thing, just slammed down on her lips and forced them open by licking them. They groaned together, but the kiss was fast, furious, and over in seconds. "Yes, you'll see ropes of my fucking come. You're gonna wear it on your skin, devil woman."

Diamond reached into those gray sweatpants and pulled his length out. It was so big, angry purple at the gorgeous crown that she felt feral inside. Her stomach muscles clenched, and one day soon, Joelle would be embarrassed by the sexual sounds she made when he started stroking from balls to tip.

*Oh, lord.* And as she guessed, he held off her orgasm like a villain. She begged, pleaded, and cursed for him to let her come.

"You'll come so hard for me, baby, won't you?" he taunted with a smirk. Joelle could only whimper in return. "That's it. Nice and slow, my good girl. My cock is so goddamn jealous of those fingers."

Diamond was the dirtiest talking man on earth. The things coming from his mouth should've sent them both to hell.

Joelle was utterly corrupted by a biker.

Each time he gave her permission to come, she bowed her back and wailed his name. And once they started again, the torture was exquisite.

The sexy grunts coming from his throat were born from fantasies, his eyes bouncing between her heated face and where her fingers were lazily pushing into herself on his orders. She was drenched from multiple orgasms, unable to stop despite feeling satisfied.

When the biker was grunting his way through his delayed climax, pumping into his hand at speed, she thought if his dick wasn't so large, it might break. He was superhuman. No man had ever lasted as long as Diamond.

"Are you ready to take what I have?" he rasped, hot-eyed.

He grunted her name and climaxed at the same time she did. Joelle's was an utter surprise, so sure her vagina couldn't produce any more pleasure, but her body reacted to seeing Diamond's rough handling. Ropes of come splashed on her pussy, lower abdomen, and across her inner thighs.

Marked by a biker.

He didn't stop powering his palm until no drop was left. He exhaled and sagged forward on the ottoman, laid half over her, and then pressed the bulbous head of his cock against her throbbing clit. He gave several strokes, angling his cock as if to enter her, and they both exhaled, their eyes holding. Temptation in every rugged pant. She wanted him inside her more than anything and would sell her soul. From how Diamond looked at her, he felt the same way.

"That's my good girl, fucking those lucky fingers." He continued to nibble her mouth. They moaned together at the skin-on-skin intimate contact until he pulled at her hand and took those wet fingers into his mouth while he petted her outer pussy, coating her all over with his pleasure. She juddered, then fell back on the bed. Diamond's body followed, and his mouth touched the shell of her ear as he husked. "I knew you'd be hot as fuck when you came crying my name, Joelle."

The dominance he exerted over her body was incomparable.

Joelle had done most of the touching, while Diamond brought the dirty talking and coaching, sometimes using his thumbs to spread her pussy lips to lick her. She'd felt like he'd operated every inch of her pleasure, so when she'd detonated, it was overwhelmingly good.

She'd never recover from this.

He'd ruined her.

It was a fact.

Maybe it was a mistake.

But the good endorphins were rife through her system, and there was no space for regrets. Yet.

If they came, Joelle would deal with it.

But for that moment, in a bubble with a biker who'd thoroughly wrecked her, Joelle could only smile. And smile. And smile.

## Diamond

"I think I was Irish in a past life," Tomb declared with white foam on his upper lip. "Irish pubs are homey. They've got good home cooking and cold pints of Guinness."

Five Diablos were hanging out at an Irish bar outside of Utah. It had been the neutral ground for an important meeting. The meeting was done, and Tomb was having a blast, feeling all Irish.

"I can't believe we got out of that without bullet holes. We met with the Irish mob, and we're still breathing. That doesn't seem right." Half-laughed Reno. The entire time, Diamond expected a Molotov cocktail through the window.

Axel dominated the conversation with the Irish mob's US representative. Diamond was always prepared for explosive meetings, and his nerves were still energized.

"Never mind that. I can't believe we brokered a deal for Snow. We should have hung his shriveled dick out to dry. Now I feel all dirty." Tomb scowled, rubbing his mouth to remove the Guinness foam. Diamond agreed.

"He all but begged me to intervene." Axel tapped his fingers on the table, stretching his legs out in front of him. "And taking five hundred G's off him doesn't hurt, either."

"I do like that part," Reno agreed. "I would have charged a million, though."

"We got more than money." Axel shared. Proving why he was the devious leader of the Diablos. "We have leverage over him. He made a mistake in coming to me, and now he'll pay. As we speak, Bash is storing the evidence somewhere safe. We get a speeding ticket, a planning violation, a fucking murder charge. Who do we call?"

As a collective, all the boys shouted "Snow." And toasted with their drinks.

That was a sweet as fuck blackmail.

As soon as he thought about *sweet as fuck*, Joelle bombarded his mind.

She'd been the sweetest, most addictive morsel he'd ever had.

Long days had passed since he'd put his hands and mouth all over her body, and the memory of it was haunting him. So many days since he'd licked, sucked, and mouth fucked her to orgasms and then watched her stroke more out while he sprayed his come like a dirty pervert over her pussy more than once. It had taken all his willpower not to show up the next night to repeat it. But they'd both agreed nothing between them could work out.

They'd scratched an itch in a way that wouldn't compromise either of them. The truth was, Diamond had known if he'd fucked her in the way he craved to, he wouldn't let her go. He'd corrupt the beautiful socialite in all the filthy, unforgiving ways. He'd bring her into the darkness with him.

But that taste of her had plagued him until he couldn't sleep.

He'd rode by the Snow mansion countless times during the witching hours just to be close. And since Titan was on duty, he had no excuse to hang around her place.

That night, after he'd cleaned her up and tucked her into her bed, the temptation to crawl in beside her had been so strong Diamond had forced himself to leave, kissing her on the forehead. But no matter what he'd done to stay busy since, he could not forget her taste or her sounds of pleasure.

Her kisses got a man addicted, willing to do anything for another fix.

She'd thanked him, for fuck's sake.

Thanked him for making her come.

Then she smiled and casually told him to sleep well as he was leaving, like Joelle wasn't as affected by their steamy time together as Diamond.

She hadn't texted or called. Never asked for a repeat performance.

She'd gotten what she needed and moved on.

And that blew.

He'd been hoping she'd turn psycho clingy.

He felt a kick on his boot and raised his head to see Reno watching him.

"Bet you'll be glad, huh, D?"

He cocked an eyebrow. "About what?"

"Not having to work for the slick dick anymore. He won't need security now the mob have put their little Irish shrew in timeout."

Their representative was embarrassed to be contacted by the Diablos for a woman-scorned situation. Shannon was related to one of their field soldiers and had abused the connection to extort Snow. Right there at the table, the Irish representative had made a call and ordered the soldier to neutralize his sister, or he would.

Diamond hadn't considered the consequences of resolving that situation.

Despite his squeezing gut, he forced a smile. "Thank fuck. One more day in that house, I might have started using a salad fork with my dinner."

Everyone laughed. Diamond didn't.

He would miss the rainbow Bluebell more than he could say.

He didn't like the job, but enjoyed being around her more than he should've. He was pissed about working for someone as unlikable as Snow, but Joelle had gotten to him.

To avoid looking like a brooding idiot, he said something. "My team will be happy to have some time off from shopping trips and social events."

Reno chuckled. "Different atmosphere than putting the heavy on someone at an underground boxing fight, that's for sure. And no brats to watch over."

Joelle was far from a brat.

His opinion of her had done a one-eighty almost immediately. She was so damn sweet and vulnerable, funny and intelligent.

And now he wouldn't get to talk to her one last time.

It was for the best.

She was way too good for him and from a different world.

Even if every soft curve fit perfectly into his hands, as if she'd been designed especially for him. She made him come alive. But Joelle couldn't be for him.

"We need to bring the old ladies here. Nina will get a kick out of the music." Said Tomb. Reno agreed, and Axel grunted, which could be classed as agreement. He'd take Scarlett wherever she asked to go. He spoiled the club queen and didn't hide the fact.

Diamond didn't respond. Getting in the middle of a couple's date night sounded like he wanted to stay home and watch the game alone.

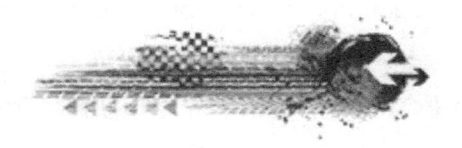

### Joelle

"What do you mean, it's taken care of?"

She blinked at her father, unsure what he was telling her. When he'd called her into his office, she thought she was in for another of his famous *do as I say, not as I do* lectures.

The bangles around her wrist jingled as she linked her fingers in her lap.

"The situation is resolved, so there's no need for tight security."

"Oh."

Joelle's heart deflated, and she felt a sick disappointment in her belly.

That meant Diamond wouldn't be around anymore. Nor the other guys, who were pretty fun to talk with.

"That also means you can drop this silly notion of moving out. You know it'll break your mother's heart."

Joelle sighed, unable to believe he was still using the same old schtick of emotional blackmail on her.

"Why do you want me to stay at home? The truth."

"I told you."

"No. You use mother as an excuse. I'm not exactly like all of you. I'm not too fond of social parties and networking. I don't fit in. Mother has to give me instructions at every public event, so I don't embarrass you."

She saw him frown. "You are my daughter, Joelle. I was the one who named you. Do you know that?"

She didn't. And was surprised by it.

"I know I don't show it, and I need to spend more time at home with my family, but you are important to your mother. And to me. You and your brother. I would be happy if you both stayed at home forever."

Joelle cleared her throat, feeling her heart soften toward her father.

"You don't need to hold on so tight. We're always going to be a family. It's not like you won't ever see us again."

His face was unreadable, which was half of the problem of not being close.

"Just give it some thought, okay?"

"I will, if you will."

He arched a gray eyebrow in question.

"I don't profess to understand the arrangement you and mom have, and I don't want to." He scowled like he was ready to lecture, and Joelle held up a hand for him to wait. "All I ask is to consider mom's feelings the next time you... and please, not someone my age." She popped to her feet, awkwardness in every limb. This wasn't a conversation she wanted to have with him now or ever. But no one else advocated for her mother's happiness, and she felt compelled to do so.

"Joelle." He called out when she opened his office door. She turned to find him watching her pensively. "Your mother was the only woman I ever wanted to marry. I love her."

It was a strange love if he had to fuck around and bring turmoil with his reckless decisions. But she never heard her mom's side, so her thoughts were unclear. If Joelle ever got married, an open marriage would not be on the table.

She shrugged and departed.

It was all the way faithful monogamy for her future relationship, or she'd bury him in the backyard and plant tulips on his cheating ass.

She found Reeves in the grand family room playing on a video game. She plopped down on the couch beside him to annoy her baby brother and ruffled his hair.

"Leave off, Joelle. You nearly made me die." She doubted it, not with the hours he played on that thing.

"You better make the most of me bugging you, little brother. I won't be here for much longer."

His gaze snapped into focus. "Are you going somewhere?"

"I've decided to move out, probably in January, if I can find somewhere. I'm downsizing from this mausoleum."

"No way!" he replied. "And Dad is okay with that?"

"It's my decision. And it's well overdue."

"Shit."

"Are you going to miss me?"

Their sibling relationship was decent, considering the age difference.

"No. Because I could move in with you, sis." He grinned, making her laugh.

"I'll let you stay in the spare room once a month. It's the best I can offer." She ruffled his hair again and climbed to her feet.

"Hey," he called out, already back into the video game with his eyes on the TV screen like an addicted zombie.

"What?"

"Mom said we don't need those bikers around anymore."

She couldn't keep dwelling on Diamond and the dirty things they'd done. She didn't need his repetitive orgasm sounds in her head.

"Yes, that's right. You can be a sneaky punk again without being watched."

He chuckled. "He was pretty cool, you know?"

She knew instinctively who he meant, and Joelle's stomach tumbled over.

"For a biker, I mean. According to Dad, they're scum. But I thought he was okay."

Yeah, Diamond was an okay guy. More than okay.

Especially if he'd made a positive impression on her baby brother.

He called out as he frantically slaughtered a monster by pressing buttons on the control pad. "I might join his club one day. It'll give Dad a fit."

Joelle burst out laughing, leaving him to his fun.

Wouldn't that be a sight? Her family and Diamond's biker family united in a peaceful conflict.

To illustrate, he occupied her thoughts as she entered her studio and saw five additional paintings of him leaning against the walls. She had an unstoppable urge to paint his face in every color and position. For days since their midnight tryst, painting was the only thing to keep her focused.

Joelle pulled out her phone and sank to sit on a stool.

What could it hurt to message him?

**JOELLE**: I hear you've been set free from the Snow drama. Congrats, Diamond. Don't miss us too much. XX

*Crap*. The two kisses at the end of her sentence were a bad habit she'd picked up from an English college friend. The Brits were notorious for it.

Grabbing her painting smock, she pulled it over her head. She had a sexy face to paint.

What was one more for her biker collection?

## Diamond

Over the years, Diamond witnessed his patched brothers and their old ladies having several arguments. They rarely kept their marital fights quiet. It was usually over some dumb stuff that Diamond wouldn't even care about.

And then harmony would resume once again once the lovers made up. Most often, Diamond would hear them going at it like sex-crazed animals behind a locked door.

As he sat at the bar in the Diablos clubhouse, drinking strong black coffee, he understood how his brothers were moody in those moments because they missed their soft-bodied women.

He couldn't say it was the same because he hadn't claimed Joelle. She wasn't his woman and never could be.

But he *missed* her.

He felt a void without her disjointed conversations that hopped from topic to topic without a smooth transition. He missed how she'd smile at everyone like they were all her friends, even if she didn't know them. He missed the way she couldn't hide how her eyes followed him. He'd fucking loved her attention. And he missed how she'd laugh so effortlessly and look his way to see if he found it equally funny.

He missed her taste. She was like nothing he'd had in his mouth before. And one time with her shouldn't make him an infatuated addict, but here he sat, unable to think about anything else.

"Why so glum, chum?" asked Scarlett as she restocked the bar.

"I'm not glum." He brooded into his coffee. What the fuck did glum mean, anyway?

His curt answer didn't deter Scarlett.

They'd all taken on the role of being her big brother ever since Axel dragged the waif into the clubhouse after trying to steal from him. From then on, it became clear Axel was keeping the woman for himself. The club queen was younger than most, smaller than a mushroom, and probably weighed less than those boxes she was hauling out to the recycling, but she sure did like to poke her nose in everywhere if she sniffed out drama.

"You look like someone painted unicorns on your motorcycle."

He raised his head and playfully arched an eyebrow at Scarlett, his lips twitching with amusement.

"That would be so cool, wouldn't it? If I can talk Axel into letting me ride a motorcycle, I'd paint unicorns all over it."

God help them. If she ever rode a bike, they'd have to climb up on the roof so she didn't run them over.

"Is something wrong, Diamond? Anything I can help you with? You're usually one boy I don't need to worry about. But here I am, worried about you."

That was the club's First Lady; she had a soft heart, and he flashed a smile.

"I'm good, babe."

"You're a boy, so you're a liar," she smiled with empathy, "but I'm here if you want to talk."

What would he say? That he was pining after a woman who couldn't be his, even if their chemistry was like nothing he'd ever felt before. He could imagine how that vote would go when he asked to bring Joelle around as his old lady. The daughter of a shady Judge, they'd never trust a Snow. They'd say it would be like having a fox in the henhouse. He understood because he would make the same choice in their position.

Decisions that would put the club at risk, especially from enemies, were consistently voted down. Joelle was not his enemy, far from it, and he felt his mood plummet even further.

He got her first text while discussing the Riot Brothers with Bash over lunch.

**JOELLE**: I hear you've been set free from the Snow drama. Congrats, Diamond. Don't miss us too much. XX

Shit.
Why did his gut have to tighten with a thrill?
She was only a woman.

A woman who had a claw hold on his attention.

He thought about ignoring it.

But he had rogue thumbs.

**DIAMOND**: If I ever say I miss your father, have me committed.

**DIAMOND**: Don't get into trouble, and you won't need my services, Bluebell.

**JOELLE**: HEY! It wasn't me who hired you.

**JOELLE**: I'm a good girl.

Diamond's mind was pure filth for what that sentence conjured.

"Why are you smiling at your phone?" asked Bash across the table. "Shit, is this another Ruin situation? It creeped everyone out when he'd hunch over his phone while he was romancing Rory. Or whatever he called it."

Fuck. It was precisely like Ruin.

He did like all men and deflected like a pro.

"Don't you have a nurse to chase, brother? Is little Lottie succumbing to your charms yet?"

As hoped, Bash's attention switched, and he scowled into his chowder. "I fucking wish. She's stubborn."

"You know, you can move on, right? There's..."

"Don't say plenty of fish in the sea," he growled. "I get enough of that shit from Denver. He saw Casey and latched on like a barnacle, so he has no room to talk."

Diamond smirked. That was true. Denver picked up his hitch-hiker, moved her in, and she'd been there ever since.

For the rest of the week, Diamond sent texts back and forth with Joelle.

**JOELLE**: I wish Christmas was over.
**DIAMOND**: You're not a fan?
**JOELLE**: It's okay. There are fifteen trees in my house right now. Fifteen! There were three in the therapist's waiting area. It's forcing festivity.

He observed that her suite at the mansion lacked any festive decorations. Weren't all women crazy about the season? Axel had stupidly given Scarlett the green light for anything she wanted to do, so the old ladies have gone all in with decorating shit.

**DIAMOND**: Who knew someone so colorful would be a Grinch?
**JOELLE**: Bah Humbug.

Diamond knew what the beeping meant while he iced his busted knuckles in his home bathroom. It was late. He'd been sorting out an issue for a client all day and only just got home to boil himself in a shower and treat his hands.

He parked himself on the side of the bed and smirked, reading her message.

**JOELLE**: I had to be social all night.

**JOELLE**: How does Santa Claus cope? I'd retire and take my cookies with me.

**DIAMOND**: Poor girl. You can retire from being a Snow.

**JOELLE**: I wish I could. It was the Christmas party at my father's office. Hell would freeze over before we were allowed to opt out of attending.

**JOELLE**: Reeves got high in the bathroom, and I got stuck talking with Trent for hours.

The little fucking suit-wearing pen pusher. Diamond's jaw cracked as he stared at his phone and thought of twenty-six ways to kill a pompous twat.

Was she trying to make him jealous? Because it was working so efficiently.

Lock her up.

Tie her down.

Keep her at his mercy until she only knew his name.

Christ. His thoughts had jumped into crazy town.

He didn't want Joelle to feel alone, but he was murderous at the idea of another man trying to make her happy. They would dim her sparkle and drain her vibrant soul.

Just thinking about it made Diamond want to punch a wall.

He couldn't help himself.

Though he had no rights here and didn't want the answer, he still asked.

**DIAMOND**: Did the monotonous dick ask you out?

**JOELLE**: LOL, you don't like him, huh?

**JOELLE**: Your assessment is correct, though. He droned on about lawyer stuff all night.

**JOELLE**: And he kept asking me out for a date.

Motherfucker. He should ride to that guy's place and stick his head under the fridge.

He had no intention of responding.

They weren't gal pals to talk about this shit.

He only discovered he was a jealous maniac over the right woman. No fucking way did he want to hear about Joelle's dating life. It would turn him into a serial killer.

He finished slathering his knuckles with ointment to heal faster, and he marched back into his bedroom to pull on a pair of boxer briefs.

He'd made his way into the kitchen to grab a beer and to crash out in the lazy-boy chair in front of the TV when the phone beeped again.

**JOELLE**: I didn't say yes.

**JOELLE**: Anyway, it's late. Goodnight, tough guy. Hope you're staying out of biker trouble.

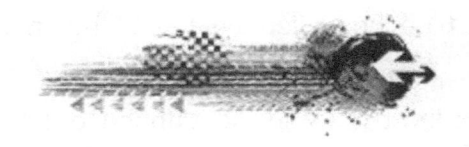

**JOELLE**: I saw all you guys today! You were riding in formation like a pack of ducks. It looked cute!

**DIAMOND**: Bluebell, bikers aren't cute.

**JOELLE**: A few are!

**DIAMOND**: Which bikers do you think are cute so I know who I'm killing?

**JOELLE**: <laughing emojis> I plead the fifth.

The answer caused him to scowl.

The next night, fueled by Joelle's comments about other bikers, he beat up a guy for being late with his Diablos debts.

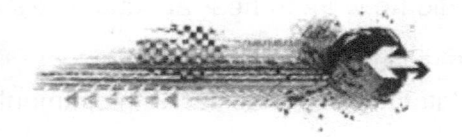

**DIAMOND**: I saw you on the local news with your Snow clan tonight.

**JOELLE**: Ugh, did my smile look real or fake? My jaw was aching by the time I got home.

**JOELLE**: Worst night ever.

She'd looked fucking spectacular in a bright yellow and peach dress, and her blue hair piled on top of her head with wispy bits around her face. Diamond had come to a complete stop seeing the news bulletin on the big TV in the clubhouse. Like she'd welded his feet to the floor, he hadn't moved until the next item came on, and he could breathe again.

**DIAMOND**: Your smile was fine.

**JOELLE**: Stop with the compliments, tough guy. You'll give me a massive ego.

**DIAMOND**: Why are you awake so late?

**JOELLE**: I'm wrapping Reeves' gifts.

**DIAMOND**: Did you spoil him?

**JOELLE**: Of course. He's a little devil, but I love that devil.

**JOELLE**: I didn't get him the sports car he begged for.

**DIAMOND**: What did you get him?

**JOELLE**: Some gamer stuff. A new monitor and clothes.

**DIAMOND**: You have spoiled him, Mrs Claus.

**DIAMOND**: Get into bed, Bluebell. Santa sees you when you're sleeping. He knows when you're awake.

**JOELLE**: You just sang the song, didn't you?

**JOELLE**: Cute biker.

**JOELLE**: Goodnight, tough guy. Wish me luck tomorrow. I have two events to attend.

**DIAMOND**: Be like a biker and get drunk. It'll make them more tolerable. Sweet dreams, Bluebell.

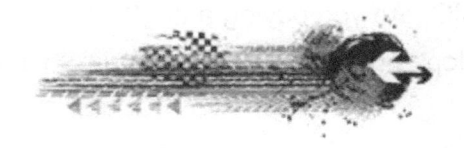

**DIAMOND**: Did you survive?

**JOELLE**: The parties? Thankfully, yes!

**JOELLE**: An old lady wearing Chanel and pearls looked me up and down and queried if I got dressed in the dark. LOL.

**DIAMOND**: Stupid old crone. Give me her name and address.

**JOELLE**: OMG. Will you put a biker whack on her?

**DIAMOND**: I'm not the Italian mafia, Bluebell.

**JOELLE**: Don't burst my imagination. That sounded cool. And hot.

**JOELLE**: Anyway, I'm about to go to my grandparents for mulled wine and more socializing. I swear, I'm hibernating in January.

**JOELLE**: What are the bikers doing?

**JOELLE**: Especially the cute one <winky emoji>

The deep breath Diamond took stretched his Henley t-shirt across his chest. He wasn't a praying man, but that woman made him ask for patience almost daily.

"Brother, you coming?" called out Devil, striding to the door in his leathers. Diamond grunted affirmatively and grabbed his leather jacket. Swinging it on, he thumbed out a reply as he headed for the entryway.

**DIAMOND**: We're going to see a man about a dog.

**JOELLE**: OMG, are you buying a dog?

**JOELLE**: Adopt one instead, Diamond. So many older puppies need homes.

**JOELLE**: But I want to see him immediately!

**DIAMOND**: Woman, it's an expression. I'm not getting a dog.
**JOELLE**: Oh. Now I'm sad.
**JOELLE**: Send me a picture of the cute biker instead.
**DIAMOND**: You're asking for it.
**JOELLE**: I'm begging for it!
**JOELLE**: I meant the picture <grin emoji>

Shit. They were flirting.
And he liked it.
Diamond grinned and pocketed his phone.
She'd put him in a good mood, and now he had to crack some Riot Brothers skulls.

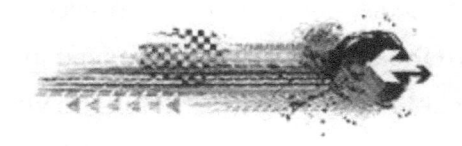

**JOELLE**: Merry Christmas Eve, Diamond.

The bike beneath him idled on the corner of a private street as he frowned while looking up at the brightly lit windows.
Could she sense he was creeping outside the Snow mansion?
There was no disguising or excusing his behavior this time. He'd gone all in with the stalking, led solely by his addiction to her.
What was his end game here? Knock on the door like a boyfriend, and give her the gift, burning a hole in his pocket?
He was acting like an infatuated, out-of-control fool.

Two weeks had passed since he last saw Joelle and their most fantastic night.

He wasn't the club muscle only because of his size. Diamond's fuse was short in intense situations, causing him to detonate quickly. But somehow, these past few days, while he'd been neutralizing some issues the Riot Brothers had been causing for the MC, having Joelle constantly on his mind meant Diamond kept his head together and didn't pummel someone to death. He only left them bruised instead.

Just picturing her in her bed, surrounded by a sweet scent, or in her paint-filled studio with her hair tied up, helped him handle the situation calmly.

Almost like he'd envisioned having an old lady waiting at home for him.

Giving his head a disgusted shake, he revved the engine and did a U-turn to go down the street the way he'd come in.

He needed to get his shit together before he went full-on stalker, or worse. He'd kidnap the woman and keep her for himself and not give a shit what anyone else thought about it.

Then where would he be?

Heaven. For sure.

Also in jail.

He rode into the night and forgot about the Bluebell broach in his inside pocket, reminding Diamond of how reckless he was.

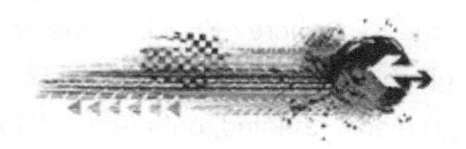

**JOELLE**: Merry Christmas, Diamond.

**JOELLE**: I haven't heard from you. I hope you're spending the holidays with your family and having a wonderful time.

**JOELLE**: What did Santa bring you?

**JOELLE**: Are you in a post-Christmas hangover?

**JOELLE**: Diamond, are you busy?

**JOELLE**: I hope you're being safe, tough guy.

**JOELLE**: Diamond, are you getting my messages?

**JOELLE**: Happy New Year, Diamond. I hope it's the best one yet.

Over the past week, he repeatedly read their texts and felt like a cruel prick for not responding. He didn't want to be another person in her life giving Joelle the cold shoulder. She deserved the fucking world at her feet. He wanted to be at her feet, worshipping her.

But his silence was for the best.

For them both. Eventually.

Even if it was tearing him apart.

She didn't need someone like him, bringing the dirt and the dangerous.

And he couldn't have someone like her in his world.

A clean cut was needed.

So he sighed, shoved his phone away, and hooked up the whiskey glass to toast to the New Year, wishing his Bluebell all the good shit in her life she could ever want.

And that didn't include a biker who couldn't stop thinking about her.

## Joelle

How many sex dreams were too many?

For the ninth morning in a row, Joelle woke up sweaty, tangled in the cotton sheets, and frustrated with unsatisfied horniness after yet another Diamond centric dream.

She huffed as she flung back the covers, trying to banish one man from her life, which was proving more challenging than ever when his filthiness infiltrated her unconscious mind every night.

Diamond had stopped replying to her texts before Christmas.

That was fine.

It was the right thing to do.

She agreed they couldn't be a thing, but it still stung he couldn't have told her farewell, Merry Christmas, and have a glorious New

Year. Manners cost nothing, so now, along with being horny all the time, she was mad at him.

Her shower took longer than usual because she had a problem to attend to. At least she could still rely on B.O.B. Her battery-operated boyfriend never let her down and always brought his A-game to the table, eh, shower.

She was a new woman when she eventually climbed out to towel dry. A biker was banished from her mind with one melty orgasm. And good riddance.

"Why so moody, sis?" she heard and turned to scowl at Reeves as she shut the bedroom door behind her. Thankfully, fully dressed, or she would have kicked her brother's scrawny ass.

"What have I told you about just walking in? I could have had company."

The little shit started laughing, sprawled out on her couch. "Yeah, right. Did pigs decide to fly? I didn't see it on my socials."

"I'll tell our parents you had a girl sleeping over several times over the holidays."

Her brother's face blanched, and Joelle smiled.

"You wouldn't dare."

"Then rethink being a sassy little shit to me so early."

Reeves swung off the end of the couch and followed Joelle into her kitchen. Because her brother was a bottomless pit, she pulled out the fixings to make him breakfast, even as her stomach gurgled. She felt unwell last night and hoped she hadn't caught her mother's winter flu. There was a painting she wanted to finish by this weekend.

"So, I'll ask again, why so moody, sis?" Reeves had his hand in the cookie jar, feeding two into his mouth. It was a wonder that the boy didn't weigh four hundred pounds. She'd believe in Santa if she could only have a teen boy metabolism.

"Nothing, I just have things on my mind."

A stupid, handsome biker who plagued her dreams and left her wanting more. She missed talking with him, feeling him looming and watching her.

"Is it Trent?"

She sent him a speculative gaze as she whisked eggs to make him a ham omelet. Eggs she could just about cook without mishap.

"Why would you ask that?"

"He's been by the house more, always panting around you at parties like a lovesick dickhead. Don't you ever notice him watching you? I thought you might get back together."

"No, that's not happening."

"Thank fuck. I hated that guy, Joelle." In went another cookie. Reeves towered over her at six feet, so she made him grab the glasses from the overhead cabinet.

"You did? You never said." She rolled her eyes with a grin. Reeves never stopped complaining about how much he hated Trent when she was with him.

"You deserve someone who pays attention to you, not someone who sucks up to Dad."

She blinked. "Are you... is my baby brother being nice?"

He smirked. "Shut up. I can be nice. Besides, you're feeding me. You are feeding me, aren't you?"

"These eggs aren't for me. I don't feel like breakfast today."

In no time, she cooked the food and served it on a plate for Reeves, who hungrily consumed it, continuously shoveling it into his mouth until the plate was bare.

"If you don't have classes, do you want to come out with me today?" she asked. "I'm viewing a few places with a realtor."

"Fuck yeah." He agreed enthusiastically. "I gotta see what room will be mine."

"I told you already, you're not moving in with me, Reeves."

"But I'll have a room, won't I?"

She relented, admitting she'd forever spoil the blue-eyed brat. "Maybe. But no girls are staying over."

"Joelle! Come on, don't be a prude. I'll buy you noise-canceling headphones so you don't hear her calling out to God." The tall brat smirked, and she forgot he was no longer a cute, toothless kid who would follow her around. He was a grown man, taking college classes, and had a better dating life than she ever had.

"Forget it. You're not coming with me."

"I am." He grinned, hopping down. "I'll meet you outside. I need to grab my sneakers and call one of my girls to let her know I'm busy today."

Joelle gaped at him. "*One of them*? What does that mean, Reeves? You better not be a man ho!"

He threw her a grin.

Lord above, her brother was definitely a man ho.

She'd need to talk seriously with him later because her parents would freak out if their nineteen-year-old son became a father before finishing college and finding a suitable wife.

After walking around several properties, Joelle was ready to sit down and drink a gallon of lemonade. None of the houses the realtor had shown her were the right fit.

"What was wrong with that one?" asked Reeves as they climbed into her car. "I liked my bedroom." He smirked.

"If I bought that house, the biggest room would be mine, you turd. And I don't know what was wrong with it, except it didn't feel like my house." *It didn't feel like it would suit a biker*. It was absurd for her to have it as a consideration. Diamond wouldn't be living with her. Or even visiting. He'd shown he was done with her for good.

"Women are weird."

"Says the man who multi-dates."

"There's a lot of me to go around."

"Just be careful, okay? I mean, use condoms if I wasn't being clear."

"I always am," He answered. "And I never use a woman's condoms. I'm not having her poking holes in them so she can become a Snow." He shuddered.

Nobody in their sane mind would be eager to become part of their family.

"Can we stop to grab some lunch? I'm starving."

"You ate a couple of hours ago."

"I know. It feels like days."

Joelle rolled her eyes and headed toward a favorite cafe. Although she was hungry initially, the smell of the food cooking changed her appetite.

"Aren't you having anything?" he asked after the hostess took their order.

"I think I'm getting the flu. It's a great start to January."

"Don't give it to me! I have a dating life to be present for."

The little shit. She crumpled a napkin and tossed it at Reeves' face.

When she woke up the next morning tired and achy, the flu had gotten to her. Feeling completely drained, she spent a day in bed, indulging in her favorite vampire-themed comfort shows.

By day three, she was fed up with the flu and compelled herself to get out of bed, shower, and change into regular clothes. At least, feeling under the weather, her X-rated dreams had stopped.

She missed him, though.

But she had to chalk up that surreal moment with Diamond as a fond memory she'd look back on in years to come. She'd call it the wild night with a biker.

It was difficult to picture The One coming into her life one day when she knew no man could ever compare to Diamond in how he lit up her heart. Was it fair to another man if Diamond was the standard now and they'd never live up to him?

A biker had come into her life, ruined her, and then disappeared just as fast, leaving her feeling unmoored, missing him more than ever.

With some of her energy returning, Joelle spent a few hours in the studio finishing a commissioned painting. Even though she didn't sell many, every time she sold a painting, she felt more confident because she had earned it.

Toward the end of the following week, she dined with her parents, viewed several more properties, and painted like a madwoman. Most of those paintings were of Diamond and for her private collection, not for sale, but she went where her muse led her. His face haunted her, but her creativity was loving it. The fact he'd momentarily eased her loneliness made it feel even more awful. Like he saw her, the real Joelle, and he'd liked her.

"You look exhausted. Are you sleeping?" Sadie remarked that night at her friend's house. "You haven't touched your wine."

"I've been battling the flu, and it's zapped my energy. I could sleep for a month."

"Tell me your symptoms." Demanded Sadie.

"Oh, here she goes, Voodoo Medicine woman," Molly said, sipping on Merlot.

Joelle shared an amused glance with Molly. Sadie was their self-appointed village healer. She'd diagnose and devise a solution in minutes if anyone became sick. Her bathroom cabinet was bulging with medical supplies.

"It's just the flu, lack of energy, and wanting to sleep."

"Loss of appetite?"

"Some, but not a lot."

"Maybe you're pregnant." Molly wiggled her eyebrows over the lip of her glass, and Joelle nearly rolled her eyes to Saturn at the absurdness of the suggestion.

"I'd need to have sex for that to happen."

"Trent didn't manage to get you back together?"

"What is it with everyone mentioning Trent lately? Do I give off a pining vibe? He's no one important and never was, and I'm never getting back with him."

"I'm joking, sweetie. Trent looks hot in a suit, but it's the only hotness he brings. You need a stallion in the bedroom and the living room." laughed Molly.

"What's my diagnosis, witch doctor?" she asked Sadie, changing the subject from her non-existent love life.

"You have the flu. I prescribe lots of vitamin C and plenty of sleep."

Joelle toasted her friend with the undrunk wine. "Thank you. I'm pleased I'll live."

"You better not die before my birthday!"

"Or my Fourth of July party."

God, she loved these girls. Emotions overwhelmed her, causing tears to well in her eyes, but she composed herself with a deep breath. It was January blues. A fresh start and the uncertain times ahead for her this year.

Her low mood had nothing to do with not seeing or hearing from Diamond in five weeks.

She wasn't missing the bodyguard biker.

And she wasn't wondering if he'd moved on to a new woman.

By the end of the week, Joelle was feeling more like herself again. She was considering two houses as her options. Also, she decided to improve her diet, cut back on sugar, and prioritize her health, prompting her to schedule a doctor's appointment for Vitamin C injections. Before anything else, she had to undergo a complete blood panel to rule out any other deficiencies that could account for her fatigue.

"What's the verdict, Doctor Gio? Are you sending me home with a bag of drugs?"

She hoped not. Modern medicine was great, but she hoped to fix her tiredness with a healthier diet.

"Not many," her doctor smiled, "just prenatal vitamins."

Joelle gaped, sure she'd heard wrong. Suddenly, she wasn't feeling so well. "Excuse me? What did you say?"

"You're pregnant, Joelle. About six weeks, according to your last cycle."

Prompted by the stunned expression on Joelle's face, the doctor asked. "Were you aware you were pregnant?"

"Oh, sure, Doctor. This is the face of a woman who came in knowing she was pregnant. You must be wrong. I can't be pregnant."

"Your hCG levels are over twenty-five, Joelle. It's a sure sign of pregnancy, but we can schedule an ultrasound for you."

Joelle's mind had been transported to another dimension. That had to be it. She'd been watching too much fantasy TV lately.

This wasn't happening.

Women didn't have immaculate conceptions, for goodness' sake!

The doctor launched into her explanation about what would come next. What came next was Joelle would have a complete breakdown in her car and then seek a second opinion!

She wasn't sick.

She didn't have the flu.

And she didn't need vitamin C injections to improve her energy.

Pregnancy hadn't even been on her list of possibilities.

Her mind was like a flip book, trying to figure out when and how. And then it hit her like a ton of bricks.

The fooling around with Diamond.

There hadn't been penetrative sex, but there certainly had been insertions and body fluids. The air whooshed out of her lungs, and Joelle felt the room spinning.

Dear lord.

This was not happening.

It had to be a dream.

Wake up. Wake up. *Wake up.*

While the doctor continued, Joelle nodded in the right places. She hoped, but her heart was beating too fast, and she was holding onto her sanity by a loose grip.

She was pregnant.

Oh, shit. That meant she'd have to tell Diamond.

And how would a man believe he'd gotten her pregnant when Joelle couldn't believe it herself?

Plot twist: Reeves didn't bring home a surprise baby. It was her.

## Joelle

After five days of walking around, all dazed, Joelle had to face reality.

She was pregnant and couldn't bury her head in the sand.

However, accepting and sharing it with someone else were two entirely different things.

How could she explain it? People knew she wasn't dating right now. She considered pretending she'd been inseminated just to stave off the embarrassment, but that was farfetched since she'd never mentioned wanting children.

But she couldn't burden this alone, so she'd spilled her woes on a three-way call with her friends. After a quick-fire round of screaming and questions, they'd advised her to talk to Diamond.

After several pep talks, she decided she could do one of two things. Tell Diamond or not tell him.

She wasn't cruel, so keeping that from him wasn't an option. It was too important to conceal. Joelle needed someone equally responsible to share the burden.

Joelle was prepared, as best as she could, for Diamond to tell her to go to hell and to deal with it alone. Yet, she had to allow him to choose.

Texting him was off the table. What could she say? *Hey, remember me? You came all over me last month. How is January treating you? Oh, by the way, you got me pregnant.*

"Stop being a chickenshit, Joelle," she scolded. "You're a twenty-eight-year-old woman who is independently wealthy, still in the process of moving, but you have perfect eyesight and good skin. Besides, you're not asking the guy to marry you or even for a relationship. Take a breath and get in there." She was rambling aloud.

The property in front of her was intimidating, but she couldn't sit in her car all day, so she started the engine again and approached the Diablo Disciples MC compound. A young man stood by an imposing steel gate, and she pulled up alongside him, whirring the window down just enough.

"Am I allowed to go in?" she asked.

He cocked a pierced eyebrow. "Depends on what you want."

*I'm here to tell one of your biker friends that he's going to be a daddy. Or not a daddy, depending on his level of involvement.*

"I'm having car issues and thought the mechanic could look at it."

He narrowed his eyes and darted his gaze over her white Denali SUV. When she expected him to challenge her, he simply nodded. "Go on." He clicked a button, and the electronic gates opened.

Breathing a sigh of relief, she drove the long distance, and the MC red brick building made her gape. She hadn't expected their headquarters to be so large.

She didn't have many expectations about where Diamond worked, even so, she was curious. It stood tall, spanning multiple floors and featuring an abundance of windows. Smaller structures surrounded the main building, and there was a sprawling mechanical shop on the left that she had lied about needing. With caution, she parked near the central structure with the double doors.

The door was propped open, and she observed two men transporting large boxes. She took advantage and waited for them to vanish before slipping into the entrance. With no prior experience with an MC, she was filled with anticipation, and her curiosity grew.

The first person she saw was a blonde woman emptying a coffee machine into a small trash can.

"Excuse me."

The woman glanced up from her task and thoroughly scanned Joelle from top to toe. "Who are you?"

"Oh, hey. Is Diamond around? Could you tell him Joelle is here to see him if he is?"

The blonde woman rested an elbow on the bar and smirked. "I'm Sonya. Me and Diamond are together."

*Oh, shit.*

Of all the scenarios she'd envisioned about this moment, Joelle hadn't factored him having a girlfriend. How did she proceed now?

"So, whatever you have to say, you can tell me, and I'll let him know later."

"How long have you been dating?"

Her glossy red lips spread with a smile. "For forever, girl. I wear his property patch, and we'll get married soon."

It was worse.

And now Joelle wanted the floor to open up and swallow her whole, not even chewing her trembling bones.

"What did you wanna see him about? Do you need a bodyguard? Because my baby is the best."

Bile rushed up into her throat. How could she tell him now and ruin his life?

"No, it's nothing like that. I should get going. Sorry to have bothered you."

"Hey, no bother, girl. You take it easy."

Joelle couldn't get out of there fast enough, and she didn't take a breath until she'd driven out of the compound gates and back onto the main road.

Regret was a wasted emotion, but it was sitting heavily in the car with her, leeching all the air from her lungs as she drove without destination.

It was bad enough that she had to drop the P bomb on him, but to do it, knowing he'd cheated on a girlfriend, soon-to-be-wife, made Joelle sick to her stomach.

She'd never gotten that vibe from him, and she'd dated a few sleazy, suit-wearing men in her time.

But Diamond had seemed like a decent guy.

But he wasn't so decent when he was instructing her through many orgasms.

Oh, god, did that make her an unintentional home wrecker?

No. She would not be that woman who took on the blame for a man's mess.

This catastrophe was on Diamond's toes.

He cheated.

Joelle knew nothing about it.

The regret remained anyway.

It stayed with Joelle right into the next day, after a restless night. She'd half decided that telling him face-to-face was out, and she'd have to resort to a text.

What he did with the information was up to him, but she had to get it off her chest.

Joelle decided to do it over a coffee. She found a corner table in a local restaurant where she usually brought Reeves to eat.

With an untouched pastry, she toyed with her phone, waiting for a spurt of courage to send the text to Diamond.

The minutes ticked by and she people watched as they stood in line to order.

Then she scrolled through the newsfeed, ordered a few items from Amazon, and answered an email. While mentally counting to ten, after which she would send the text, she saw a broad back, recognized it, and waited for Titan to be finished being served before she gave the security man a little wave.

Seeing his furrowed brow, she anticipated him walking right by her.

"Hi, Titan."

He grunted in reply.

"How are you? I see you have a takeout coffee, but would you like to join me?" He hesitated, staring down at her. "That is, if you don't have anywhere to be."

She almost told the guy to forget about it because he took so long, but then he pulled out the opposite chair and sat down.

"Aren't you eating that?" he asked.

"So you can speak!" she smiled and shook her head. "No. It's yours if you want it."

He took the plate, and within three clean bites, the pastry disappeared.

The phone in her hand taunted her for not doing what she should have done an hour ago or yesterday.

"Are you a biker?" she asked, latching onto a distraction, if only for a few minutes.

"No."

"Oh. I thought the guys working for Diamond were all bikers."

"Some are. I'm an independent contractor."

"I wanted to thank you for taking care of my mom. Your stoic silence impressed her." Joelle chuckled, and she saw Titan crack the tiniest corner lip smile.

She wished to ask him about Diamond, yet wouldn't mention his name.

"She was the easiest job I had," Titan shared. "Lots of shopping." He grimaced like he'd rather face bullets than go inside a boutique again. She couldn't relate. Shopping for clothes was one of her favorite sports.

"You haven't had any more issues from the Irish?" he asked, sipping his coffee.

The Irish? Did he mean Shannon? She popped up an eyebrow, about to ask him to clarify when he went on. "The mob isn't something you want to get messed up with, for future reference."

Excuse her, what?

Joelle blinked, sure she'd heard him wrong.

Was he talking about actual mobsters from Ireland? Crime lords and gangsters?

No, that couldn't be why her father had hired Diamond. It was because of his mistress.

But then it all fell into place.

Shannon was Irish.

Was Shannon part of the mob?

Oh, damn him. She had convinced herself that she no longer harbored anger towards her father, but it all returned instantly.

Titan didn't realize he had just revealed the information her father wanted to keep secret, so she quickly covered for him. "Yeah, that's good advice for sure. I should keep your number on speed dial," she tried to laugh, but it fell right out of her mouth when the object of her sleepless nights was striding through the door.

He had a mean look on his face, and Joelle gripped the table, fearing that the world might go topsy-turvy after Diamond's presence took all the air away.

But she realized, though he'd swept his gaze over her, it was Titan he was staring daggers at. If looks could kill, his employee would be sipping coffee as a corpse.

"We have company." She whispered, right before Diamond reached the table and Titan looked up to see his boss towering like a menacing war statue.

"What's this?" Diamond asked.

"It's a bistro." Answered Joelle flippantly.

No *hello*?

No, *sorry, I have a girlfriend, but I jerked off on you*.

Charming.

"If you head over there, it's where you buy coffee and food."

"Don't get smart with me, Bluebell."

Oh, she was Bluebell again, was she?

It made her feel worse because he didn't realize she knew about his other woman, so calling her a cute nickname felt like a stab to the heart.

The same heart that skipped a beat when he took his stare away from Titan and focused it on her face. Joelle wasn't prepared for this.

But she couldn't stop the sass as she pointed her chin in the air, meeting his ferocious glare.

"It's rude to stare."

"I told you already about that smart mouth." He dared warn, and she saw Titan move to stand up. Her hand shot out and landed on his arm. "Stay. Your boss has the manners of a lettuce."

"*Leave*," Diamond growled, and though he was staring at her, she knew he didn't mean her. Her poor heart pitter-pattered like crazy.

What a situation to find herself in.

All she'd wanted was a coffee and a chance to work up to sending him a brief text.

She was caught in a stare-down.

"Stay." She kept her hand on Titan's arm, and the poor man looked like he didn't know what to do.

Diamond's stare got Joelle thinking some wild thoughts. And he had no right to look possessively at her. Not when he was taken.

If her assumption was correct, he was acting jealous because of Titan. But that couldn't be right. He'd already told her Titan was in a happy relationship.

Before she knew what was happening, he bent his solid body in half, leaning over her, and his lips came for hers in an attack she didn't see coming.

A hand went to the back of her head and then to the front of her throat, holding her steady. But Joelle, weak where he was concerned, didn't even try to evade Diamond's seeking mouth.

After pining terribly for weeks, she withered under his forceful lips instantly.

Her brain emptied of all thoughts, of anything she knew was right and wrong.

His lips angled dominantly. Every flick of his tongue dared her to push him away. The kiss was like a storm unleashed, and despite her surprise, Joelle didn't hesitate as his kiss demanded she take it.

Even though she had only a limited history of kisses, her body remembered the taste of his mouth and hungered for more as he sensually moved his lips, enticing her with brushes of his tongue. Diamond's passionate kisses caused her insides to riot, and his seductive grip around her throat made her weak as a kitten, so easily foldable against his magnetic touch.

His tongue was so irresistible and skilled. It made Joelle long to follow him anywhere, as long as he never stopped kissing her.

When she heard Diamond grunt, she was overcome with a sudden clarity, causing her to wrench her head back. Instant regret sank in for her poor actions.

Labored and harsh, Diamond's breath echoed in her ears. With her hand on the center of his chest, she encouraged him to move backward, even as the heavy tapping of his heart bumped on her fingertips. He moved, although not willingly, and then gave Titan a piercing look.

"Leave."

"Boss, whatever shit you're thinking..."

"I said leave. *Now.*"

It was hissed, but there was little room to mistake the command as it rattled out of his mouth.

Titan gave Joelle a *good luck* shrug, climbed to his feet, and exited without saying another word.

She stared up into Diamond's darkened, angry eyes. Feeling shaken not only by his appearance but by that kiss.

Why had he kissed her like that?

Why didn't she hesitate to kiss him back?

"Do you feel better now you've exerted dominance?"

Diamond pulled out Titan's chair and put himself in it. Then he gave his lips a quick lick. "Why are you here with him?"

She ignored his question. "What the hell, Diamond! What do you want from me? Because you're sending a bunch of mixed signals. You ghosted my last messages. Fine, I got your dismissal loud and clear. You're here, sticking your nose where it doesn't belong and blowing things out of proportion."

He narrowed his eyes. "Blowing what out of proportion?"

Her eyes challenged him to say it. "You tell me."

"Were you on a date with him?"

Laughter bubbled up inside Joelle's throat.

Was he jealous?

Now, that kiss made sense.

But he had no right to be jealous.

None at all.

She didn't know whether she should be angry or feel flattered that he'd lost his cool, assuming wrongly that she was dating his employee.

"Because there are bigger things about to happen, I won't drag it out, though, for that caveman act you just pulled, I shouldn't tell you the truth. But no, I was not on a date with Titan. I'm not a cheater!" She aimed her chin high. "We happened to be in the same bistro, that's it."

That didn't appease him, and she watched his eyes narrow. "Why were you together?"

Some part of her wanted him to be green with jealousy, to feel the same shaking possessiveness she had felt over him.

Her answer was petty. And she didn't care. "That's none of your business, Diamond."

He was the man in the wrong here. With a girlfriend at home, he had no right to force kisses on her or to act jealous.

"That's no problem. I'll break his legs and find out that way." He smirked, a tinge of darkness around his eyes, kinda sinister but hot.

Even when she was mad at him, he affected her.

She'd been wrong about Diamond, trusting him from the start. But needed to give her intuition a reboot.

"You came to the MC." He announced, sweeping other thoughts out of her head, derailing her breath.

Joelle blinked. "Did... did you track me down?"

"I was on the way to your place, and saw your car outside. And then I find Titan all over you." he scowled.

"He was not all over me. For god's sake, he'd only just sat down. Stop overreacting." She snapped. She hated how much of a thrill his open jealousy gave her. Most men would keep their jealousy hidden from a woman. It would have been refreshing if he hadn't been a cheater.

"Did you come to the MC to see me?"

*Oh, boy. Here we go.* Her poor emotions were like a pinball, crashing from wall to wall.

Heat crawled up Joelle's chest and flushed her cheeks. Grimacing, she sipped her lukewarm decaf coffee before setting the cup aside.

"Who told you I was there?"

She waited for him to say *my girlfriend* so it was out in the open, and her heart cringed, not wanting to hear those words.

"The prospect on the gate described a blue-haired bombshell dressed like a rainbow. It could have only been you."

Oh. *Oh.* She smiled.

"He was pretty cute. Bombshell, you say?"

Diamond's eyes flashed, and his forehead creased. "Don't start that shit, Joelle."

"What shit?" she asked innocently, with her tongue in her cheek. "Is the boy single?"

"I'm already going to break Titan's legs. Do you want to add another man?"

Oh, god. He had to stop that.

"I was at your MC to speak to you about something, but your girlfriend said you weren't around. As you can imagine, it was a tad awkward." She revealed. She could tell the truth, even if he was incapable of it.

He pulled a face. "What fucking girlfriend?"

*What?*

So, he was straight-up lying?

Joelle scowled and shook her head. "Listen, there's no need to lie, Diamond, okay? If you cheated on her, that's something private between you two. But please don't insult me by lying right to my face. We're not anything, and what happened between us was an obvious mistake."

If anything, he frowned even deeper until she could count the etches on his furrowed brow. Diamond held her stare for so long that she nearly squirmed in her seat.

"I don't have a girlfriend." He spoke finally. "Who told you I did?"

"She did." Joelle fired back, remembering to keep her voice regular because of where they were. "Sonya."

"Fucking Sonya? Are you serious?" he snapped. Suddenly, Diamond was on his feet. "You're coming with me."

"Like hell am I getting in the middle of your mess. No, thank you." She protested, but Diamond already had a hand underneath her arm and was helping her up, her body moving to his demands instead of listening to her logic.

He got in her face so close she saw all the different shades of blue in his irises. When he dropped his head lower, she held her breath. "You won't believe anything I say. I see that shit on your face, Joelle. Do you think I have an old lady even when I put my mouth between your legs? Even though I sucked orgasms out of you like a dying man, you won't take my truth."

"For heaven's sake, shut up." She hissed in a whisper.

"You'll follow me back to the clubhouse."

This situation was getting worse by the second, and if she thought he wouldn't forcefully chase her all over town, she would have refused point blank.

"Fine, but this isn't necessary. I don't care if you have a partner, Diamond."

"You do, or you wouldn't be looking at me like you are. And you wouldn't have taken off from the MC without waiting to see me. Let's go."

Diamond didn't touch her. He didn't have to; she followed him like an invisible line connecting them. She watched his formidable back as he strode out of the restaurant. Every pair of eyes, including hers, was on the dynamic man.

"Wait up, there's something I need to say." She said, a step behind him on the street.

He turned and pinned her with a stare. "You can say what you want to say to me once we do this."

"This is stupid, Diamond."

He ignored her, waited for Joelle to open the door, then sighed and pressed her against the car. Diamond's head canted down, and he pinned her with a laser-blue stare.

"Because you want me to be honest, Bluebell. Let me tell you, we might have agreed that me and you couldn't be anything more, but that night together? It was not a fucking mistake. Far from it," he breathed, holding her gaze before he stepped back, and she watched him striding to the Harley Davidson that gleamed under the midday sun. The way he climbed on was so sexy she was awestruck, gaping at him. Until he pointed a finger at her car, telling her to get in and follow him.

Sighing, she shook her head. But what could she do? The sensible thing by going home? Nope. She got behind the wheel and waited for Diamond to pull out in front of her.

And then she followed him back to the MC.

Oh, goodie, round two of her humiliation.

She figured telling him she was pregnant with his baby would be the most embarrassing thing ever. Little did Joelle know it would come with two crushing side quests first.

## Joelle

It was a pity the journey didn't take longer.

Joelle couldn't remember a second of it because her eyes had been pinned to the back of Diamond the entire time.

She knew they wouldn't work for many reasons, but it didn't alter how captivated he made her feel. In another life, they could have been perfect together.

And then she saw him on that impressive machine, handling it like a pro. No wonder she was a trembling idiot when she parked next to him. He swung his leg over the seat, pulling off the half helmet. And then he came for her with a steely stride.

"I'm not going in there." She told him when he opened her door. He gripped her hand and brought her out, and like a puppet, she let Diamond take her without the slightest struggle. He could lead her to hell, and she'd go without question.

"You don't have to." Over her head, he whistled, blistering the air with a shrill noise, and seconds later, footsteps jogged closer.

"Whatcha need, Diamond?" the guy asked. He wore a similar leather vest over a white t-shirt, but his vest stated he was a prospect.

"Go tell Sonya to come out to me."

Oh, great. Joelle rolled her eyes and pulled her coat tighter around herself.

"This way, you don't think I've instructed her on what to say to you," he stated in a strained voice.

"I don't care, Diamond."

"Yes, you do."

She did. Ugh, she cared too much.

They remained silent, though his eyes roamed over her face, and Joelle watched as the woman from earlier came out of the main entranceway, smiling as she swished her hips from side to side. The smile dimmed when she clocked Joelle standing with Diamond. Her walk got sassier as she approached.

She smiled up at him, pouting her pink lips. "Price said you needed me, Diamond."

"Are we dating?"

She turned red. "Excuse me?"

"Answer the question, Sonya."

"Why are you asking me this?" she said, then shot Joelle an accusatory stare.

"Answer." His tone was deeper, rougher.

"Is this because *she* took off earlier? It's not my fault she can't take a joke, D."

"Explain." He demanded from the other woman.

"She came asking about you earlier."

"And?"

Sonya huffed and rolled her eyes. A hand on her jutted hip. Still sending Joelle hate-filled stares.

"She clearly complained to you about me claiming we were getting married. It was a *joke*. Anyone would know that. Her humor is lacking as fuck."

"You lied. Are we getting married?"

"No." she pouted.

"Are we dating? Are you my woman?"

She took longer to answer but fired Joelle a stare that would have curdled custard. "No, I'm not his woman or his girlfriend, but we have fucked." This part she sent with a smirk toward Joelle before asking Diamond. "Can I go back inside now?" A scowl etched lines around her mouth.

"You can apologize to her."

Joelle finally spoke up. "That's unnecessary."

Rather than expressing gratitude for Joelle's reassurance to the other woman, she glared at her even more intensely. Well, no sisterhood here, even though Sonya lied.

"Fucking apologize, Sonya. Now."

"What the fuck for? Because Rainbow Brite here can't take a fucking joke, and she ran off with hurt feelings? Bikers need a bitch with a backbone. All she had to do was tell me to get you; she would have known already. But no, she ran off and cried to you." Under her breath, she murmured, "fucking bitch." It wasn't something Joelle could mishear. It was loud enough, and Diamond growled.

But that's where she'd had her fill of this woman.

She would've let all the lying go, but no one called her a bitch. She cut in front of Diamond and went up to Sonya.

"Call me a bitch once more and see what happens." She threatened.

Diamond's arm came around her waist, and he pulled her away and tucked her into his side.

"You will tell her you're sorry for fucking lying to her right now, Sonya. Or your ass is out of here for good."

The other woman's eyes widened and pooled with worry.

"You can't do that."

"Can't I? I'll take every goddamn last thing away from you after this stunt you just pulled. Now fucking apologize."

"Fine. I'm sorry." She huffed and then turned around and strode back toward the entrance.

"Well, how fun was that?" Joelle snarked. "Just what I wanted to do with my morning."

"Would you have believed me if I'd told you she'd lied?"

Joelle shrugged. "As I keep telling you, it doesn't matter. I need to go now."

"I don't think so," He lassoed her wrist. Not tight enough that he was hurting her, but unless Joelle wanted to yank her arm, Diamond wasn't letting go, so she jutted her chin to stare at him.

"I have to go, Diamond."

"Why did you come looking for me?"

"I'll tell you another time. After this Sonya saga, I'm maxed out on drama."

His eyebrow shot up, and she laughed.

"There's no need to panic. I'm not stalking you for your body, far from it. I got the hint super clear when you ignored my messages. I deleted your number and blocked you, if you must know."

He smirked then, and the whole sternness of his face changed. "Who's lying now, Bluebell?"

"I am. But only so I can leave already. I have very important things I need to do at home."

One: Freak out. Two: Ask Google where to buy diapers. Three: Freak out because she didn't know how to change a diaper.

One facial feature she'd become accustomed to in their brief acquaintance was the one he was giving her now, as if to tell her he had all day to wait for the answer he wanted.

"Why did that woman lie about you?"

"Who knows why women lie?"

"Maybe so. But you know why *that* one lied." She pressed. If they had slept together, Sonya wanted more.

"Why did you come looking for me, Joelle?"

Joelle let out an annoyed sigh, her lips pursed. She would have preferred a quieter setting to break the news, but since she hadn't come here willingly, she blamed Diamond for the situation.

"Fine. I planned to tell you somewhere quieter when I wasn't annoyed, but whatever, you won't let this go. I'm pregnant." She said, rolling her lips inward.

*Oh no.* She hadn't even softened the blow by giving him the birds and the bees talk, about when daddy bees jack off on mommy bees, and then somehow it made baby birds.

His jawline was so tight she didn't want to know what he was thinking.

"I'm..."

"Shut up, Joelle." He gruffed and pressed a fingertip on her lips.

Okay then.

Fine.

Great.

He was taking the news almost as well as she had.

Now, they could both be in misery.

It sure loved company.

## Diamond

By having Joelle follow him to his place, she continued to glare at him with an intense desire to punch him in the junk.

He was not having an *I'm pregnant* conversation in the middle of the forecourt where all his brothers could overhear. They loved nothing more than gossiping.

"Sit down." He'd told her, showing her inside his condo. The gated complex of ten apartments belonged to him. With three bedrooms, his place was the largest. However, his entire place would fit inside Joelle's bathroom.

"I'll get you a drink."

"I don't want to sit. Or have a drink." She sighed. "I shouldn't have told you like that, but I was annoyed. I was plucking up the courage to text you when you stormed into the restaurant."

"Sit down, Joelle." He growled.

"Does this bossy act work on everyone?" she huffed, but he was pleased when she chose the high-back armchair to perch on. "No wonder Titan took off with a sprint. He feared the big evil boss's angry voice."

"Titan isn't scared of me, and neither are you. What do you want to drink?"

"A whiskey sour. Hold the rocks. And keep them coming."

Her answer had him swallowing, and both his eyebrows winged up. Was she serious? As clueless as Diamond was about all things babies, even he knew a woman shouldn't drink when she was pregnant.

"Tell Sonya I *can* take a joke." A small smile tugged at her lips, as some of the anxious feeling rode down off his back.

"I don't want a drink. Thank you for offering."

"How are you pregnant?" he asked, leaning against the breakfast bar that separated the living room from the kitchen. "We didn't fuck."

"Oh, good. I get to tell the birds and the bees story after all." When he only stared at her sarcasm, she sighed and rubbed at her temple like she had a headache. "I'm sorry for how you found out. I should have been more diplomatic. I also wasn't thrilled to hear the news. So whatever you're feeling, I'm there with you, buddy. We didn't have sex, as you put it. But we did things, Diamond. And your stuff was all up near my stuff. I guess your little guys were determined to follow the map, no matter what they had to do to get there."

There was laughter in the back of Diamond's throat at her description. She glared at him when he let it out.

"So, what you're saying is, babe, I jacked off on you. You were fingering yourself, and that's how you got pregnant?"

"I don't know, okay? *Oh, my god.* Could this day get any more mortifying? I wish I had a time machine; I never would have texted you that night. I should have called, *I don't know*, a porn line. Do they still exist? Don't answer." The exhale she let out could have blown his hair back if it was long enough.

He had never witnessed Joelle being so easily rattled. She was fucking adorable.

"I went to the doctor and..."

"Why?" he interrupted.

"That doesn't matter."

"*Why*, Joelle?"

"I thought I had a persistent flu, but she gave me this news instead, so yeah, I'm a little unsettled. And I don't know what to do or what you're thinking, so I'm freaking out even more."

Diamond moved swiftly across the room with long strides and crouched before her. The second he put his hand on the front of her throat, she snapped her gaze to his and switched from breathing rapidly to not breathing at all.

"Take a breath, Joelle."

"No, I don't want to." She frowned, and he smiled. He'd missed her sense of humor.

As soon as the prospect described the bombshell who'd left the clubhouse, he'd known it was her, and he'd about bolted to find her. He devised a weak excuse to justify what he did, thinking she was in trouble, but Diamond could've easily found any reason to see Joelle again. For weeks, he'd been stalking her just to catch glimpses. He was drawn to the woman who had an undeniable power over him, and it had slowly been driving him to insanity, not being near her.

If only he'd known she'd needed him, he would have punched his way through the brick walls to get to her again.

"Tough shit, you'll breathe anyway." He stroked the front of her throat until he felt it expanding with air. "Good girl."

"Please don't pander to me right now, Diamond. I'm seconds away from crying, and I hate crying. Are you mad?"

He frowned. "Why would I be mad?"

She rolled her pretty eyes. "Oh, I don't know. Maybe because a woman just told you that you're going to be a father, and you're not behaving how other men would. It's freaking me out."

"There's no point in flipping out over shit that's happened, babe." He said, rising to his feet.

"I'm not asking for anything. Before that's your next question. I don't want your money, and you don't need to be involved. But it's only right that you know."

"It's my baby, too." He growled through his teeth.

Did she think she could keep it from him? She was in for a hell of a fight if she tried. Kidnapping her was not beneath him. He'd fucking love any reason to do it. She'd finally be his, and Diamond didn't care about coming up against her powerful father. No one would keep him away from his child.

"I know that. *I* told *you*! There's a baby, and I'm not aborting it or having it adopted. I'm going to have it. There, you have all the information I have." She tipped her chin defiantly.

"You're not getting rid of it," he said, ready to spring forward to lock her up somewhere. The unhinged feelings she brought out in him were fucking ridiculous.

"I just said I wasn't! *Oh, my god*. Can we sit in silence for a minute? My head is spinning. I feel like I'm in an episode of Days of Our Lives." She then sat back in the chair and closed her eyes.

The most important thing on his mind when he woke this morning was how long he wanted to work out.

Now, the whole trajectory of his life had changed.

And it changed in an instant.

He was going to be a father.

And Joelle was the mom.

Christ, the universe loved laughing at him.

For all his magnanimous reasoning for not pursuing a woman out of his league, the universe had already conspired to put Joelle at the center of his life.

Now what the fuck did he do?

It was a no-brainer.

All his life, he'd been a doer.

He jumped in with both feet, never knowing the outcome.

It was how he came to the MC. He hadn't known that would work out as well as it had.

It made sense he'd have a kid like this, not in the usual way with a wife and a life plan.

"You've had your say, babe. Now it's my turn." He said, witnessing Joelle's eyes reluctantly open, locking onto him with a skeptical gaze.

He couldn't blame her for the look.

Plenty of men would have denied her claim.

After all, they hadn't fucked.

And if it were any other woman who was telling him this, he would have insisted she come back with a paternity test.

But it was Joelle. Sweet, mouthy, trustworthy Joelle.

And she wasn't the vindictive type of woman to trap any man.

He sensed that in his soul, even without knowing every detail about her.

Never in his wildest thoughts had Diamond considered getting a woman pregnant without fucking it into her. And he was feeling cheated of the pleasure.

"You said you're keeping the baby. You'll be its mom. So, I wanna be his dad."

"Do you even want children?"

"I never thought about it, but it's happened now, so that isn't a question for me anymore."

"That's a fair point." Her face was pale and melancholy.

He was still percolating the news, but he knew one thing for sure. He would be in this with her all the way.

"We co-parent everything. That means it starts today, Joelle. Doctor appointments. If furniture needs building or buying, or you need to go places, I'll take you."

She seemed frazzled. "Diamond, that's not..."

He cut her off. "This is how it'll be."

She blinked. Her brow folded in the middle. "But, we're not together. That's very coupley."

"Do you want to get married?"

"Jesus." She breathed. "Do I want to marry a man who ghosted on my messages? Thanks for the offer, but no thanks. I didn't tell you just so that you'd take the lead."

"Lucky for you, babe." He half-smiled, and her scowl became more prominent.

"Maybe you need time to think about it. These are big decisions. I'm still processing it, too. I haven't figured it all out yet."

"But we're keeping the baby, yeah?" She nodded at his question, which appeased something in Diamond, and his tension unfurled. "That's the major decision done. All the other shit will fall into place. I wanna be involved, Joelle, at every stage."

"This went a lot different in my head." She said, rubbing at her temple again.

"It's gonna be okay, Joelle." Diamond rarely had all the answers, and things usually worked out, even when they didn't. He was still standing, so all his life decisions couldn't have been that bad.

"Will it?"

"People become parents every day. I'm sure they're scared shitless about it, too. We're nothing special." He watched her face flip through a gambit of emotions, and then she announced.

"Okay, we should do this together, but I'm not sleeping with you again. Sex will only make matters more confusing."

"Baby, we haven't slept together a first time yet, let alone again," he chuckled.

He should be losing his mind, but surprisingly, he wasn't. And he found her declaration adorable. There was a stirring of darkness in his soul for how right this felt. And if he'd known this would have brought

Joelle into his life permanently, Diamond was confident he would have deliberately got her pregnant.

"People will never believe an immaculate conception. I'm like Mary. Only I'm not a virgin." She whined and then put her head in her hands to continue moaning.

Diamond never considered himself a possessive guy. Nor a jealous one. Until Joelle came onto his page, and he wanted to tear every other man's gaze off her with his bare hands.

One little dramatic statement reminded him she'd slept with others in the past before him, and his veins wanted to expand with possessiveness. *She belongs to me.*

"Who was the last guy you went to bed with?" Diamond narrowed his eyes, but he already knew the answer. He'd been witness to how Trent, the limp dick in his bow tie, couldn't stop staring at her.

She rolled her pretty eyes. "That hardly matters now."

It mattered to him. He needed the names of men he would toss into Kylie's cremation machine.

"The party jerk with his tongue dragging on the floor for you, wasn't it?"

She spluttered a giggle.

That fucking prick.

Diamond felt a surge of anger, remembering how he'd imagined the satisfying crack of that jerk's head hitting a table. Now, he wished he had followed his gut that night.

"Diamond, are you jealous?" she sounded so pleased that he snapped his head up to see her smiling.

"No. It's *my* baby inside you. Doesn't matter if it was fucked there or not."

"*Ugh.* Did you have to remind me?" Her smile fell. "You are so crass."

"Babe, I'm a biker."

"Yeah."

"Reality crashing in for you, huh? You realized you got a biker kid inside you."

"I have my baby inside of me."

"Ours." He rasped.

"Yes," she smiled with a radiant blush. "He's ours."

"Will this make things complicated for you?"

"Oh, I'm sure. But I don't care right now. What will be will be. I'm going to be a mother. I need a minute to get my head around that before tackling other people's opinion." She inhaled and blew it out slowly. "I'm going to end up on Page Six, aren't I, like Jesus' mom?"

Diamond felt the rolling of a growl surging up his throat. "Don't mention that party prick again, Joelle."

She blinked, all wide-eyed and lovely. "I never mentioned Trent's name."

Another heated growl. "You talk about not being a virgin, and it puts that paper-pushing prick in my head and reminds me he slept with you, and I haven't yet. It makes me want to snap his weak bones and make a pie out of his dust."

"*Diamond.*" She giggled, and then it was full-out belly laughing until she had to brace a hand on the arm of the chair. Then, before Diamond knew what was happening, she jumped to her feet and dashed off down the hallway. He followed instinctually and was in time to see her slamming the bathroom door shut.

Did he say something to upset her?

"Joelle, what's happening? Are you sick? Are you crying? Open this door." He was about to kick it in when he heard a flush, followed by the faucet.

The door whooshed open.

"Okay, new rule. Don't make the newly pregnant lady laugh because I nearly piddled on the chair."

Diamond's head was whirling from all the different directions they were taking at full speed. "You laughed and nearly pissed yourself? Is that something?"

"It must be. It's my first time being pregnant, and I don't know how the hormones are mixing in there. It's like a giant amalgamation pot."

"How many rules will there be?" His brow arched high on his forehead.

She shrugged. "That's another don't know. Maybe a million? We'll have to play it by ear."

A million rules to have a baby together?

And no sex on top of those rules?

Fuck that.

He'd get his dick in this woman.

If they were going to be co-parents, they deserved the pleasure of making the baby.

Even if it happened after the conception.

## Joelle

Joelle was going to smack her baby's daddy.

The man had no filter. Whatever he thought came right out of his mouth seconds later, and he was making her head spin like the exorcist.

The news bomb changed his life, and he took it all in his stride.

Joelle was sure he was not human.

"Come on, tell me, Joelle. Co-parents don't have secrets." He coaxed, repeating his earlier question, smirking. Knowing he'd made her cheeks flame when he'd casually asked if being pregnant had made her hornier.

"Don't be cheeky. I'm trying to have a meltdown. Would you care to join?"

"I'm not freaking out."

"I know. It's weird! You can't stay cool when a woman says she's pregnant. You didn't even ask if it's yours! That's insane, Diamond."

"Of course, it's mine."

"How can you be so certain?" she squinted, convinced of his madness. In his situation, Joelle would have doubts.

"Because it's you."

What did he mean by that?

"Because I have so few options, and you're the only man I've touched recently?" she snapped, jumping to conclusions because did she mention she was mid freak out? "Charming! I could snap my fingers and have several men in my bed within the hour. You don't know."

He moved like an apparition. One second he was across the room, then the next, he was crowding into Joelle's space, sucking all the air out of her lungs with his proximity. And he made it worse by grasping her chin.

"You listen to me, Joelle. One: shut your little mouth because you're freaking out and projecting your fears. Two: I said because it's you, because it's *you*. You're not someone who would pin a kid on any guy. So yeah, if you say it's my baby, it's my baby, I trust that. And Three."

"How many are there?"

His eyes flared. "Three: who the fuck are these guys who you'd snap your fingers to? I want names. I want addresses."

He was so deadly serious, with his thunderous eyes and flat lips, that it loosened some tension in Joelle's shoulders.

*Yay.* Although it took Diamond a while to arrive, thankfully, he was also irrational about two separate things. Yet a girl still enjoyed having company in her time of misery.

"I can't tell you that."

"Why not?" he growled, giving her chin a little shake, which made her smile for some obscure reason.

"I don't take the names of my booty calls. I get serviced, then kick them out once I'm done with them."

"*Joelle.*" He growled a warning again, and she outright laughed as he paced away and then turned. The darkened hue had drifted from his features. "You're fucking with me."

"Duh. Of course I am. You wounded my female pride."

"How? You're fucking stunning. Why wouldn't I think you have men lining up to climb into your bed? I was there within seconds, if you remember."

Oh. Wow. If she had feathers, they'd be fluttering now.

However, during her panic, she couldn't feel flattered.

"Can we focus on this crisis, please?"

His eyebrow angled high. "Is it a crisis? Or is it a surprise?"

"Both? It's certainly a surprise."

"It's nothing we can't deal with."

Had he been huffing bath bombs? She couldn't be the only one panicking about how this would turn out. She didn't know the first thing about taking care of a baby. And as for keeping it alive for eighteen years, she was not a wizard.

"I've been fertilized, Diamond! Don't you get that? It's a big deal for a woman when it happens unexpectedly."

She didn't expect him to laugh and not to laugh as hard as he did. For a full minute, she scowled and waited for the raucous good time he was having to come to a stop.

"Are you done? I need to go home to paint. It's the only time I can think clearly, and I need to think when I'm not looking at you."

"Thank you, Bluebell." The biker smirked, and she rolled her eyes.

"I wasn't complimenting you."

"Yes, you were."

*Dammit.*

"Walk me to the door, Diamond."

They were connected forever now; she'd have to get used to his cheeky humor, or she'd end up digging a grave, and he was a big man. She'd be digging forever.

She wondered how proficient Kenneth was with a shovel. Something to consider at a later date if needed.

He followed her out to the car.

"I guess I'll call you?" she was uncertain how they proceeded from here. After all, she hadn't thought this far ahead. And then, when she'd told him the news, she hadn't expected Diamond to jump on the daddy train as fast as he had.

"You'll have to unblock me," he smirked knowingly.

"You know I didn't block you. But I should have."

An arm touch focused her eyes on his serious face. "I know you're scared, but you're not alone in this, Joelle. I won't leave you to deal with anything by yourself."

Her heart thudded hard.

As much as she longed to believe what he said, nothing had changed. Diamond hadn't suddenly pursued her. Without this hiccup, he would still be living his carefree biker life, free from her.

As positive as he was today, their conversation only happened because of an oopsie baby they'd made together. Otherwise, he'd still be ghosting her. She had to remember that before her heart took over.

She couldn't become hysterical because of his presence. She had to keep reminding herself if he'd wanted to be with her, he would have made it happen before this.

Joelle unlocked the car door, and Diamond pulled it open for her. She slid behind the wheel and glanced up, feeling vulnerable under his piercing gaze.

"Thanks for being so positive today, Diamond. I never expected it."

"We're in this together, babe. Drive safe. We'll talk soon."

Diamond seemed genuine in what he told her, but she didn't wholly expect to hear from him so soon. People said things they didn't mean. So her heart thudded as she saw his name illuminate her phone screen later that night while she was relaxing in the tub.

"Hey, Diamond. Is something wrong?"

"No, babe. I said I'd talk to you soon." There was a hint of amusement in his voice.

"Can you hold on for a minute? I'm in the bathtub. I'll get out so we can talk."

He gruffed something inaudible. And it was the wrong time for her to remember how deep his voice sounded over the phone because the distraction made her crack her knee against the marble bathtub.

"Ow, goddammit."

As she limped towards her robe, she could hear him calling her name. She slipped it on without bothering to dry off, knowing Diamond was waiting.

"Sorry about that."

"What happened? Are you hurt?"

"I banged a knee on the climb out."

He grunted on the other end, and she could hear him making noises.

"Are you at home? What are you doing?"

"I didn't want to sleep yet, so I'm baking."

Had Diamond told her he was giving a cat a manicure while wearing a pink leopard onesie, she couldn't have been more stunned by his answer.

"You're a baker!?"

"Yeah, babe." He answered, a smile in his thick, rusty voice. "Is that a surprise?"

"Yes. You're a roughened biker who grunts and scowls. I never expected to hear you bake."

"I can knock people out with a punch and make chocolate eclairs."

Joelle positively whimpered. "Oh, please, don't say that. You're talking to my weakness."

Suddenly, his voice turned to pure smoke, and Joelle had to latch the belt tighter around her robe before she started groping herself like a pervert.

"Oh yeah? Do you have many weaknesses, Bluebell?"

"Mmhm, at least a thousand, but I shan't be telling you any of them. Tell me why you called before I ask to lick the mixing beater."

"Babe," he laughed. "You can't say that seductive shit to me and not expect me to react."

She turned as red as the color on her toenails, curling them into the thick, plush carpeting. "I wouldn't know how to be seductive, so you must be imagining things."

"Babe," he said again. That one word conveyed so much. "You asked me over the phone to talk dirty to you so you could get off. That's about the most seductive shit ever."

"Oh, please, don't remind me of that," she groaned. Mortification setting in like concrete.

"We're always gonna have a reminder," he said.

Yeah, he was right. And she placed her hand on her covered belly. Soon, there would be evidence of what she'd set in motion that night.

"Why did you call, Diamond? I'm sure it wasn't to make me blush."

"I enjoy seeing you blush."

"River! Concentrate."

He laughed on the other end, and for a few seconds, she listened to the sounds of him cooking, trying to picture him in his kitchen. Was he wearing a black apron around his waist? Was he bare chested with a little spatter of cake mixture right on his manly pecs?

Oh no, her thoughts were ready to spring forth and become filthy if she didn't back them up.

Rule #4: Don't think about the biker being half-naked. She was firm on that.

"You were all over the place earlier. I wanted to check you were doing alright now."

"I'm fine. Thank you for asking. How are you feeling now?"

"So polite." He chuckled.

It probably would feel awkward between them for a while. For Joelle, at least. Diamond seemed well-adjusted.

"It's happened, babe, and now we deal with the things that need dealing with."

"Did you tell anyone?"

"Not yet. You?"

"Perhaps we should keep this to ourselves for now."

"Anything you need, babe."

God, he was being nice.

"I need to make one thing clear, Joelle."

"Oh?"

She caught the sound of mixing and inhaled in a slow stutter because she wanted to lick the beaters. Not sexually. She just liked cake batter.

"Your father is high up on the power ladder. I want you to know as powerful as he might be, so am I. Us having a baby is between you and me. He's not gonna jump for joy and offer me a congratulatory cigar when he knows a biker knocked you up. But Joelle, his approval means jackshit to me. This is our baby. You and I make all the decisions. No one gets a say in our baby. If he tries anything..."

"He won't." She rushed out. Not knowing for sure, since this was the first time she'd been pregnant by a biker.

"If he tries anything, Joelle, I won't fight cleanly. I need you to get right with that because nothing will come between me being that baby's father."

The passion in his voice leeched down the phone line and curled warmth in her lower belly.

He wasn't finished.

"And that goes for you, too. If he comes at you with nasty shit, I won't sit by and let that happen."

"Stop." She wheezed. "Diamond, stop being nice or..."

"Or what, babe? You'll ask me to come over with my mixing beater?"

"You are rotten," she half-laughed, "say goodnight so I can cream myself."

His grunt was unmistakable. "Now, who's being seductive again, Bluebell?"

"Put lotion on." She corrected, so damn red she could have set fire to the carpet.

He only laughed. "Goodnight, Bluebell."

"Goodnight, you big bear. Save me a cupcake."

Once they'd hung up, she flung herself back on the mattress and sighed.

*Whoa.* The biker needed to come with a clit warning.

She knew, logically, she shouldn't ever flirt with him. It would lead to places they shouldn't go.

If she could have a life with Diamond, if they thought about it, how would it even work out?

He was a criminal, and she was the daughter of a Judge.

Could she trust him? And would he ever trust her?

That's why she had to take flirting off the table, even if he made her smile more than anyone else.

The biker was the father of her unborn baby. He baked and had ink all over his body. He made sexy grunting sounds that shouldn't be sexy but were. And he'd just declared to protect her and the baby from her father's future wrath.

He wasn't even trying, and he was already the perfect man.

Sighing and banishing crazy thoughts of throwing herself at him, Joelle didn't think about Diamond while she creamed her legs.

And she didn't imagine him half naked while he was baking when she attempted to sleep later that night.

## Diamond

The clubhouse was bouncing with celebration, loud music, and booze in endless supply.

And Diamond's mind was elsewhere.

It didn't stop him from toasting a drink to his recently patched-in brother.

Mouse looked like he was about to burst with pride wearing his new cut.

"It looks good on you, brother," Diamond told the other guy and watched how he grinned.

"Shit. You're the first to call me that."

"I didn't know I was taking your virginity, Mouse. We'll always have this." He laughed and slung a meaty arm around his shoulder. Mouse was a stand-up guy. Loyal, hardworking, and a good dad to his two kids, raising them almost single-handedly.

Diamond recently understood Mouse's challenges with managing a job, the club, and raising children.

Nothing made a guy focus like having a kid.

Diamond had never been so organized in his life.

Since Joelle informed him weeks ago, he'd been extra worried about their safety. He ensured his peace of mind by driving past her house at night. It also meant that, around his club duties, he spoke and saw Joelle almost daily.

He was turning into someone he didn't know but wasn't hating it, far from it.

Because of Joelle's morning sickness, witnessing how fierce it was, he was stressed that if she were alone, she'd choke to death.

While celebrating with his brotherhood, he sent her a text.

**DIAMOND**: Everything okay?
**JOELLE**: No. I'm hanging off the chandelier and need rescuing.
**DIAMOND**: Are you serious?
**JOELLE**: Of course not. How would I even get on the chandelier? Everything is fine. The same fine I was this morning.
**JOELLE**: How is the party? Is Mouse happy?
**DIAMOND**: He's like a pig in shit.
**DIAMOND**: And I won't forget these lies you tell me, Bluebell.
**JOELLE**: Ooohhh, is the big bear bodyguard keeping a tally in his little black book?
**DIAMOND**: Might be.
**JOELLE**: I'm not scared.
**JOELLE**: Hey, did you bake today?

**DIAMOND**: No.

**JOELLE**: Oh, okay. I was craving a little treat.

She had an addiction to his cookies, *not a euphemism*, unfortunately. He'd baked a few tasters for her several times, and now she was a gorgeous little begging thing when she needed a treat.

Swinging his legs down from the table, he fist-bumped Mouse, leaving him alone just in time because Sonya snuck her way over and climbed onto his lap. The new brother laughed and grabbed onto her barely covered ass. Diamond didn't need to see what happened next.

He was pulling out pans in the kitchen when Axel came in, his arm tucked around Scarlett.

"Yo, Prez, Mrs Prez."

"Hey, Diamond," she beamed. "Are you baking... at a party?"

"Yeah," he half smirked, checking the club pantry had the ingredients to make mini lemon chess pies. Joelle had been craving anything citrus lately.

"I think this is what it must have been like to watch Picasso painting." Remarked Scarlett an hour later, once the miniature curd pies were assembled on a cooking sheet to go into the oven.

"Prez, control your old lady. She's objectifying my spatula."

"I've never seen a man baking until you, Diamond. Axel, why don't you bake?" She accused her husband.

"I prefer eating." He told her. "Speaking of, move your little ass, wildcat. I've got an appetite, and I've had enough of you drooling over D."

The club's First Lady jumped from the stool and squealed like she was about to be chased throughout the clubhouse. She ran out, and Axel smirked, following her slower.

He was glad he could facilitate someone getting laid since he'd slipped into celibacy.

They weren't in a relationship, and Joelle had actively told him there would be zero sex between them, but he felt like he'd be cheating on her if he fucked someone else.

Not that he had the urge to. The only woman he wanted was her.

So now he was baking to avoid thinking about the real problem: he wanted to sleep with the mother of his unborn child.

The hunger hadn't come on suddenly. It wasn't brand new. The need had been percolating and growing for months. The attraction had been rooted in his gut the day he met her and had crawled around his organs ever since.

The shit was way more complicated now than it ever was. But now, he wasn't holding himself back from having her.

With the packaged chess pies in his saddlebag on the side of his Harley, he left the Diablos party in full swing sometime later. Just before midnight, he parked at the back of the Snow mansion, as he always did.

"Sir." The butler blinked in confusion at the back door. Despite the late hour, the guy was still pristinely dressed in his butler suit. In case of a social emergency, maybe. He had no understanding of the difficulties experienced by the ridiculously rich. If not for Joelle and the extraordinary pull she had on him, he wouldn't be caught dead at the mansion.

"Were you expected?"

"Nope, Kenny, and you haven't seen me, either." He winked, making the old man grin and usher him in.

He looked at the plastic box in Diamond's hand. "I believe I'll make myself a hot chocolate and retire, but I'm sure this door will be unlocked for a while."

Kenneth was a good man, Diamond decided. He hadn't even made it to the staircase when he heard the noise of male laughter along the hallway where Snow's office was situated. He paid little attention when another male voice joined him until he realized who it was.

Stepping out of sight but close enough he could listen in, he didn't have to think long to wonder why the jackshit Harvey, the leader of the Riot Brothers, was having a late night tete-a-fucking-tete with a crooked Judge.

The two men were shaking hands and looking chummy as fuck.

Before he was discovered, he trekked through the mansion up to Joelle's suite of rooms. He knocked lightly and leaned against the doorjamb when she yanked it open.

"Reeves, I swear I told you... oh, it's just you." She smiled, and Diamond felt a direct impact on his solar plexus.

She wore an oversized shirt that had once been white but was now stained with paint splatters, and a bandana held her hair back. Her legs were deliciously bare.

She looked good enough to eat, and Diamond had brought a full appetite.

He didn't know what this new feeling was, only that it was *intense*. It drove him forward every damn day. It felt like an addiction, how it only settled down when he was near her.

He'd always been attracted to Joelle. She had the kind of body that made a man look twice and then a third time. It made him think of sheets and seeing her tangled around them while he pumped into her.

But now that he'd gotten her pregnant, it was like his hormones were the ones changing because the chemistry between them was electric. Her breath alone made his erection strain against his jeans. He had to restrain himself from mauling her when she smiled at him.

It was out of character, a first for Diamond.

He noticed her lowering eyebrows and responded by holding up the plastic box.

"Did you bake?" she asked. Excitement in her voice.

"Might have." He smirked. "You won't know until you let me in."

"You and whatever smells so good can come in. I need to wash my hands. I've been painting all night."

"Yeah? Did you do good shit?"

She'd only let him see a few pieces she'd painted. Diamond didn't know art from his asshole, but he could see talent when he looked at it, and Joelle was incredible.

"It was a productive painting day. Whether it's good shit is up to the client. Now, hand over the goodies." She smiled, turning his stomach to boiling water as she wiggled her fingers at him. She was mid-bite, moaning around the pie when she asked. "I thought you were at Mouse's party?"

"I was, but you wanted something sweet."

She blinked, turned pink in the cheeks, and then she smiled. "You didn't have to do that, but these are exceptional, so I'm very grateful you did."

Diamond parked himself on the couch. "Do you know the guy your father is meeting with?" he asked.

"I didn't know he was. It's a bit late for a meeting. Do you know him?"

"Yes."

"Ah. And your lack of words tells me it's not someone you like? Or approve of? Or he's a bad guy?"

She was his child's mother, which changed things for Diamond. He'd protect her with his all from people like Harvey or the Riot Brothers. One of theirs was already hounding Denver and his old lady, Casey.

Joelle wasn't his old lady, but maybe she was something *more*.

"Remember that day you were eavesdropping on your father's office when we were here?" she grinned at his question, not an ounce of guilt. He liked that about her.

"Maybe, why?"

"Do you wanna go do the same again?"

"Ohh. Espionage? I'd love to." She agreed too readily, and Diamond knew he'd made a mistake.

At the door, she turned and nearly smacked into him because he'd followed her. "How did you even get in here, anyway?"

"I have my ways, Bluebell."

She laughed. "I'm sure you do. Wait here while I get my spy on." The saucy minx even winked at him before she closed the door behind her. And like a puppy waiting at the door for the one who owned him, Diamond remained there.

The minutes went by. And he wished he hadn't asked her to eavesdrop. He went for the door, but it opened first, and there she was, bringing him relief.

"I need another little treat. Have you heard of the British dessert Jam Tarts?"

Diamond's brow puckered. "No."

"Well, look it up. I think the baby would like it next week. I saw it on that British cooking show. Anyway," she slipped off the painting smock, revealing she was only dressed in a pair of yoga shorts and a floaty pale blue tank top, leaving Diamond's tongue bone dry when he could see the swell of side tits.

Christ, he was hard up if the sight of a side tit was getting his engine revving.

Joelle tucked herself up on the couch with the many pillows. He avoided temptation by choosing the armchair.

"I don't know who the man is, but he's been here before. I recognized his voice. They were talking about property investments. Father cuts through red tape for people. He doesn't know I know that. Anyway," she continued. "I bumped into Mom on the way back and casually asked what Father was doing. She's had a few tipples," she said, "that means she's likelier to talk openly. She said Harvey is an old family friend, and he'll be coming for dinner next week."

"You won't be here for that, Joelle." His snapped remark came gruffly. "He's not someone I want you around."

"I'm rarely invited to his stuffy business dinners, anyway. They're a snooze fest. I'd rather watch you baking."

"Are you inviting yourself over to my place, Bluebell?" He was close to begging to get her there.

She was a temptress by licking a crumb from her thumb. "If you want me to stay out of the way, you must provide adequate shelter to hang out. And what appeals to me currently is watching my private baker."

Diamond chuffed a laugh.

"I put a baby in you, and look how you're turning out. A con artist."

"I know. It's good doing business with you, big bear."

*Big fucking bear.*

She'd started calling him it recently, and each time she used it, he wanted to show her how he could bear attack her down to the floor while he pushed his hand into her pants and got his fingers nice and soaked.

He knifed up from the chair. "Lock this door behind me and don't let anyone in you don't know."

"I'm safe, Diamond. Father won't let anyone in the house he didn't trust."

"Listen to me, Joelle. I don't trust him. That means I don't fucking trust him around you. Harvey is known to the club, and he's bad news. Don't put yourself in his eyesight for any reason. I don't want him to be aware of you or my baby."

Her smile dropped, and he saw she had understood his meaning.

Thank god she was not combative, or he would have revisited his kidnapping idea. It was becoming more appealing by the day when being away from her was driving him fucking crazy.

"Okay. I'll be careful. And besides knowing this cool baker, I also know a bodyguard. Oh, and a rough biker!"

She waited a beat and said as he was about to open the door.

"I'm sure Titan would come over if I rang him."

"Bluebell, don't start with the mouth." He growled low, only for the saucy brat to burst out laughing.

"You're too easy."

If she only knew how easy he was for her.

But he figured they were talking about different things.

## Joelle

Time flew when you were pregnant and puking up a spleen every morning.

Joelle's modesty quickly faded as she realized her medical care team required greater access to her body than she had ever granted to so few people before.

Diamond came to each doctor's appointment with her but disapproved of her being touched so much. However, grabbing his hand neutralized the big, growly bear. He was absolutely incredible, like a god. They could have had a great friendship if her feelings for him weren't so potent.

The sight of the gray blob on the screen confirmed the reality of it all.

"It's all real now, huh?" he asked across his truck's console, and Joelle turned her eyes his way. "I was just thinking that. I knew I was pregnant."

"But seeing it on the screen makes it real." He spoke her thoughts.

He drove in silence for some time. Because his face was relaxed, she couldn't gauge his feelings.

But her mind was still churning out the questions.

"Do you hate me for trapping you?" she let drop.

It hadn't been the question she was going to ask, but it was the one that pushed itself forward, and she sat with her hands clasped in her lap, dreading the answer.

She'd given him the out already, but he'd insisted on being involved.

Should it be offered a second time?

Although they weren't a romantic couple, she believed that parents should have a civil agreement for the sake of raising their child. If he started resenting her, she didn't know how she would handle it.

"Babe." He communicated as if he assumed she would delve into his thoughts and decode that one word. Diamond kept his eyes on the road until he reached a stop sign, then he looked at her. "You didn't trap me. I came all over you, remember? Or are you getting the details of that night mixed up in that head of yours?"

"No, but..."

"You could have asked me to fuck you if you were planning to trap me," he explained, and she felt her anxiousness slackening a tad. Then he smirked. "Maybe I trapped you."

Joelle was so stunned. For the entire ride back to his place, she sat in the cab of his truck with her mouth agape. She finally reacted when he pulled into his private parking spot and approached her door to help her down.

"You totally trapped me," she laughed, not taking him seriously.

That was the blessing about Diamond.

He truly was a nice guy.

He meant what he said, and he didn't give veiled responses. He'd done many lovely, thoughtful things for her in the last weeks. Bringing her medicine to soothe the sickness, making her pots of soup when all she could keep down was the broth. He changed her car tires for better traction on snow and ice. She'd lucked out in the baby daddy department.

"Told you," he smirked, spanning her waist to help her down. "I had a devious plan that night, Bluebell, and it worked."

"You are so rotten," she chastised, watching him striding to his front door, trying to ignore the zip of electricity his touch had caused. It didn't stop her eyes going up and down him, though. Gracious, that biker had such a delectable walk. So masculine and powerful, so sexy and hypnotic.

*It's the hormones, Joelle.*

They were going to be purely platonic.

"Get in here, baby mama." He told her, holding the door open for her. "Gotta feed you."

"Yes, please." She nearly swooned. What that man could do in a kitchen ought to be illegal. She was considering funding his baking show.

Before pulling out a pot, Diamond slid the sonogram photo from his back pocket and pinned it to the fridge with a magnet.

Joelle's heart instantly flooded with love.

It was *platonic* love.

While she stared at the gray blob on his refrigerator, her world suddenly grew small. *It's just us, bubba. I hope you're ready for two parents who don't know what they're doing.*

An arm came around her, and Joelle realized Diamond was unzipping her coat. He pulled it off her shoulders.

"I could have done that."

"But I got there first." He half-smiled so handsomely that he swept the air from her lungs. Then, he jutted his chin toward the breakfast bar, where she liked to sit and watch him. She'd learned early on that Diamond didn't like help in the kitchen. But he didn't mind her volunteering for spoon-licking. A task Joelle was excellent at.

Her phone pinged, and she saw her mother asking where she was. Ignoring it, she was about to fix them a drink when Diamond did it first.

"I could have done that."

"Let me take care of you," he said in an even tone. His head was bent over several mixing bowls. Still, he sent her a look from underneath his hooded eyelids, and the tension seemed to snap like a visible crackle in the air, and it only dissipated when she buried her mouth in the glass of fresh lemonade.

Whatever she was thinking, she had to be imagining it.

And Joelle decided she needed to stop looking at Diamond so much.

Though it was so lovely to watch him.

But her hormones didn't care that they were becoming friends and parents-to-be. They were constantly on horny alert when he was close by.

And even when he wasn't near.

It was awful.

It was like her body missed him. Her heart screamed for him.

Not only was she a close second to Bible Mary, sans virginity, but she was the only woman to develop a greater crush on the man after he'd impregnated her.

Joelle was an ethics study waiting to happen.

"I need that spatula once you're finished using it, and make sure it's ladened down with cakey goodness." She grumbled, leaning on the breakfast bar.

It was the only pleasure she had left.

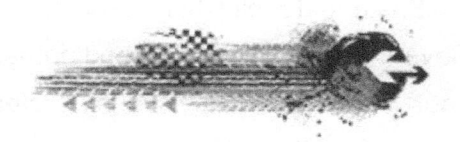

Of course, she was avoiding telling her parents.

The sonogram was nearly a month ago.

After telling Reeves but swearing him to secrecy, he'd laughed for a full five minutes and then announced that he could do anything now because he'd never be the one who got sullied by a biker.

She'd nearly walloped him for saying that.

Diamond was so much more than only a biker, but even so, he was damn good at it.

She hadn't seen Diamond in a few days, but they spoke on the phone several times.

Was it weird to miss him?

It was weird.

She'd said as much to her friends.

They were crazy, too. As soon as they'd found out, they'd jumped into action by insinuating strongly that Joelle and Diamond needed to be together like they were a fated love match.

"It's not like that," she'd insisted.

"Girl, don't feed me lettuce and tell me it's chocolate. The man got you so pregnant even without trying to! That doesn't say platonic. And you wanted to jump his bones, too. Your face says you still do. Get to it."

Molly and Sadie had been relentless for days.

"It's lucky I love you both, or I'd sell you on Craigslist and get two new best friends." She'd told Molly this morning.

"That would never happen. We took blood oaths."

Joelle burst out laughing. "Molly, we all tested our blood sugar levels. That's not the same thing."

"Yes, it was! Don't try to get out of it. Terrible things happen if you go back on a friendship blood oath. Tell me, when do we meet the daddy biker? He needs my stamp of approval."

"He needs nothing. And I don't know yet. We're still navigating."

"Just jump into bed. The rest will fall into place."

That would be sound advice for two people trying to sleep together.

She and Diamond were not those two people.

He was attentive and caring, but he wasn't trying to get into her pants. And for the man she knew, who was bossy and driven, he wouldn't sit on the sidelines if he was feeling her that way. He'd make it happen.

She had more pressing thoughts today, though. She'd distracted herself with as many errands as she could. House hunting was still not going well. Nothing seemed right, and now she had the baby to think about. So, the search continued.

If she waited any longer, her parents would realize she was expecting. Perhaps that was a possibility? She thought about it for an entire minute.

She was nearly thirty and didn't need their approval or their shame.

But like any child, regardless of age, she wanted their blessing.

It had taken her many weeks to accept the fact she was single, unwed, practically having a biblical pregnancy, but she was excited at the idea of becoming a mom. She went as far as purchasing books, which was unusual because she never bought self-help books. The only books she owned had hot, sweaty men on the front. Hot, suited mafia men. Or aliens with two dicks.

There was just this one hurdle to go.

A well-known saying said that once you choose hope, anything else is possible. Joelle would have liked to believe it, but the look on her parent's faces when they heard her news gave her anything but hopeful thoughts.

She'd told them the basics. She was pregnant and keeping it.

Her father's eyes were like ice, and his lips were tight. She could only imagine what he was thinking.

But she didn't have to wait too long.

"Whose is it?"

"The baby is mine."

"You didn't have an immaculate conception, Joelle." He snapped. Oh, how close he was to the truth.

"You aren't even dating anyone." Her mother said, fret in her eyes like it was the biggest scandal to hit their family in decades.

"I know it's a shock. It was to me, too. But it's happened. It's happening, and I'd like it if you could support me. If not that, give me your blessing for your grandbaby."

Her mother cleared her throat and came forward. Her face was still strained, but politeness had been trained into her. She hugged Joelle. "Well, of course, dear. You always have our support, doesn't she, darling? We're always here. And we will love our grandchild."

That was fair. She hadn't expected them to jump for joy.

They weren't the jumping-for-joy type of parents.

She looked toward her other parent.

"Do you have anything more to say, Father?"

"I want to know who did this to you," he demanded sternly.

"No one did this to me. It was quite mutual."

"And you'll be raising the child alone?"

"No. We'll be co-parenting."

His brow raised. "This mystery man is in the picture, then?"

Joelle sighed. "Yes, Father. And you will meet him one day, I'm sure. But this is about your daughter letting you know you'll soon be a grandfather."

"Is it Trent?"

She'd had enough. Joelle kissed her mother on the cheek. "I'll see you later."

"Sweetheart, don't go. We haven't even discussed anything yet." Her mother implored, but she knew what mood her father was in. He was already calculating how this would affect his Snow empire.

It shouldn't come as any surprise to Joelle. And yet, it did.

She hoped her parents would one day react purely based on their emotions, disregarding societal expectations.

"Joelle, I asked you a question." He said sharply. And she turned to glare at him.

"No, it's not Trent's baby. He and I broke up a long time ago. You'd know that if you took one iota of an interest in your children's personal lives. I'm not here asking for your permission, Father. I thought for a silly second you might be happy for me."

"Happy that you're unwed and having some strange man's child?" he narrowed his eyes like she'd committed the most heinous sin, and she felt the stab of his scathing opinion hit like a physical blow.

"It's the twenty-first century. Look around; a woman doesn't need marriage to have children." She said icily, holding onto her tears.

Emotion rushed up her throat. And for a woman who wasn't much of a crier, she blamed her influx of hormones.

"Joelle, I would like answers, please." He said in his usual authoritative tone. Her father's grave flaw was expecting obedience from everyone.

"And I would like supportive, understanding parents. But we don't always get what we want, Father. You don't have to be happy about this, but I am."

His frown lines relaxed, and he chose to remain silent. Joelle sighed and left the family lounge. She changed her mind about going up to her suite.

Kenneth was holding her coat when she went to the coat closet. He was a mind reader.

"Thank you, Kenneth."

"I can drive you wherever you want to go." He frowned as she slipped into the white coat. "Or I will call for a driver."

"I'm fine. You heard all that then?"

He nodded. "He'll come around. Your father always needs time to process."

"This isn't for him to process," she told the family butler, who'd always been like a grandparent to her and Reeves. She knew Kenneth loved them like family, and she loved him back. However, his loyalty would always be to Judge Snow above all else.

There were several people she could turn to.

Joelle wasn't without people who cared about her.

But she drove herself to the only place where she wanted to be.

Diamond wasn't home, and she didn't want to call and disturb him.

She was in no rush, so she sat on the two steps outside his front door.

And waited for her biker haven to come home.

## Diamond

With her blue hair, patterned leggings, and the snow-white coat with its fur trim, it was hard to miss Joelle as he turned his bike into the apartment complex and saw her resting on his steps. But his body would have sensed her before his eyes because his heart sped up.

Immediately on alert, he parked, ignoring the prospect who came riding up behind him. He jumped down and crouched next to Joelle, who hadn't moved. Her head rested on the wall, a hand cradling her cheek.

And she was fucking cold when he rubbed the back of his knuckles on her face.

"Baby?" he palmed her thigh, trying to rub warmth into her.

"Is there a dead chick on your doorstep, boss?"

Her little puffy breaths told him she was only asleep, but it didn't stop Diamond from worrying. Why was she here? How long had she been sitting outside in the cold, for fuck's sake?

"No, she's sleeping." He answered the probie, who was hovering behind Diamond. He rubbed Joelle's thigh again, and she stirred. She'd fallen asleep a few times at his place, so he knew she slept deep. Only the smells of cooking sugar could ever get her alert in seconds. "Come on, baby, wake up."

She stirred some more, and her eyes fluttered open.

The lazy smile she sent his way nearly broke his fucking heart. Had anyone ever been that pleased to see him?

"River." She murmured his name. "Hi."

He kept rubbing her outer thigh. The thin fabric was freezing. She never dressed appropriately for the weather. That had to change, he decided. He'd make sure of it.

"She has wicked blue hair," chuckled the probie. That's when Joelle shifted her gaze to the other man.

"Hi," she smiled at him, the smile she gave everyone like they were already old friends. "Who are you?"

"I'm Price, ma'am."

"Ma'am!" she chuckled, eyes twinkling, "such lovely manners. You need to take lessons from this one, Diamond."

"I'm a good boy, ma'am." The probie dared say, and Diamond swung a deadly stare over his shoulder.

"Thin fucking ice, probie. Get gone. I'll come and check on the painting in a while."

"Got it, boss." He smirked and ambled off around to the storage shed. Diamond had roped in the probie to touch up some paintwork around the complex.

"What are you doing here, Bluebell?"

"I nodded off. I was only going to wait for thirty minutes."

"Let's get you inside. You're fucking frozen." He said it harsher than intended. Over the weeks, he'd become obsessive about ensuring Joelle was well cared for. She was cooking his baby, and he'd worried that she wasn't eating the proper nutrients, getting enough water, or sleeping the correct number of hours for a pregnant woman. Because she stayed up all hours painting and ate whenever she got hungry, which could be hours between, he'd turned into a one-person health coach, checking on her several times a day.

She was unruly, he'd found. She always sent him pictures of her drinking from a gallon water bottle to prove she was hydrating. Then she'd update him on how many times she was peeing. Sassy baby.

He unlocked the door, turned off the alarm, and led her inside.

"Sit down," he told her. "Or do you want to shower to warm up?"

She chuckled. "I don't have a change of clothes, Diamond." Her eyes sparkled like she thought he was an over-pandering papa bear. Taking care of Joelle was like trying to keep a stick insect alive. Most of the time, he had no idea if he was doing the right thing.

Though the heat was on in his apartment, he pulled the blanket from the back of the couch and draped it over her legs. Still frowning, he told her, "Get comfortable. I'll make you a hot drink."

"I'm fine, Diamond. I shouldn't have taken that long blink."

"You were asleep on the fucking doorstep, Joelle." He scowled from the kitchen area. "What if I hadn't come home yet?"

"Then I would have woken up from my power nap and headed home."

"Why aren't you at home already?"

It was her turn to scowl. Stirring shaved chocolate into a pan of simmering milk, he made her hot chocolate so sweet it made his teeth ache just looking at it.

"I told my parents about the baby."

"And it didn't go well?" he guessed. Fucking snob assholes.

"Not quite. He thought Trent was the father."

Diamond's head snapped back, and he glared. "Do you mind if I shoot your father?" he meant it, but she spluttered with laughter like she thought it was a joke. It was far from a joke. That boiled his blood. *He* was the dad, not that skinny piece of crap.

"Did you tell them it was mine?"

The way she colored told Diamond the answer, and he grimaced. When ready, he poured the mixture into a white mug. He brought it to her and sat in the leather chair. Pinning Joelle with a stare.

"You don't want me to tell my family or friends. You haven't told your folks about me. I'm not liking what I'm thinking, Bluebell."

She frowned and buried her mouth in the cup, moaning when she sipped. He loved it when she moaned. He needed those sounds pushed down his throat while she clawed him up.

"I needed time to process it, Diamond. You know that. People assume they're entitled to an opinion."

"No fucker's opinion matters but yours and mine. Let me deal with people, and I'll put them in their place." He let her drink until he was appeased she wouldn't get hypothermia. "You're ashamed a trash biker made you pregnant?" It needed to be asked so he could figure how to strategize her deeper into his life. He wasn't giving her up now, not when life itself had put her in his path. As far as Diamond was concerned, possession was nine-tenths of the law. And being a trash biker, he'd break all the rules for her. Joelle belonged to him.

That got her attention, and he watched Joelle's head crank up. She pinned him with a feminine stare, her pink lips pursed.

"Don't be obtuse, Diamond. Take this cup off me so I can punch you in the eye!"

Her threat made him smirk, and the tightness around his chest gave way until he inhaled and kicked back in the chair, legs spread in front of him. He didn't miss how she checked him out with interest and lust right in the open for him to enjoy.

"It's nothing like that. You're not a trash biker; don't repeat it. You're a foul-mouthed biker, an unfiltered biker, and a biker with no manners."

"Thanks, baby." He sent her a grin.

"You're welcome." She scowled, and the hot chocolate stole her focus.

They didn't speak again until she'd finished.

"I know about the Irish mob." She announced, stunning the fuck out of him.

"How?"

"That doesn't matter. So my question to you, mister biker, is, if my father is messed up in people like that, what can he do to you if he knows you're the father of our baby? Tell me honestly. I don't want you to protect me from the answer because I know you will have thought about this."

"He's only a Judge, Bluebell. He isn't a god. Sure, he has contacts who could cause issues for my MC or me, but that's not unusual; we always have some sector of the law working to put us behind bars. But unless he's into planting evidence, he can only throw his power around so much. As I keep trying to tell you, I'm not without power, too."

She sighed and nodded. "That's what I thought. Now, do you understand my reluctance to tell him? It's nothing about being ashamed. I am far from ashamed of you, Diamond. You've been wonderful this whole time. No woman could ask for a better co-parent. Bubba isn't even here, and I already feel supported by you."

His chest burned.

He was in prime shape for a man his age, but it felt like a heart attack or something equally daunting, his heart swelling with pride.

No, it was the dreamy way she was looking at him. Like if they were a couple, she'd be crawling into his lap and showing her appreciation.

Fuck him. He wanted her to do that. He'd shape her hips with his hands until she moaned because he'd squeeze a little too hard, but she'd get off on him handling her roughly, beg for it, even.

Diamond continued to ignore the pounding through the top half of his body.

"Do something for me."

"What's that?" she asked cautiously. Diamond smiled.

"You only worry about cooking our baby, and I'll take on the worry of everything else. Deal?"

"That doesn't seem equal."

"There is no equal in this, Bluebell," he explained and watched her frowning. He went on. "You have the most important job, yeah? That's something only you can do. So you let me do the rest. You and me are in this bubble, Joelle. If outside disruptions stress you out, therefore stressing out your pregnancy, I'm gonna be pissed. You get what I'm saying?"

"Yes," she replied softly, a sereneness and acceptance in her eyes.

"You don't need to tell your folks anything else," He stated. But then added, "I'll do it."

"What?" she yelped. With eyes wide open, she was unbelievably arousing.

"I'll deal with your father."

"Oh, great. So, what you're saying is hunker down for World War Three?"

Diamond only smirked at her adorable dramatics. She didn't know he'd faced tougher opponents than Snow and survived to recount the story.

Diamond climbed to his feet, and for a second, she looked like she was waiting for a kiss, with her head tipped back, watching him. His lips tingled before tossing her the remotes for the media wall. "Find something for us to watch. I'll check on the probie and then make dinner."

"What's Price doing?"

"He's looking at some maintenance around the complex."

"Invite him in for dinner. He's a cutie."

"*Joelle.*" He growled in warning and saw her eyes twinkling. Sassy, tempting thing. "Do you want me to go out there and break his arms? Because I will."

"Big bear, you're too much," she giggled and curled up on the corner of his couch to watch TV. She looked so at home, like she'd always belonged there. Soon, she would.

Diamond inflated his lungs with cold, fresh air once outside. Plans percolating in his head. Once he'd gone all in with Joelle, he'd known it wouldn't happen overnight. He'd need endurance, but he was coiled tight, his patience wearing thinner by the hour.

It took him a while to head back inside because the prospect needed help to move some outside furniture into the storage shed.

With his skin cold as ice, he shrugged out of the leather jacket, hung it up by the door, kicked off his boots, and discovered a cooking show on the TV. Joelle was fast asleep.

Quietly and carefully, he took the remote out of her hand, slipped both arms underneath her, lifted Joelle, and started for his bedroom. She came half-awake when he was almost there, and fingers clung to his shoulders.

"Are you carrying me? You'll break your back, Diamond."

"Hardly." He answered. It had been a while—months since he'd been this up close and personal with her goddess body, and he reacted to her nearness by hardening in his jeans. It worsened when she dropped her head on his shoulder, nuzzling his neck.

So this was what agonized ecstasy felt like then.

Putting Joelle on the bed, he uncovered it and directed her to move into position. She was instantly cozy in his bed.

Another slash of heat went through him.

"You're staying the night," he told her firmly, ready for her to fight, but she only hummed and closed her eyes. "I'm gonna put you a toothbrush out in the bathroom."

"Okay, River." She replied sleepily.

She was fast asleep when he came out of the en suite. Smiling, he crouched on her side of the bed and brushed back a few strands of blue hair. He enjoyed this woman's company, which had nothing to do with the project they were working on together. He liked her humor and her sass. She was never short of words, so their time together was seldom filled with uncomfortable silences.

"Mmm, nice." He heard her murmur. Her eyes were closed, but her lips were turned up with a smile. And Diamond realized he'd palmed her belly. The only time he'd been this close to his baby was at the ultrasound, and they'd seen the small flickering blob. That was weeks ago, and she now had more of a prominent bump underneath his hand, and he was fucking mesmerized.

His kid was in there.

The kid he'd made with this blue-haired beauty with a smile to launch a thousand ships.

"Mm, River?"

He continued to roam over her covered belly. "Yeah, Bluebell?"

"Kiss me."

He glanced up in a hurry.

Diamond had one of those *'fuck it'* moments and raised to his feet before he leaned over Joelle and pressed his mouth to hers.

Without hesitation, he took action.

As his tongue touched hers, she let out a surprised breath, her body shuddering in response. Even if she was asleep, she knew he was there because she opened her lips, and her tongue sought his. When she groaned, he groaned back, and he kissed her the way he'd been hungering to do for weeks and longer.

The warmth and sweetness of her lips only intensified his desire for more.

Need clenched his muscles as he lingered over Joelle, his arms bracketing her head. To rule over her fuck-hot body was his only screaming thought until she was so sopping wet, she'd beg him for an orgasm, and he'd deliver.

After drawing back from her siren's mouth and swallowing his groan when her eyelids flickered, her mouth split into an enticing smile. "Am I dreaming?"

"Yeah, baby."

It took herculean effort to tuck her in and leave the bedroom.

Sometimes, relationships defied logic for everyone else. It was a million intangible things.

Relationships didn't always have to make sense to anyone else. They were about impalpable things that felt right.

Every time he looked at Joelle, he had the undeniable sense she was for him.

He didn't live in a black-and-white world.

He was shades of gray.

But Joelle, he realized, was all color.

That meant he could make the rules.

And right now, he wanted to be painted with her rainbow.

## Joelle

"Who's bedroom are you in, you tramp?" asked a nosy Molly.

Joelle should have known not to answer a video chat when her friend called.

"That's not important. Why did you call? Is it another witch-in-law saga? Just banish her to a hole in the backyard."

"I wish I could, but Joe likes his mother." She rolled her eyes, but then came closer to the screen. "Now stop trying to distract me. Where are you? That's not your bed."

"I'm at Diamond's place. Do not overreact, Molly." She warned and counted to three in her head before Molly shrieked.

"You're in the daddy biker's bed?" she looked ready to combust with glee.

"It's not how you're thinking, so calm down."

"Since when do women calm down when we're told to? Now tell me everything. Don't leave out one dirty detail, or I swear I'll send the witch-in-law to you."

"You're mean," laughed Joelle. "And it's nothing, I promise. I crashed here last night. It didn't go well with my parents, and I came to Diamond's place like an orphan, and he took pity on me."

He timed his entrance into his bedroom well when he came through the door and arched his eyebrow at her statement. She instantly turned red, and Molly noticed.

"What are you looking at? Is he there right now? Let me meet him, Joelle! You know it's my right as the baby's favorite auntie. He needs to meet me."

Naturally, Diamond could hear everything, and he smirked as he reached into his closet for a shirt.

Oh, yeah, he was shirtless, and Joelle was nearly drooling on his bedspread.

She tried to pull her gaze away, but his insane body was made for staring.

So tanned and solid all over. He had valleys and ripples that made her tongue ache to explore them.

On went his shirt, and Joelle nearly groaned, wishing he'd walk around half naked, if only for an hour or a week. Was it too much to ask for?

He glanced over at her again and winked.

Oh, wow. Her stomach swooped with feelings.

"No." she finally answered.

Joelle found her friend's campaign to meet Diamond amusing, but her laughter turned to shock when he approached the bed. Joelle was almost gasping as she tilted her head back to get a better view of him.

"What's wrong with you?" inquired Molly, but who could concentrate with a shower-fresh, good-smelling Diamond standing over them?

"Hand over the phone, Bluebell." He spoke, and Joelle shook her head.

"Ohh, is that his voice?" squeaked Molly. "It's deep. Hi, Diamond!"

She was incorrigible, and Joelle laughed.

All he did was wiggle his fingers at her, and she immediately caved and handed him her phone.

"So, you're the daddy." Molly proclaimed.

"I am," He rumbled proudly. And Joelle squirmed beneath the covers with warmth, especially when he kept flipping his gaze to hers.

"I'm the baby's auntie and also Joelle's best friend. When you meet our other friend, she will claim she's the favorite auntie, but what you need to know, daddy biker, Sadie is a liar."

"Oh, my god, quit calling him daddy biker, Molly."

Diamond arched an eyebrow at Joelle. "You don't want to call me daddy, Bluebell?"

Oh, he was teasing her. In front of her friend!

She was going to expire in a puddle right this second.

Molly hooted with laughter.

"Give me that phone," she insisted, but he kept it at face level.

"Are you taking care of Joelle and our baby?" asked her friend.

"Trying to," gruffed Diamond, sending his eyes to her again, making her all mushy. Feelings that were impossible to hold back. "When she does as she's told." He added and fired her a wink.

The cheeky boy.

Molly hooted. "I love this. Anyway, give my girl a kiss; I need to go. I'll call you later, Joelle." She said, and the call ended.

"She meant nothing by what she was saying."

Diamond stared, an unreadable look in his concentrated eyes. "She cares about you. Nothing wrong with that, babe."

"If Sadie calls next and insists on talking to you in a few minutes, you have no one to blame but yourself."

"I'll talk to her, too." He acted as if being interrogated by her closest friends was no big deal.

The man was so confusing.

Nothing seemed to faze him.

"Sorry for zonking out on you."

He shrugged. "You were tired."

She wanted to ask where he slept, but kept the question to herself.

"I should get going soon."

"I made breakfast. Get ready and come into the kitchen."

Who was she to turn down breakfast?

After washing up in the bathroom and using the facilities, she dressed in yesterday's clothes, and thankfully, she had a hairbrush in her purse.

"I'm gonna follow you home." He told Joelle before she even took one bite of the cinnamon-drenched French toast he'd made. The fork paused to her mouth, and she gaped.

"Are you sure?"

"Told you I'd handle your parents. Not gonna keep sneaking into the mansion, Joelle."

"But you're so good at it." she grinned, filling her mouth. His eyes tracked to her lips, making the food turn to sawdust.

She could not come up with a counter-argument. She didn't want to deal with her father's anger, so if Diamond could handle him, she'd appreciate it. They'd likely come around unless they didn't. Her life would no longer revolve around their needs.

The baby reminded Joelle he or she was there when the last mouthful of toast went down, and the nausea hit like a train. She barely climbed off the stool, made it to the nearest bathroom, and landed on her knees before she threw up.

She emerged only after rinsing her mouth, dabbing her face with water, and nearly colliding with Diamond. She hadn't known he was waiting outside.

Just seeing him made Joelle cry. And he took her into his arms immediately.

"I wasted your French toast." She sobbed, not even sure why she was crying, only that it felt like the end of the world.

Diamond held her tighter and caressed a hand along her back, but his comfort made her cry harder.

"It doesn't matter. I'll make you more food. How do you feel now?"

"Empty."

He chuckled. "You threw up for a long time."

"Were you listening the whole time?" she cringed.

"I didn't want to be far away in case you needed me."

If he continued to be kind to her, she would fall in love, and that's when things would get complicated.

But knowing that, Joelle didn't brush off Diamond's soothing comfort. Just having him near made everything that much better. They embraced for a while before he offered to make her a warm drink to settle her stomach or to make more food. She declined both, but he insisted she drink water, which she complied with.

He was such a sweet biker.

Joelle wasn't looking forward to seeing her parents again, but it had to be done. When she pulled into the circle driveway, she waited in the car until Diamond pulled up beside her. Pulling off his helmet, he turned his head and gave her a reassuring smile that said to trust him.

Her belly did that slow dipping again. It had nothing to do with feeling nauseous and everything to do with how nice he was being with her. Even as she fought them, Diamond made it easy for Joelle to catch genuine feelings.

It was Diamond who opened her car door. "You can't sit here all day, Joelle." He half-smirked.

"Does anything ever bother you?"

"Nope." He answered. She wanted to be as unconcerned about others' opinions. "Out you get, woman. Let's get it over with and see where shit lands, yeah?"

"Yes." She agreed.

"Let me handle it." He warmly folded her hand into his, instantly giving Joelle peace.

She was okay with that.

They'd only taken a few steps together.

Joelle wasn't sure what happened, only that her ears were ringing and Diamond had thrown her to the ground and was laid on top of her. Protecting her from the booming explosion that had gone off inside the mansion.

"Keep your head down, baby." She caught him saying, his hand cupped around her head.

Confusion stained every blink as she tried to figure out why she was on the ground and what had happened.

The house alarm was whirling loudly. Debris was scattered across the lawn like broken confetti, and the acrid smell of smoke burned the inside of her nose.

"Let me up. I need to see," she wheezed, and Diamond's weight lifted off her as he helped her up. Keeping her in his arms, she tried to make sense of the half-house she was staring at.

It was unbelievable.

Like a dream.

Or a nightmare.

Disorientated, the ringing in her ears made her hearing fuzzy, but fortunately, Diamond was entirely in charge, already on a call to the emergency services.

"My parents! Diamond, they're inside! Reeves! Where is Reeves?" she screamed, trying to pull away from him. But he wrapped both arms around her from behind.

"You're not getting any closer to that fucking house, Joelle. I mean it," he said darker, his voice penetrating through her shocked system, and she looked up at him with her tear-filled, terror-filled heart. "I'm putting you in the car, and you will stay there. Got it?"

She nodded. Looking at the house, it was a wreck.

One minute earlier, they would be there, too.

Instinctively, her hands covered her belly.

It was seconds when some of the staff started pouring out from around the back of the house. They looked terrified and disheveled, like they'd dug through a bombsite. Joelle attempted to climb out of the car to help them, but Diamond growled.

"Stay put, baby."

"My parents, Diamond." She cried.

*Please be okay.* They might not always agree or understand who she was, but they were her parents, and she loved them.

"I'll go search. Do not move from this spot." He issued a warning, looking her in the eye. "Think of our baby, Joelle. You protect bubba first."

He was right.

It didn't mean she liked it, and her heart thudded hard as she watched him stalk toward what used to be the front door.

The police started arriving.

They came in droves.

Naturally, they did. The explosion at the house of a well-known Judge prompted a massive response from all emergency departments, including the chief of police.

Ambulances came.

It was utter pandemonium.

Small fires appeared in broken windows. Smoke clogged up her lungs. From what she counted of heads, all the staff had gotten out unscathed; paramedics were looking them over.

The fire services were working on putting out the fires, and the police had already closed the street.

But her eyes remained locked on what was left of her family estate.

She was feeling overwhelmed as her heart and mind raced in various directions.

And then she saw someone emerging.

It was Diamond carrying her mother.

Joelle didn't even recall shouting for her mom, but her lungs burned, and her heart beat so hard. She didn't get far because a cop stopped her from crossing the barricade. She rooted to the floor, watching Diamond placing her mom on a gurney. The paramedics took over from there. Right behind Diamond was her father. He was in a much better state, though coated in black smoke. He stayed close while the paramedics were with his wife.

He returned to her, and she threw herself into his arms, overwhelmed with gratitude that he was safe.

"Thank you," she cried. "Are you alright? Is mom?"

"Found her at the bottom of the stairs. I'm not sure if she got thrown by the blast, but she's out cold, still breathing. They're taking care of her. Your father was trapped in his office. He was screaming your mom's name. The fucker broke himself out like the Hulk." He almost sounded impressed.

She clung harder to him.

"What about Reeves?"

"Your old man said he stayed at a friend's place last night. I need to get you out of here, Joelle. It's not safe to hang around."

"What?" she blinked, tear-streaked face. "I can't leave now, Diamond."

"Listen to me," he gruffed, cupping her face. "Houses don't just explode, Joelle. Some shit has gone down here, and I don't want you or our baby anywhere near it, you hear me?"

She got it, she did.

But how could she leave?

So many emergency services kept coming. Even the press vans and helicopters arrived to report the news.

She cried again in Diamond's arms and waited until they loaded her mom into the ambulance.

"What on earth happened here? Was it a gas leak?" she asked her father.

He looked withdrawn, like he'd aged fifteen years in moments. For the first time, Joelle realized he was an old man. And not the dynamo he'd always been. They'd rarely been a family that hugged, but she immediately put her arms around him, and he instantly hugged her in return. "Mom is going to be okay."

"She will." He agreed hoarsely. When they parted, she retook Diamond's outstretched hand as her father ran shaken fingers over his snow-white hair, his eyes locked on their connection. His team had already arrived and was handling the gathering of journalists.

"I need to talk to the police." He told her. "But first, let me have a minute with Diamond."

She frowned and looked toward Diamond. His face was unreadable.

"Wait in the car, Joelle." The biker told her with a reassuring smile.

Curious about the situation, she was about to decline, but Diamond's tense reaction made her retreat to the car, where she observed their brief exchange. Diamond stood with his arms folded, nodding in places.

Their conversation went on for a few minutes.

They both headed toward her car, and she jumped out again.

"You'll stay with Diamond for a while, Joelle." Her father announced. Had he said she was adopted from an alien race, she would have been less stunned.

"No, I'm not. I'm needed here."

"Listen to me, honey." He'd never called her honey, and her panic intensified. "I need to focus on sorting this mess."

"But mom..."

"She would say the same. The father of your child is going to ensure you are kept safe until this is dealt with." Though he looked more fragile than ever, some of his authoritative demeanor returned, and he held Joelle with a parental look. "He's the child's father, isn't he, Joelle?"

"Yes."

"Then he's the one to take care of you. He's already agreed. I'll feel better knowing you're safe, Joelle. Now, I must get to the hospital to be with your mother. I'll be in touch, honey." He kissed her on the cheek and then strode off. With his team of people following, he looked once at their fallen house and climbed into his blacked-out SUV.

Nothing made sense anymore.

It was like walking on a film set and not having the script.

Diamond returned her to the car and said he'd follow behind on his bike.

To ensure her safety, her father placed her in the care of a biker. The biker seemed cool with it, even working closely with her father, which she thought hell would freeze before that ever happened.

Once the news hit the airwaves, Joelle's phone blew up with messages and calls. After a brief talk with Reeves, she reassured Sadie and Molly that she was fine and would contact them later with updates.

That was if someone told her first.

## Diamond

Tonight wasn't a regular church meeting.

Only three men were sitting at the table.

Diamond was with Axel and Chains. The president and VP. The two most influential men in the Diablos.

The pair remained silent while Diamond recounted everything from the Snow mansion explosion. He got Joelle settled and tucked into bed, emotionally drained, and then came to the club to chat with Axel.

This shit was too much for him to bear on his shoulders alone.

"Snow knows for sure it's the Irish mafia?"

Diamond answered Axel. "He says so. Said he got a cryptic message from the Shannon chick that he wouldn't be able to silence her. Then, less than an hour later, his house blew up. It's too much of a coincidence."

"And you've knocked up his daughter?" Interjected Chains. "You kept that quiet."

"It was her choice." His jaw felt like glass. If he gritted his teeth any harder, his face would shatter. He didn't want to leave her alone, but things needed cementing before he could return home. "Joelle didn't want to tell anyone yet."

"How did the old man take it?"

"Not well. But he all but begged me to look after her tonight. He wants her far away from him like he expects some other shit to happen."

During the silence, Axel and Chains exchanged a wordless glance.

He knew this shit didn't look good.

But he couldn't abandon Joelle.

Even if she weren't carrying his baby, he still would have dragged her away from that bombed estate, screaming and kicking, if he had to. As soon as he'd heard the fear in Snow's shaken voice, and the old man had begged him to take Joelle with him, Diamond had wanted to turn around and get her far away to safety. Fuck the rest of them. His total focus became about protecting her. It hadn't even happened suddenly. It had been happening over time, little by little until that was all he could think about.

"It makes little sense," Chains finally said, drumming his tattooed fingers on the table. He then ran a hand over his shorn mohawk. "We talked to the Irish, and they weren't aware of the bitchrella's revenge plot. They shut her down."

"They didn't shut her down enough." Shrugged Diamond. "That's as far as I know. And I don't care. I don't give one shit about the Judge and what happens to him. I hated working for that fucker."

"You didn't hate all of it if you got into his daughter's panties." Smirked Chains.

His jaw worked tight again, and he shot the VP a stare across the table, trying to remain calm. He wasn't one to rattle easily when provoked by the boys, but he was finding out Joelle was his weak spot.

"Joelle isn't up for discussion, Chains." He bit out.

"But she is, isn't she?" asked Axel, scrutinizing from the head of the table. "You're here because you want us to protect her."

"Not exactly. But I'll be absent because I know she's gonna want to poke her nose in, and I have to be close to intercept the nosiness. I already said I don't give a shit what happens to Snow. Or how he handles his disaster."

He was uncertain about what he wanted.

Understanding?

Acceptance?

These men were his brothers. Not by blood, but they might as well be. He respected his patched brethren. They'd fought side by side for a lot of years. You couldn't go through economic wars and not forge strong friendships. It was built on trust and loyalty.

His guilt stemmed from that.

The club shared every piece of good news as if it were their own.

He'd kept Joelle and the baby a secret, which hadn't sat well with Diamond.

"This isn't our drama, Diamond," Axel stated in his totalitarian voice. "Snow hasn't paid us to get involved. And we're not wading in against the Irish fucking mob on a whim. We have enough on our plates already with the Riot Brothers. The Murphys know more than we do about them, and they said they're fucking lunatics. My house was bombed once already. I don't want a second go-around. I have my old lady to think about now. We're trying to dig out of shit, not ask for more."

"I know that," agreed Diamond, somewhat frustrated at what he was hearing, but he got it.

"You know the rules, D," added Chains. "We don't throw the club's weight behind just anything. We have a lot to lose. Is Joelle your old lady?"

"No." he grimaced. It was fucking complicated. "But would you abandon your kid's mother at a time like this? Could you leave her in a place that would get her hurt or worse? Sometimes rules have to be shifted for extenuating circumstances."

"Listen," Axel stated. "We agree with you. Snow can fend for his fucking self. He has enough cops on his payroll to take care of his ass. If he gets blown up, he is one less jackass to worry about. As for your situation." He said, pinning Diamond with his presidential stare. "Your *not* old lady, had it right. Keep things close to your chest for now."

Diamond could feel himself heating under the collar, and he had to clench his fists on the tabletop.

"Before you blow a gasket," he continued, "It's for your kid's safety. The fewer people know she's pregnant with a Diablos biker, the better. These mad fucks wouldn't think twice by dragging her into the mess, using her to get to Snow. So, as far as it goes, this talk didn't happen, yeah?"

Diamond climbed to his feet. "Yeah, got it." He'd do whatever he had to do. Even if he did it alone.

It was funny that bikers got into the lifestyle, so they didn't have to live by society's rules, yet the MC still had rules in place and expected everyone to follow them. Until now, Diamond had been a good soldier, always following the MC bylaws, and had agreed with many of them. Especially about who the club waded into trouble for.

He wanted to say so fucking much. That he'd protect their old lady's without a second thought.

Officially, Joelle wasn't his. But she was *his*. Underneath everything, he felt it in his soul.

Somewhere under his pissed-off anger, he got what they were saying. But he didn't like it. Not one bit.

He wouldn't allow Snow's bullshit to touch Joelle or their unborn child.

And if he couldn't rely on his brotherhood, he'd do the protecting alone.

"Diamond?" he heard when he reached the door and turned at the sound of Axel. Diamond lifted an eyebrow, and waited. "You're gonna be a good dad. Pleased for you, brother."

He gave a brief nod and left. And he didn't stop to talk to anyone on his way out. The ride back to his complex didn't take very long, and when he let himself in, locking up behind him, he found Joelle where he left her. A tear-streaked face, asleep in his bed. She woke when he opened the bedroom door, sitting up.

"Is there any news? Has my father called?"

"Nothing yet." He answered, slipping out of his cut. He hung it up in the closet and turned to find her watching him. "Are you hungry?"

"I couldn't eat."

"Let me rephrase that, Bluebell. I'm making something, and you'll eat. The baby needs it."

She sighed, but nodded. "Okay. Have you been out?"

"I needed to do something. I'm back now, not going out again."

"I should be at home. Or at the hospital."

"You're right where you need to be."

She followed him into the kitchen, but he motioned her into the living room, where he heard the TV switch on.

"It's all over the news," she gasped.

That wasn't a surprise. It would remain breaking news for days.

"They're saying it's a terrorist attack. Do you think it was?"

He was mixing and chopping. Monitoring Joelle and not the TV screen. "If that's what they say."

"But you don't think so? Or you know differently already. What did my father say to you exactly, Diamond?"

"Just what I told you."

He saw her eyes narrow as she stared at him over the back of the couch. "You're lying."

"Withholding info for your safety isn't the same as lying." He clarified, and she pursed her lips, making her fucking adorable. But he didn't think she'd appreciate being told that right now. So, Diamond stuck to putting ingredients together.

"Okay, let me fill in the blanks."

"Joelle, leave it alone."

"No, I can't leave it alone. My mom is in the hospital."

"She's not seriously hurt. She's only there for observation."

"An entire house exploded around her!" She blew out her next breath and turned back to the TV, doom watching her family life exposed on the screen. "One crazy bitch couldn't have made that happen, could she?" she asked, guessing at the truth. And then. "Diamond?"

His gaze shifted toward her. She was understandably upset. But she had to grasp that her family was not his priority. Joelle was.

"Can you trust me on this?"

"I do trust you. But I still need to know who's trying to kill my family."

"It was more like a warning, Joelle. You must know your father isn't squeaky clean."

She blinked. "He's a Judge. Of course, he makes enemies from people he puts away."

Diamond was building the sandwiches, but couldn't pull his gaze away from Joelle for long. Unable to bear her upset voice, he left the knife and joined at her side. After he took her hand, she immediately latched onto his fingers.

"Trust that I'm gonna ensure you and the baby are safe, Joelle. That's all you need to know. Your dad and his staff, plus the whole police division, have everything else."

"But..."

"No, Joelle. You're not getting in the mix of this."

She huffed and pulled her hand from his.

He could deal with a stubborn woman who hated him. But he couldn't deal with her getting hurt. So he'd be the asshole as much as was needed. He rose to his feet, leaned down, kissed her forehead, and then returned to making sandwiches.

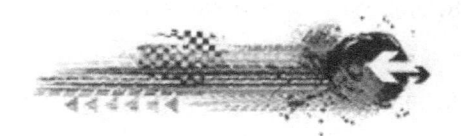

Joelle hardly talked to him for two days unless he asked her something.

It wasn't precisely animosity, more like she'd crawled into her shell.

And on day three, he realized what it could be.

She'd only been wearing his neutral-colored sweats and t-shirts.

So that night, while she was watching a show, he said he was going out for food. He couldn't check out the mansion while the cops were there, but they were done with their investigation. Despite the destruction at the front of the Snow mansion, Joelle's suite and that side of the house remained undamaged. He had to make four trips between her room and the truck to bring out the items he packed for her.

His girl needed her colors.

Upon pulling into his complex, he became alert as he noticed another Harley parked outside, knowing exactly who it belonged to.

Diamond was pissed, and his face showed it as he used his key to get inside and faced Axel, sitting on his couch across from Joelle.

"Hey," she smiled. The first smile she'd given him in days.

"Why did you open the door?" he bit out.

His abrupt words surprised her, but he didn't care at all. The Irish mob was targeting her father, yet she still opened the door to a stranger and welcomed him in.

It didn't matter that it was Axel.

Axel was watching him with a raised brow. Diamond would get to him in a second.

"I'm waiting, Joelle."

She pulled a stubborn face. "I heard the bike engine and thought it was you."

"It wasn't me. It was someone you don't know."

"Relax, brother," Axel said. Smiling.

The asshole would smile on the other side of his face in a minute. But his stare still zeroed in on Joelle and her blatant lack of self-preservation.

"It could have been anyone, and you just invited him in and made him a coffee." He narrowed his eyes, seeing the cup in Axel's hand.

"It was polite to ask." She dared to say as his fury fucking skyrocketed. "He said he knew you."

"So would a fucking lunatic carrying a shotgun."

In an instant, her eyes widened, filled with tears, and she gasped.

"D, take it easy," Axel warned quietly as he climbed to his feet. "I told Joelle who I was. That's the only reason she let me inside. Why don't we talk outside?"

"Yeah. Why don't we?" He snarled and waited for Axel to walk by him before he turned to the door. But her sweet, uncertain voice stopped him. "Diamond?"

"You are in so much trouble." He told her, and this time, when her eyes widened, it was with no distress.

"Me? What did I do? It's not my fault all motorcycles sound the same, and I thought it was yours. This is your fault!"

"Bluebell..." he warned.

"Don't Bluebell me, big bear. Now I'm angry with you all over again. Axel dropped by to check on us. It was a kind gesture and made me reevaluate talking to you again. Well, I've reconsidered." She huffed and turned her back on him, sitting like a debutante with her back straight and chin high to stop her crown from slipping.

Christ, that woman was going to put his ass in an early grave. But he lost his anger with her as he glanced at the side of her blushed face and fingers latched together in her lap. Beautiful fucking queen.

She was still in trouble. He'd come up with an adequate punishment later. A nice little spank over her full ass would downgrade his fury.

Outside, he walked to the end of the complex where Axel was waiting. The prez turned when he heard Diamond's approach.

"Big bear and Bluebell," smirked Axel.

"Don't," grated Diamond, folding his arms. "What are you doing here? You gotta know I'm pissed you've ambushed Joelle."

"It wasn't an ambush. I assumed you'd be here."

"You should have waited outside when you knew I wasn't here." He shot back.

He felt frayed at the edges.

The uncertainty of Joelle's safety affected him, but not being able to communicate with her was messing with his mind. Smelling her scent every day aroused him to the point of madness until he had to stand on the back porch several times a night to clear his head. He'd known having her so close would build this need in him until he wanted to punch walls to distract his dick from wanting to fuck a woman two bedrooms away from him.

"You said you wanted nothing to do with this, Prez. I respected your decision."

"You wanted to tear my head off," smirked Axel.

"You don't get to stroll into my house and ambush the mother of my kid."

"That's fair." Axel conceded. "My old lady saw all the shit on the news earlier. She sent me on an errand to check if Joelle needed clothes or other feminine stuff. She'll run into town tomorrow and pick anything up for her."

Diamond's eyes narrowed. "You told Scarlett after telling me to keep my mouth shut?"

"Brother, when you have an old lady, there isn't much you don't tell them. She wanted to help."

Yeah, Scarlett would want to help. That's what she did.

But he felt oddly possessive about Joelle and didn't want to share her with anyone.

Axel may have been right about keeping it a secret. This way, he got to be the protector and have her to himself longer.

"I've got everything sorted."

"You said she wasn't your old lady."

Diamond snapped his eyes up. Said nothing.

"That in there didn't look like she wasn't your old lady. She lit up when she heard you coming home until you yelled at her. Even then, your connection is clear."

For two nights, Diamond had hardly slept. Between the sexual frustration and worry, he couldn't close his eyes for long. He sighed and let the tension roll off his shoulders. He leaned into the house wall and faced his friend and MC leader.

"It's complicated."

"I can see that." and then the fucker smirked and added. "Big bear."

"Shut up, asshole." He said, but did it smiling.

"Call me a nosy fucker, but I needed to see it with my own eyes."

"See what?"

"You and her. If she'd been a one-night hookup, you wouldn't give a shit about bringing the issue to the church table. That's not you, Diamond. Even if a kid were part of the equation, you'd do right by them but not involve the brotherhood." Axel explained. "I had to see for myself if she could be trusted, being a Snow and all. She's your old lady."

Diamond exhaled and didn't know what to say. "It's complicated."

"The best ones always are, my brother."

"She's not my type. And I'm sure I'm not hers either."

"But?"

"Can you see me with someone like her? A socialite and a bruiser. It's laughable."

"We could all say the same about our women. But when it works, it works. You can't pigeonhole feelings, D. Shit never makes sense. It's what feels right that matters. I never expected to find a waif trying to rob me for sandwich money and how seeing her would affect every decision after that," Axel said. Then he smiled. "Ruin is with America's popstar sweetheart. You couldn't have written that shit and made it believable. But it happened, and for Ruin, it's righter than he's ever had."

Axel pushed off the wall and faced Diamond.

"I made some calls."

Diamond lifted a brow in silent question.

"It's got the mob's fingerprints all over the explosion. The info comes from the Murphys, so I know it's not just rumor and gossip."

"You didn't have to do that."

"Yes, I did. You came to me, and I shut that shit down because I want nothing else touching the club right now. I was wrong to do that, D."

"I don't want shit to touch the club, either."

"But you have other priorities now. For what it's worth, I don't think they intend to pursue the vendetta. They made their point clear to Snow. But for the sake of your old lady and unborn child, we're at your back, brother. And the Murphys said they can weigh in if talks with the mob need to take place."

Diamond was stunned.

He had expected none of it.

"She's changed me, Axel." He breathed.

"Yeah, I can see that," his buddy stated.

"I don't even know what to do. But seeing that house wreckage and knowing if she'd been in it and hurt... it would have destroyed me. It sounds so fucking bad that I wasn't thinking of my baby. *Just her.* I would have lost everything if she'd been taken from me."

"I know. That shit, when it grabs you, it's like a fucking noose, but a happy one you want to put your head into."

Diamond chuffed a laugh at Axel's description while agreeing with him.

When Axel turned to walk to his bike, he paused.

"We learn a lot of shit in different ways in our life, don't we? No person is better than another, Diamond. Your socialite in there is quirky. She's different, but I can tell she's so fucking loyal to you. She's someone my Scarlett would rope into her gang in a second."

Diamond groaned and rubbed a hand down his tired face. "That was fucking cruel to say to me, Axel." He could only imagine the female carnage.

The prez laughed because Axel indulged his old lady in all her whims.

"We don't get to live a long time in this life. There's no point in wasting the time we're here second-guessing what we don't deserve. Grab on and take your slice of good."

With that cryptic message, the prez turned and strode to his bike.

Diamond was already letting himself into his place before the engine roared and powered out of the complex.

He faced an angry woman holding a sofa cushion to her chest like a protective barrier. Tears were filling her eyes, but not yet spilling down her cheeks.

He frowned. Confused.

"So we are clear. You're not *my* type either, River Durant!" Without another word, she shot off down the hallway, and the slam of her bedroom door made his back teeth rattle.

*Fuck.*

He exhaled like a gust and locked the door, slipping out of his jacket.

She'd heard what he'd said and got it all twisted.

Parking his ass on the couch, he groaned like his bones were five hundred years old and looked down the darkened hallway as if he could see into her bedroom.

He was the only biker in the world who'd fucked up with his old lady before he could even attempt to make her his old lady.

## Joelle

The biker was an asshole.

A purebred, leather-wearing asshole of the highest caliber.

Tired of reading the same line because of lack of concentration, Joelle closed the Kindle app on her phone. Wishing it was a physical book so she could slam it shut for better effect. She was feeling restless. No surprise there.

It had been a hell of a few days.

Her family home exploded, but thankfully, there were no fatalities, and her mom was okay and staying in their townhouse, heavily guarded.

And then the cherry on the shit sundae. She had to overhear Diamond telling his biker friend she wasn't his type.

For days since that night, she'd woken each morning pissed off.

Hurt, but worse, *mortified* that he even had to qualify it to his friend. He was probably embarrassed she was even pregnant by him.

But unlike another type of woman who might have gone off the deep end by throwing a tantrum at every turn, Joelle hadn't done that.

She'd been treating Diamond with cordial civility.

If he spoke to her or asked a question, she replied.

But she no longer sought him out.

The day after, he'd tried to address it.

"About last night," he'd said when she walked out of the bedroom after not sleeping a wink. She'd held up a hand to him and told Diamond. "There's no need. Can I fix a cup of ginger tea?"

And that was all that was said about it.

Days later, she was climbing the walls.

Diamond wasn't home much, but when he was, all she saw, felt, and smelled was him. He'd brought her clothes from home, and she was grateful for that, but she needed to go somewhere else.

Sadie and Molly wanted her to stay with them, but she gently declined. Having all her money was pointless if she was trapped in an unwelcome condominium.

Once Diamond went for his morning run, she sat on a breakfast bar stool to make a call.

"Do you have any suites available? Immediately, if possible. Oh, you do! That's great." She smiled. "Can I book..."

The phone was plucked out of her hand, and Diamond, staring at her, pressed the button to cut the call.

"What did you do that for? That was rude! I'll have to call them back. Can I have my phone, please?" The rude biker ignored her outstretched hand.

"A suite where?" his voice came out in a dark rumble. Standing in his running gear, she avoided moving her eyes away from his face because the form-fitted workout muscle tee and running shorts could turn a statue on.

Sadly, knowing she wasn't his type didn't make her any less attracted to the biker. Blame it on the hormones. It had to be. They were raging lately. A gentle breeze could turn her on. That he was right there made it worse.

"The Cedar Regency."

"No." he bit out.

"What do you mean, no? This isn't your decision to make. I'm leaving today."

"Try again, Bluebell."

"Why are you even here?" she snapped.

"I live here." His eyebrows folded in a little deeper.

"Funny. I meant, you just went for a run."

"And you waited until I was gone to book a hotel."

"It's time I left." She answered.

"Says who?"

"I say. I've overstayed my welcome. You only agreed to take me in because of the situation. You could hardly tell my father no while his house had just fallen on him." She huffed, brushing her hair from her face.

"That's enough." He exhaled an angry sound, and before Joelle knew it, Diamond was towering over her, grasping her chin, holding it firm so she couldn't pull her head back from his touch. He forced her to look at him.

She was in agony being near him, but not being able to touch his chest.

"I've given you enough time to sulk. Now you get to listen."

"I have not been sulking!" she hissed. And he jostled her chin a little.

"It's time to listen, Bluebell. And you hear everything I say, not translate shit in your female mind until it's all twisted up."

Of all the nerve.

She'd turn her fucking ears off, see how he liked that.

Her heart was beating so fast it wouldn't be a surprise if Diamond could hear it rattling around inside her ribcage.

"You heard me say you weren't my type."

"We don't need to talk about that."

He shook her chin again, so light it was almost playful. "It's listening time now."

"Fine," she grumbled.

"Did you hear me tell Axel I wasn't your type, either? I'm not a stick-in-the-ass country club fool with a Ferrari and a house in the Hamptons. I'm a biker, a criminal. I use my fists often in my line of work. You're so far out of my fucking league, Joelle. I should be shot just standing near you. That's what I told Axel, because he was grilling me about you."

She attentively listened while her mind buzzed with questions and emotions.

Diamond released her chin but remained near, his mammoth chest almost touching hers.

"We're having a baby together, Joelle."

Yeah, of course, the baby. She frowned. He would try to be a nice guy because of that.

"But the baby has nothing to do with my feelings for you."

Oh.

He looked so severe, his brow furrowed, and his usually smiling mouth pulled into a straight line. "I want you to hear exactly what I say next, Joelle. And to know it has nothing to do with our baby. It's all about me and you," he stated seriously. "We might be from different worlds, two people who never would have ordinarily met. But if we were at the same bar one night and I saw you, I would've been inside you ten minutes later."

Oh.

Her world tilted, and Joelle didn't know if she was breathing.

Diamond wasn't finished.

"It wouldn't matter where it was. In a bathroom stall, in the alley around the back where I could make you all dirty, or in a dark corner, as long as I got my hand up your colorful skirt. It would have happened, Joelle. We're not each other's types on paper or in lifestyle, but that doesn't mean jackshit when the chemistry has scorched us down to the ground from day one."

Lord. When that man declared his attraction, he went in and didn't leave a crumb behind.

Was the floor swaying?

"And if you weren't so determined to run away from me, we could have been fucking the bad mood out of you for days."

Sweet goodness in a cookie jar. She flatlined right there in Diamond's cozy kitchen. Unsure it was her turn to talk, she struggled to move her tongue. It was currently bone dry and clinging to the roof of her mouth.

"You were coming home with me that day regardless of your father asking me first. Even if I had to toss you over my shoulder, you would only end up in this house. And had he got in my way, he would have had to fight me to prize you out of my arms. Bluebell? I fight dirty when it's something I want."

Oh.

So this was what an out-of-body feeling was. Joelle was on the ceiling looking down at the woman, hearing the hottest declaration from the most sizzling and sweetest bodyguard biker.

Diamond dropped his head, and she stole a breath, anticipating a kiss, but he still had things to say.

Sheesh, she thought men didn't like to express their thoughts and feelings?

"As for you leaving. That is not happening. If you want to stay in a hotel, somewhere bigger than here, I will take you somewhere else, but we will go together. You could have been buried beneath the rubble at the estate, Joelle. Has that even crossed your mind? It's all I've fucking thought about. I need you close. I need to be near you, so I know you're alive." His voice shook like thunder, and Joelle reacted, trembling down to her toes. "I would have dug through brick by brick to get to you, Bluebell."

It was one of the most significant declarations.

She was so hyped it felt like her skin was charged with electricity.

"You and me, I can't explain any of it. And if all we are is co-parents for our bubba, it won't stop me trying to get under your skirts, Joelle." He confessed with a raspy voice that was so sexy she had to press her knees together because, yeah, she was growing soaked and aroused. "I'm done trying to do the right thing. I wanna do the dirty thing all the fuck over you."

Damn those pregnancy hormones. She'd read the second trimester was the horniest time, and boy, was it not wrong.

"Ten years down the line, if I was dropping our boy off from football practice, and I saw you framed in the doorway, looking so fucking edible that my mouth watered, I'd wait until our kid was out of sight, and I'd corner you, Joelle. Like a dog in heat, all I'd need is to scent you, and I'd be ready to go. That's how bad it is for me."

The silence was palpable before she forced her lips to frame some words.

"Um, can you explain what this means?"

He smiled—smirked, more like. "It means we have an insane amount of chemistry bouncing between us, ready to set fire to every inch of us. You feel it, Joelle. And I'm gonna chase it. I won't hold back now. I don't give a shit if the world thinks I'm wrong for you. Or we're not a match on paper. I'm gonna chase you so fucking hard until you're mine. And I keep what's mine, Bluebell. You need to get right with that, because there's no escaping me."

Oh. Well.

She exhaled and squeezed her knees even tighter.

She didn't expect him to back up and then trek to the front door, where she jumped down from the stool and followed. He was stroking his eyes the full length of her body, and when he reached her face, she nearly died on the spot from the amount of lust staring back.

"As mad as you've been this week, you've been eating me up with your eyes, Joelle. And if I hear you pleasure yourself tonight, I will kick the door down. Do you get me? Do you feel how insane I am about you? I will hold your legs apart, and my mouth will be buried between your thighs so fast, licking all your arousal until I'm drunk on you. But if you wanna watch me stroke one out in the shower while I groan your name, walk into the bathroom any time." He smirked like he was swapping recipes, not stirring her blood to a raging boil. "I've looked it up. I know you're horny as fuck right now during this trimester. If you need a hard and willing body to use and abuse. *A very hard* body, Joelle, for the biggest railing of your life, I'm right here."

And with that, he pulled open the door, told her he was going for his run, and left her there, with her mouth gaped open, her hormones a screaming mess, and her panties so damp, she had to change them. When her legs regained function.

## Joelle

There had been a lot to process after Diamond took off for his run.

The first order of business was to dig into Diamond's freezer and pull out the pint of blood orange sorbet he'd bought for her because she mentioned she couldn't get enough citrus to satisfy her cravings. Now, the fridge's salad drawer was overflowing with various oranges.

That man was crazy sweet.

And apparently, he was into her!

She wouldn't overreact.

Instead, Joelle sat at the breakfast bar and took small bites of the super sour, super delicious sorbet. The cold richness melted on her tongue, and she got lost in her deviant thoughts.

Did Diamond actually offer himself up to her? That part of the conversation was not something she imagined.

Was she considering it? Oh yeah, one hundred percent she was.

Her peaked nipples and throbbing clit were on board.

Joelle might have been on the wrong page with Diamond almost always, thinking he wasn't interested in her, but he'd said it in terms she couldn't misinterpret. Hormones did not govern her actions. She had desired him from the moment she'd seen him.

Over the next hour, her thoughts were diverse and deviant. Each one centered on riding a biker into fucking oblivion until he had no dick left. The time went by quickly because before she knew it, the door opened, and there he was. Larger than life, wider than the frame, and his eyes zeroed in on her instantly.

There were moments in life that robbed a woman's sanity. Watching Diamond walking through his apartment toward her was one of those times.

He ate her up, and he did it blatantly. It was so hot she wanted to purr like a kitten. Joelle had to compose herself, unsure what to say, but Diamond wasn't stuck for words as he rested both hands on the island.

"Give me a bite," he said, voice rough like gravel, though his eyes weren't on the ice cream; they were pinned to her blushing face.

"Let me get a clean spoon." His hand on her inner wrist stopped her, though the zapping electricity along her arm would have rendered Joelle motionless. Diamond wasn't unaffected; she saw his pupils dilating, and when he spoke, it was with the same gravel-thick tone. The kind of tone that said he wasn't thinking about ice cream.

"Your spoon is fine."

Digging into the tub, she loaded the spoon and held it up to Diamond's mouth. He leaned forward when she offered it to him, and she watched like a pervert as his kissable lips opened and latched on.

Clog-wearing butterflies exploded in her belly. No, it wasn't butterflies. It felt like birds manically flapping their wings. She was so strung out by his proximity that she nearly moaned as he met her gaze and did something obscene with the spoon, licking it clean.

Joelle tried to suppress her moans as she ladled the spoon into her mouth to cool her off, imagining the flavor of Diamond on her tongue.

"Aren't you going to shower?" she asked.

"Not yet. I'm sharing your treat." He smirked, touching her wrist to direct the next spoonful into his mouth.

Could he feel the pattering of her pulse under his fingertips?

This food sharing felt like hot foreplay.

One spoon for her. The next for Diamond. On and on, she fed him, and it was the most erotic thing she'd done in a long time.

Diamond took the spoon off her and licked it clean. She was all too aware she'd been the last one to use it, so he was licking her from it. "Delicious," he rasped.

Holy crap, the air was so thick, like trying to breathe through cherry jam, and if she got any more turned on by his sweaty features, she'd freaking explode and disintegrate right in his kitchen.

"Did you have a good run?" she asked hoarsely, lightheaded.

Diamond angled his chin down, his lips twitching like he knew exactly the state her mind was in because of him. He reached into the fridge and drank directly from a water jug.

"Yep." He wiped his mouth with the back of his hand and then pinned Joelle with a stare. "Did you give some thought to what I said?"

Oh, jeez. He was so blunt. She kind of loved it.

She just nodded, and he smiled. "Good girl. Gonna jump in the shower."

And he left her there, dazed and fidgety.

She hadn't told Diamond yet, but she loved being in his apartment. It was everything she thought a home should be. Warm and welcoming. It was spacious but small enough that she heard the shower water coming on and then turning off ten minutes later.

Without thinking, she jumped off the stool and stumbled along the hallway. She hadn't outright decided with rational, ordered thoughts, but her body knew what she was doing and urged her to move faster.

When she reached Diamond's bedroom door, she pushed it open, making a whooshing sound on the thick carpet.

And then there he was. Standing in the middle of his room, a white towel was held low on his hips, so low that it dipped below the enticing V-shaped grooves on his abdomen. And he was rubbing his hair with another towel.

He turned instantly when he heard the door.

Then they both just stood there, staring at each other.

Diamond was eyeing her like a dessert he wanted to sink his teeth into.

The desire felt brand new. Something so right, burning through her veins, urging her to take what she hungered for. All she had to do was take the first step, and Diamond would do the rest. She knew that much. There was nothing else she craved more than being owned by him.

Everything clicked into place, and she exhaled.

It gave Joelle the confidence to take a step into his masculine domain.

His smile came slowly until it pulled his lips wider.

She frowned. "Why are you grinning like that?"

"Because I'm happy you made the right decision before I had to come for you. Get over here and give me your mouth, Joelle."

"What happened to Bluebell?"

"You're only Bluebell when you're being a sweet girl."

"And I'm not sweet now?"

"I bet you taste sweet." And then he grabbed her around the back of the neck and crushed Joelle's lips, stifling any more words she might have said.

Her mind emptied. Her lust intensified. And she put her whole self in the hands of a biker who wanted to devour her.

She was only sensations and tingly skin as he kissed her with a single-mindedness to ruin her.

"What is it you want, Joelle?"

"You know what." She panted against his lips, aching for more.

"I do. But I want to hear you say it."

"Can't you figure it out yourself?"

Her cheeks burned, and she avoided making eye contact.

She nearly lost her nerve, but realized his hands were clasping her hips, squeezing, massaging, and his touch felt too good to withhold anything from him.

She cupped Diamond's face, pressing her lips to his. Lost in a sex fog.

"I want to use this extraordinary body to make myself feel good." Another kiss. "I want to take all my frustration out on you until I don't ache. Make it hurt less, Diamond."

He looked pleased. "You'll get used to telling me your needs, baby. It's what I want. Where are you hurting?" he asked. "Is it here?" he stroked up her torso and helped himself to her breasts. While nodding, she suddenly felt an overwhelming urge to bypass manners and jump his bones. "I think it's here," Diamond smirked and moved a hand down to cup Joelle's mound through her leggings. "Am I right?" she leaned into his touch until she was grinding on his hand. "Are you hurting right here, baby?" he repeated, and this time he heeled harder against her clit until she had to grab onto his shoulders.

"Yes." she hissed in pleasure.

Diamond laughed lightly, and he gave her another glide of his hand before removing it. She wanted to whimper.

He reassured, "There's no need to feel embarrassed about whatever you want from me; you tell me, and I'll give it to you repeatedly until you're a shaking mess."

"I'm not good at that."

"I will help you get good with that, baby." He flashed a sensual grin. "With lots of horny practice." Diamond brushed his lips lightly across hers, coaxing and enticing her to play.

Joelle swallowed her nerves and played before he pulled away and parked his butt on the side of the bed. "Undress for me, baby, and then I can make you feel good and take the ache away."

It was the promise of pleasure that eradicated any shyness about getting naked in front of him. He watched every item peeling off her, and his admiring eyes made her feel confident as he growled low, stroking his cock while he stared at her naked body.

"Fucking incredible." He grunted. "Get back here."

She did something unexpected and bold by reaching down to knock his hand away, replacing it on his cock with hers.

He was so hot and smooth, like the silkiest encased steel. Holding it in her palm filled her lower stomach with lust. She could taste the anticipation of how it would feel inside her, the place she wanted it the most. A pulse bloomed between Joelle's legs while she played with him. Diamond grunted, but she continued to trace her fingertips along the raised veins. However, he hissed when she lightly touched the little slit on the crown.

"I want this, Diamond," Joelle exhaled undiluted desire.

Diamond's hand cupped the side of her face, drawing her in until all she saw was the dilated pinprick of his pupils.

"Ask me nicely for it," he rasped, nipping along her jaw. She hadn't known biting would turn her on, but he was making her pant and moan, and needed more of his teeth all over her body.

The moment her hand flexed, trapping him in her palm, he hissed and shot a narrowed gaze her way, but there was nothing but longing, looking back at her, and she felt powerful.

Joelle leaned forward, almost touching his mouth with her quivering lips, and whispered, "Please, can I have this now, River?"

He made an agreeable, lovely noise and took her mouth with a kiss, which was so consuming that she felt changed when he set her free.

His eyes were lazy and darkly hooded as he arched up and pulled off the towel. The heat from his skin radiated down her arm as she hovered nearer, drawn like a magnet to his incredible body, and she watched him grab his erection at the base. The raw, scorching action sparked a newfound fire within her and a thirst in the back of her throat. Before she knew what she was doing, she dropped to her knees and pressed a little kiss to the crown of his cock.

Diamond grunted and held his cock up for her attention.

"Go on then," he said, "suck me in, Bluebell. When you dropped to your knees, you wanted to be a bad girl, so do it."

She didn't hesitate; she was dying to taste him, but he didn't let her go more than a few sucks at the crown of him before he threaded his fingers through her hair and pulled her head back.

"It's too good, but I don't come before you do, baby."

She was flush all over and getting warmer when he spanned her waist and drew her to stand between his knees so he could nuzzle her breasts. He licked around her areole and then grazed his teeth until she hissed in suffering bliss. The pleasure went right to her core.

Diamond palmed between her legs, encouraging them to open.

She knew what he was telling her to do.

Hesitantly, she sat on his lap, straddling him with her legs. She steadied herself by placing her hands on his shoulders. Then she pressed her lips against his throat.

When she looked up and gasped for air, his eyes were blazing like twin flames.

"I've waited too long for this," He shared huskily.

So had she. Forever. Eons. Light years. Too long.

Joelle was so desperate for him she couldn't handle it.

"Please, Diamond." She whined.

"I'll please you all day, baby." He brought two fingers up to her mouth. "Get these wet for me." Without shame, she latched her lips around them, snaking her tongue on his pumping fingers, mimicking sex until he grunted and she let them go. Diamond took his wet hand between them, and if she weren't holding onto his shoulders, she would have catapulted to the ceiling when he started rubbing her clit.

It was pure bliss all at once, and Joelle moaned. And the more she moaned, the faster Diamond worked his magical fingers until she rode out an orgasm so ferocious, she thought she blacked out for a second.

The guy with the ocean eyes smirked and captured Joelle's mouth.

It was hard not to notice the thick length of him arched up against his stomach, squashed between them. Joelle was itching to play with him, but Diamond had other ideas when their kiss ended. He tasted minty, but the longer the kiss went on, she tasted a spicy man, and she groaned to take more of him onto her tongue.

"I'm gonna fuck you, baby." He announced, and she shuddered, enjoying his special attention. "It'll be rough and probably fast this first time. I've wanted between these legs for too long to make it last. I'll savor you a thousand times afterward."

He was the type of man that women would plead with to satisfy their desires.

"Tell me that's what you need."

His voice was soaked in desire. She wanted to drown in the noise.

"It's what I need. You're everything I crave." Despite her uncertainty about sharing too much, Diamond's smile showed he appreciated her openness.

"Good, baby." He stroked, playing with her, toying with her opening, and her eyes rolled into the back of her head. She moaned his name, pleading. He grunted and cursed, fingering her faster.

"Fuck, you're soaked, baby."

She knew it because she could hear her body sucking on his fingers.

And then something much thicker replaced his hand, and Joelle nearly roared with pleasure as the broad tip of Diamond notched into place, stretching her impossibly already. She rose, her knees on the bed and his hands on her ass, guiding her.

"This soft body has driven me crazy." He grunted against her breasts, tonguing her wickedly, roaming his hands over her curves like he couldn't touch her enough.

She was mindless already and was still to get him inside of her.

"*Diamond.*"

"I know, baby. *Fuck. I know.*"

And then he was there, pushing in, going inch by agonizing inch, drawing her down by the ass cheeks. The fit was so snug she was sure he wasn't even half in when she felt so overly full of him. It was absolutely incredible. Her eyelids flickered with the raining bliss.

Unbidden, she whimpered his name, pressing her mouth to his for the connection, and he answered her plea by kissing the holy hell out of her.

Her entire being was turned inside out by the strikes of his tongue.

When she felt the vibration of his grunt, he took a tighter grip on her ass and pulled her down, and that's when her inner walls gave around his girthy cock, and she accepted the last inches in a fast exhale.

Never in her life had she felt this feeling.

It was ecstasy set on fire.

Diamond surrounded her, ultimately owning her with his desire.

They were totally in the moment, connected by his touch, scent, and cock.

"*Jesus, Bluebell.*" He groaned, cupping the side of her face, and she fluttered her lashes open to peer into his eyes. "I knew you'd be the fuck of a lifetime. My utter downfall. Now, I'm gonna fuck you the way I should have done to put a baby in you."

She'd known he'd be the same for her. It had been inevitable, moving toward this moment forever.

"This won't hurt you?"

"No," she answered. "Unless you want it to."

His eyes flared, and he started moving in her. It was fantastic. "Don't say that to me, baby." He pushed deeper after a few testing thrusts. "Or I'll wreck you."

Joelle smiled into his lips. Just as she hoped he would. "Promises, promises, River."

Before she knew it was happening, he locked onto her hips, stood up, and then flattened her to the bed, with her legs dangling over the edge until he gruffed. "Get them around me. Come on, Bluebell. I need to fuck you the way I've been thinking about for months."

He shoved home, and Joelle shrieked and latched her legs around his trim hips.

His intense gaze made her feel a surge of energy run through her body.

"This body is going to be so pleasured, you won't walk until Thursday." He promised huskily in a dark voice. Joelle chuckled, but the sound got buried in a languid moan when he repeated the movement, finding a rhythm until she was clutching the bedcovers and writhing against him.

With a hip swivel, Diamond caused air to escape from her throat, and he smirked down at her. "Like that?"

"Yes." She wheezed. "Do it again."

"My fucking pleasure, baby."

He went at her hard. Like he'd been waiting to fuck her an entire lifetime.

It was crazy wild.

Rail after hard rail. It wasn't sex, not lovemaking, not even fucking. He was rutting her so thoroughly.

It was like being fucked by her best dream on steroids.

"You feel like wet silk." He grunted, leaning in, and he took a kiss that was dominant as it was messy. It was heaven.

While Diamond was licking into her mouth, Joelle felt her lower body gather. She'd wanted to prolong it for as long as she could, but

Diamond's pistoning hips had other ideas when his hands lifted her ass from the bed, making his cock hit a part inside her that rendered her blind with sin-delivered bliss.

"That's it, baby." He encouraged, framing her face as he leaned into her, driving his body harder into that spot that was so mind-blowing. She clutched his forearms and opened her mouth to make a noise, but it was trapped in her throat. "You're gonna come for me," he growled, *pleased*.

And he was right. Her body no longer belonged to Joelle because she splintered at his command.

The incredible orgasm swept through Joelle and obliterated everything in her life, what she thought and knew. All there was left, was her and a hard man powering himself into her until she shuddered his name.

It scrambled her brain. It set fire to all her nerves, and it brought the cries of pleasure from deep within.

And while Joelle was in the throes of passion, Diamond slammed into her twice more. His grip on her thigh tightened as he came with a heavy-sounding grunt.

"*Fuck, baby*." He rasped, tenderly moving inside of her until he was spent, and he came to a stop, planted to the root.

Joelle was so full of him. Her inner muscles spasmed again with tiny aftershocks good enough to make her eyes roll into the back of her head.

"I think I'm dead." He rasped, panting in her face.

He'd never looked sexier with his hair still wet but messy and his eyes glazed from the orgasm, still shaking them both.

Joelle moved a hand between them and tweaked his nipple. Diamond grunted, and his eyes flashed.

"Nope, you're alive if you're reacting to pain stimulus."

"You bad girl, I give back as good as I get," he smirked with a hint of a promise.

Oh, she hoped so.

He'd already given her so much. It was soaking the inside of her thighs.

"No condom." She remarked, looking up at him.

It was like she was throwing out trigger words to turn the biker on because he made a sexual noise low in his throat again and shunted his hips, trying to get deeper, even though he was pressed pelvis to pelvis.

"That was the first for me."

And for her, too. She was thrilled to have that experience with Diamond. "It was?"

"Yeah. You feel so good, Bluebell. I'd die to stay right here with your grabbing pussy walls fluttering like crazy. But I wanna clean you up so I can eat an orgasm out of you."

"Oh." She puffed air in his face, and the dirty monster grinned and kissed her swollen lips. He detached slowly, and she bucked, not wanting to lose him.

"*Goddamn.*" He cursed, and she saw he was looking between her legs. Before she could ask what, he gathered his pleasure onto his fingertips, and he slid them into her.

Joelle, sensitive like she'd been fucked by a demon, whimpered and angled her hips.

"Shh, baby. I'm just..."

"You're pushing your come back into me, you dirty boy."

Why did she love it? It wasn't like her womb could get *more* pregnant. He'd already fertilized her good.

But the action was carnal. It was primal.

And the more he played with her wet, sensitive pussy, the more turned-on she became.

"Don't you have a plan to be getting on with?" she reminded him. Playfulness after rough, consuming sex had never happened to her before, and she wanted more of it.

"Get in the shower, baby. I'm gonna get on my knees and fuck you with my mouth."

Lord above and all the weeping angels. She was toast from his dirty words, but you know what? Joelle was a trooper, staggering to the bathroom with the hottest man god had ever created, fondling her ass all the way there.

And he stuck to his plan. Twice.

## Diamond

"**H**ow's your hostage?"

The question came from Chains, and Diamond threw the VP a *don't go there* glance as he took a long sip of coffee. Axel snickered and earned the same stare from Diamond.

"Forcing women to be with me ain't my deal, boys. That's your trope, isn't it?" he smirked.

"Hey, it worked. Monroe loves me."

"Monroe tolerates you." Axel chimed in, coffee in hand.

Diamond agreed, smirking. "The second you're not around, she'll take off and find a decent guy who doesn't force her into wedded misery. Poor little wife."

"Never gonna happen." A confident Chains flashed a grin. "I keep my old lady satisfied."

"Can't believe you're tangled up with a WASP," Axel remarked.

It still came as a surprise to Diamond, too.

After his last relationship ended, when the bitch did the dirty on him with almost every man in Utah, he wasn't spending his days imagining what kind of woman he might end up with because it hadn't been on his horizon. He'd deemed himself a lifelong bachelor. But even if the thought of a relationship had been on Diamond's mind, a WASP wouldn't have made the cut. A socialite with airs and graces regularly featured on Page Six gossip news outlets wouldn't have interested Diamond.

But then Joelle appeared in his peripheral.

And then she was all he saw until he was an all in, obsessed man, determined to keep her no matter what obstacles stood in his way.

Her blue hair and colorful attire didn't differentiate her from the other pearl-clutching socialites. Her graces still came through clearly in the way she spoke and moved. But she was so much more than her social position.

He was a gritty biker who had no interest in owning a dinner jacket, only acknowledged a single fork and glass, and consistently put his elbows on the table.

But with Joelle, that divide in their class differences didn't seem to matter.

She didn't care he was a coarse biker; she wasn't money motivated, and they didn't want to change each other; just share the same space.

And he was obsessed with that woman.

Every inch of him was infatuated with every inch of her.

Knowing she was carrying his baby only amplified that obsession to the point he was fidgeting about being away from her today.

But he'd left her in bed well-sated, well fucked and smiling.

A week of non-stop romps had put Diamond's sexual prowess to the test, but if there was any woman who could make a man of his age excel at sorting out her needs, it was Joelle.

She was a sweet little savage, and he'd been more than willing to sign his name in blood to have her. She'd wrung him dry and still demanded more from his body.

He didn't know what living was until he tasted her.

He realized he'd been living in a half-asleep state until she consumed his thoughts.

"Earth to Diamond." Nudged Chains.

He blinked out of his filthy thoughts of what he'd do to Joelle. "What did you say?"

"Yep, he's gone waspish, Axel. We might have to put our guy out to pasture."

"Nah, can't do that now. His father-in-law is a Judge." Axel added.

"Oh, fuck off." He laughed and rose to his feet, finishing the slurp of coffee in the mug. "I'm taking off. You knuckle-draggers can laugh to yourselves as much as you want, but you were in my place not so long ago. Now look at you," he smirked, "waiting on your women so you can take them shopping. Pussy whipped. Just don't carry their little purses and lose all masculine credibility." He laughed and avoided the swipe Chains aimed his way. "You gotta get up early to catch me, VP." He saluted his brothers with double middle fingers and took off to play the heavy alongside Bash.

But he was eager to get back home.

To the soft, willing, and so fucking beautiful woman in his bed.

Diamond had to adjust his cock along his thigh after climbing onto his bike. Before he started the engine, he pulled out his phone.

**DIAMOND**: I'll be home in a few hours. I expect you naked, Bluebell. If you want to be on the table so I can eat, that'll be appreciated.

He was such a whipped bastard. But he was smiling as his phone instantly vibrated with a message.

**JOELLE**: Not if you want me sprawled on the floor surrounded by broken furniture.

She had such a warped opinion of her body. Being a curvy girl didn't dampen her confidence, his girl had it in abundance. He adored her self-assuredness in her sexiness. But she'd get all weird if he attempted to carry her. He loved putting her places, so that wasn't going to stop. And she'd been reluctant to sit on his face when he'd told her to. That worked out well as soon as he got his tongue into her sex and lapped her into screaming, she'd suffocated him in the best way.

**DIAMOND**: For that, you get punished.
**JOELLE**: How?
**DIAMOND**: Five orgasms.

**JOELLE**: LOL. Oh, I'm scared stiff.

**DIAMOND**: I'm the stiff one. Just tell me you're naked and covered in soap so I can get through work.

**JOELLE**: Hate to break it to you, big bear, but I'm still in your bed.

**DIAMOND**: Fuck, that's even better.

**JOELLE**: The sheets smell like us.

**DIAMOND**: Fuuuuuuuck. You bad girl. I'm adding to your punishment.

**JOELLE**: I'm terrified. Hurry home.

**DIAMOND**: It's a promise, Bluebell.

Diamond had a dumb smile on his face as he revved the bike and headed out to kick some ass.

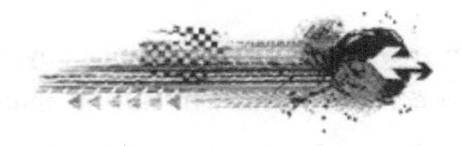

## Joelle

She was grinning at her phone, even after they stopped texting.

Joelle wasn't sure if they were officially dating, but she knew it was the best thing ever.

She had no words for how incredible being with him was. Every day, she felt a sense of joy and lightness just from their conversations and his tight embraces. It meant something to her, how he was never the first to let go after a hug.

No one man should possess the power to render a woman's body under his control, as Diamond did with hers.

He was a sex master.

His mouth was so desirable that she would sacrifice her soul to aliens for it.

If she looked up *addicted* in the dictionary, her picture would be right there wearing an in-love smile.

The sex was terrific. Out of this world. Fantastic. Toe-curling, knees knocking, womb shaking good.

But Diamond, the man, was even better.

As upside down as her life felt, he'd made her laugh more this week than she'd ever laughed in a while.

No previous relationship had Joelle as invested as she was with Diamond.

That man demanded her attention, and he got it. Effortlessly. *Entirely.* He walked into a room, and her mind spun out of control. He smiled, and she lost the power of breath.

She couldn't explain the depths of her feelings, but she knew they were stronger than anything she'd experienced, ever.

On paper, they made little sense.

But what did? Relationships were a melting pot of a lot of things.

She trusted her gut instinct and her feelings. And her feelings exploded around that man.

It was like her smiles and thudding heart beats hinged on his very existence.

It was ridiculous and wonderful.

She found out that he wasn't a fan of her comfort shows and movies, but he still watched them with her without getting bored. Since he liked action and true story adaptations, they made a lot of compromises.

Both of them enjoyed the same dishes. Despite his limited sugar intake, which she found unimaginable because sugar meant love and happiness, he found baking relaxing. He was a true talent in the kitchen, and she would gladly pay to watch him work.

As she left the bed, she sighed dreamily while looking at the crumpled pillows.

Her phone pinged, and she got excited, wondering what dirty things he was saying. But her smile dropped.

**UNKNOWN**: I can find you anytime.
**UNKNOWN**: You shouldn't hide from me, pretty.
**UNKNOWN**: I miss you, my pretty.

*Ugh.* Joelle almost forgot about her mystery texter, since she hadn't received any messages in weeks. They kept switching numbers whenever she blocked them.

Joelle blocked the number and went about her day. Showering, cleaning sheets, and not burning down Diamond's apartment. The apartment survived, and she continued her daily routine. While visiting her mother, who'd surprisingly bounced back from the devastation since she was in the throes of organizing a black-tie gala.

They were still kinda unhappy about her being pregnant, but she didn't give a damn. Joelle was getting increasingly excited as the baby started making itself known in her belly with little flutters.

Kids were not something she had considered, but a biker's potent sperm changed everything. She had a complete shift in perspective.

She was busy running errands and having lunch with Reeves, but she could only think about Diamond and going home to him.

Diamond felt like home to her.

She'd do everything to hold on to that man.

If she could get doubly pregnant to trap him in her love, she'd do it.

With a smile, she eagerly counted the seconds until she could embrace him again.

### Diamond

"You need to tell him."

It was the first thing Diamond heard when he let himself in.

He didn't recognize the Mercedes Benz parked outside. He was going to flip his fucking lid if he found Judge Snow in his house. But all he heard were female voices, and he downgraded his wrath.

"I second what Sadie said. You need to tell Diamond today."

"Tell me what?" He asked, and three pairs of eyes turned toward him. Joelle blushed as he looked at her with intense focus. Her two best friends were at her side.

"I didn't hear you come home!" Joelle said.

"Tell Diamond what, baby?"

"Oh, it's nothing."

"If you don't tell him, I'll tell him, and then I'm going home to tell my cop husband."

"You're married to a cop?" Diamond narrowed his eyes.

The woman smiled as if she could feel his repulsion. "I am. Don't worry, daddy biker, he owns a motorbike, too."

"Forget your romantic rides," the other woman said, pointing to Joelle. "Tell him."

Giving Joelle a suspicious look, he noticed her reluctance to reveal whatever it was. "Is it the baby?"

Joelle answered. "No, bubba is fine, kicking me, but fine."

"Well?"

"Oh, fine. I've been getting peculiar texts from a number I'm unfamiliar with. I'm sure it's some kid pranking me for giggles."

"No, we're not sure of that," Sadie said. "A kid who sends prank texts doesn't know things about you. Show him."

"Isn't it time for you both to leave?"

"Nope." One answered. "You said we'd get homemade treats from a badass biker daddy."

With Joelle's blue hair, her blush was more prominent, and he smirked across the room at her.

"I did not! They're lying, Diamond."

"You're lying! You've tantalized my tastebuds all afternoon."

"Have you been talking a good game about me, Bluebell?"

She rolled her eyes but smiled. It felt like a connection. Domestic as fuck. Just perfect.

"Let me get cleaned up. I'm dusty from the road, and I'll whip something up for you ladies."

"Yesssss." Her friends cheered.

"Come with me for a minute, baby." He motioned with two fingers to Joelle. "And bring your phone."

He grabbed her hand and led her to his bathroom, closing the door behind them. He held Joelle by the waist, plopped her on the sink counter, and spread her legs to stand between.

"I warned you, your back's going to hurt."

Diamond squinted. "Do you really wanna be pushed over this counter and spanked with your girls right out there?"

Her gorgeous eyes widened. "You wouldn't dare."

"Mention once more about me picking you up and doing myself harm and see how it works out for your sore ass, baby."

She huffed but looked so fucking fuckable that he smashed his mouth on hers and took the kiss he'd wanted her to fling at him when he walked through the door. She mewled and sucked his tongue until he pulled away.

"Now show me these texts."

He quickly washed the road dust from his hands and face. He expected a small number but was furious at the months that had built up. He scrolled slowly, reading each one.

"Some I deleted."

He lifted his eyes from the phone to see her face etched with worry. "*Some*? Joelle, there are so many of them here. Why didn't you let me know when I was watching over you?"

"It's happened before, but they always fade away. I thought I could ignore it."

"They say they see you. And miss you."

Nothing much fazed Diamond.

He routinely faced violence, a consequence of his job as a hired brawler and protector. Injuries were commonplace, yet he remained unfazed.

Until now.

Fury surged inside him as he realized someone was digitally frightening his woman.

*His* fucking woman.

They weren't official.

He hadn't offered her his *Property Of Diamond* patch or a wedding ring; they hadn't even talked about anything long-term, but she was his woman.

And he was her man.

Diamond went all in, envisioning forever in their future.

The idea of someone in a dark basement creating creepy messages to scare her made Diamond's vision bleed into murderous red.

Unaware, he growled until he felt her soothing hand on his chest.

"Hey, it's okay, Diamond."

"Nothing about this shit is okay. I will kill them."

She spluttered a laugh. "You can't do that."

"Watch me."

Diamond was deadly serious. And he'd take great fucking joy in ending their life.

"I'll sort it."

"How? Besides the killing."

"I'll find out who the motherfucker is and stop them."

"How?"

"I have ways and means."

The MC came with a heavy network of connections, and he'd use them all if he had to.

"Now kiss me again, and you better use some tongue to calm me down. Then sit with your girls, or I'll be taking you in here. You look goddamn edible, baby."

The look she gave him burned Diamond down to the soul.

She wanted his fuck so badly.

The flush on her high cheekbones, her nibbled lower lip, and how her knees rubbed against his waist spoke volumes.

When she landed on his mouth, she did it hungrily and with determination to make him crazy.

"There, now we're both turned on." She told him sassily and hopped down from the counter. Smiling in the doorframe, she gave him a saucy little flutter of lashes, eyeing him up and down, pausing on his erection before she called out, "Don't forget you said you'd bake us treats."

Diamond let go of his inhale and rested both hands on the counter, willing his cock to go down.

He never bought into the theory that women were created to ruin men.

But that gorgeous creature out there was.

She was his downfall.

His rise from the ashes.

His undoing and ruining.

And he was going to enjoy every second.

After changing his clothes, he baked cookies for his lady and her friends.

It was hours until he could get his hands on her again.

And when he did, Diamond consumed her.

In the living room. The bedroom, the shower, and then in his bed during the night when she'd tried going to her room, and he'd carried her right back and pinned her underneath him.

"That does not happen again," he warned, getting between her legs, notching his so-ready cock at her entrance. She was dripping and already trying to clutch him.

"I didn't want to disturb you with my restless sleep."

"Your place is here with me." He growled. "Now I have to fuck you to sleep again."

He made it seem like a chore instead of his dream.

"Yes, please." She said demurely and arched up into him.

There was nothing more to say after that.

But once Diamond had fucked her to sleep, she stayed cuddled into him all night and didn't go back to the spare room ever again.

## Diamond

The focus of all his obsessive thoughts appeared in the archway leading to the hallway, like an apparition from his filthiest dreams, and Diamond knew why.

Constant sex for weeks hadn't doused how badly he craved this woman or how he'd fold his spine in half to provide Joelle with everything she needed. Spending every spare hour with her wasn't enough.

His body heated and pulsed blood straight down to his dick. Hardening him in seconds.

"*Christ*," he muttered, scraping his nasty gaze over her floaty nightie, flirting around her knees. She looked like one of those women you'd see in an old film. There was nothing sexual about her nightwear. It was practical to keep her warm, but she was so fucking gorgeous he nearly came staring at her.

She'd told him she wanted an early night, and he'd tucked her into bed thirty minutes ago. Yet here she was, staring at him, with her hard nipples visible through the nightie.

He spread out his bare feet and grabbed hold of the back of his leather chair.

"Can't sleep, baby?"

*Say it. Tell me you climbed out of bed because you felt empty without my cock rammed ten inches deep.*

She twitched on her bare feet.

How she could be nervous after all the fucking they'd done over the weeks, he didn't understand the female mind, but he thought she was adorable when she was acting shy.

He knew ways to get her un-shy real quick. And each way was filthier and more depraved than the last.

She shook her head. Still eyeing him. His shy baby.

Diamond ignored the din of the TV. Who cared about the game when there was a goddess to admire?

The pregnancy had given her defined curves that called to his hands. When they weren't in bed shaking pleasure out of her body, he loved palming her belly to feel connected to their baby.

They'd chosen to keep what they were having as a surprise for the birth. Diamond was happy either way. The longer her pregnancy progressed, the clingier Joelle became, and he not-so-secretly loved how she needed him in every aspect of her life.

He stroked his gaze over her chest. Pregnancy had changed her tits, too. They were fuller, more sensitive, and reacted to his mouth like he'd detonated her. He'd even made her come the other night just by sucking on her nipples.

"Do you want me to make you a hot chocolate? A nice back rub?"

She shook her head and came nearer on silent feet.

"What do you need then, Bluebell?"

She was so close now he could have grabbed her around the waist.

"Why do you always make me say it?" she whined, looking like a snack he wanted to gorge on. Her hair was loose around her shoulders. She'd gone for a color change this week and surprised him with deep violet hair. He'd been so surprised by how it aroused him, and he'd fucked her over the arm of the couch before they'd even said hello. Then he'd spent the rest of the night talking and rubbing her feet.

Diamond smirked and leaned forward, close enough to run a hand along the back of her leg and under her good girl nightie. She shivered and grasped his hair, scraping her nails on his scalp. She knew that got him going.

"Because I enjoy hearing you talking dirty. I enjoy knowing you want my dick."

She snorted and scratched his scalp again while he reached the top of her thigh, digging his fingers in so she moaned. "I'm on it enough. Doesn't that tell you anything?"

"Words, not actions, baby."

"Isn't it meant to be the other way around?"

The groping foreplay continued. As soon as she told him what she needed, it was on.

"Not tonight, it isn't."

"River?" she strained closer.

"Yeah, baby?"

"I'm horny. Will you lie back while I take what I need from you?"

If Diamond had to gauge how strong his desire was, it could have powered everyone in Laketon.

He might have wanted to go gentle on Joelle, but she'd sounded the claxon, and when he grabbed onto her waist, it was with rough hands.

First, he kissed her belly. "Bubba, you need to go to sleep. What I'm gonna do to your mom is indecent."

Joelle laughed and clambered onto his lap. "You are too cute."

He grasped the back of her neck with one hand, and with the other, he got hold of her hip and pulled her closer until she was rubbing against his erection with enticing circles.

Before she'd even straddled his lap and got comfortable, she was already fishing his ready cock out of his lounge pants. She burned his world down to dust when she was desperate for him. Diamond was busy hiking up her nightie, tossing it on the floor, and leaving his woman naked for his eyes.

When he grunted and captured her lips, hers were open and ready, and he swallowed her groan.

She howled with pleasure when she fed his cock into her sweet, wet pussy. The electric sensation nearly buckled him, but he elongated his torso so he could watch her take him in, watch her struggle to settle on all of his inches.

Fuck, he loved this part, and he thumbed her pussy lips, strumming over her clit to get her wetter.

"Go on, baby, you take it all like a good girl."

"Oh, god. You make me feel so good, River."

"It's what I live for." He rasped.

He returned to kissing her, feeling the deepness of her need down to his toes. When she sucked his tongue and nibbled on his lips, Diamond's eyes blissfully rolled back into his skull.

Kisses were preludes, not the whole meal, but her kisses sent him reeling.

Diamond fingers coasted against her pussy as she rose and fell on his cock. Tentatively, at first, she was finding her rhythm while she tortured him with pleasure.

His two middle fingers were slippery and coated already. "*Fuck. You're wet.*"

As Diamond got his dick rode off by a sex siren, he watched her writhing and being the confident queen he knew her to be. He couldn't get enough of Joelle.

And what she didn't know yet, what he hadn't voiced in actual words, he was keeping her. He would lock their relationship down as tight as possible, with no refunds or returns. She was his girl to the end.

It didn't matter if he had to fight the legal weight of Judge Snow and his ilk. Even if he had to plow his truck through the entire social upper crust with their pinkies in the air, he was keeping Joelle Snow forever.

"*Ride it, Bluebell*. Fuck your orgasm all over my cock. Soak me. I want it running down your thighs. Goddamn, I need to fuck you morning, noon, and night to keep this tight little pussy satisfied, don't I? I need to fill you with so much of my come that you crave feeling it trickling out of you. How much do you love my cock, baby?"

"I love it." She moaned.

"Say it."

"I love your cock, River!"

She sobbed and whimpered, begging him as he guided her to the pinnacle, and when Joelle climaxed, it was his name she cried out, his name she moaned as she came down from the euphoria, and it was his name she whispered in amazement as Diamond released inside her.

"How does that keep getting better?" she asked, all snuggled up on his lap.

Diamond was being a dirty pervert, playing between her legs, pushing his come back into her where it belonged. Each time his fingers brushed against her sensitive clit, she jolted and moaned. He fucking lived for that noise.

"Because it's us."

She liked his answer because she sent him a devastating smile and then landed on his mouth.

Fuck yeah, he was going to own every gorgeous inch of Joelle Snow.

They were never meant to tangle their lives together.

It hadn't been written in the stars.

But there was little denying how he felt about her, how she'd made his heart burst open.

He'd do anything to keep them together, even if it meant keeping her barefoot and beautifully pregnant for years.

He was wild for Joelle. And yet tamed.

If that meant love, he loved her more than he thought possible.

Destiny didn't mean shit to a man like him.

But belonging to a woman from the good side of the tracks did.

Being her man was everything to Diamond.

A privilege.

Pure, undiluted happiness.

The whole fucking world.

"What the hell is this, Joelle?"

"Wow, did someone get out of the wrong side of the bed this morning, big bear?" She had the audacity to stick her fancy nose in the air and smirk while he glared at a table full of house listings. Houses that looked like they were English castles.

They'd been living together more than harmoniously for four months; she was six months pregnant, and the reappearance of her house hunting blindsided him.

"We both got out of bed at the same time, baby. I was wearing your juices all over my beard."

She instantly flushed. "River! Do you have to be crude?"

Diamond smirked. Flustering her was his favorite thing to do.

"I can repeat it, but hold my pinkie finger in the air if you approve of those manners."

She snorted, amused, and held out her hand. It wasn't for a kiss. Diamond passed her his full coffee mug, and he watched her nose molest it, sniffing deeply.

She stopped drinking decaf coffee because she hated the taste and now only took a sip of his coffee every morning.

"Oh, yes, that's the stuff." She moaned, having one last whiff before giving it back to him.

"Now you've had your drugs. Mind explaining what I'm looking at?"

"What do you think of this one?" she waved a mansion in his face.

"Hate it."

"It is on the big side, but my realtor included it, anyway."

"You're not moving." He situated himself at the table.

She blinked. "Not this second. These are properties to view today."

"No."

"No? What do you mean, no?"

"Exactly what no means, Joelle. This isn't happening. You live here with me."

"Diamond, it was temporary, and that was months ago. I still need a place. The rebuild started at my parents' estate, but all my things are in storage."

Diamond felt the gust of air vacate his sternum.

She looked at him, so clueless, as if she believed everything she said.

Temporary? *Hardly*. He was keeping her. Didn't she realize that?

And while he watched Joelle flip through the listings, he realized he needed a different stance with his woman. He pushed out his chair, and it scraped on the tiled floor.

"Joelle, come and sit on my lap."

She looked up, still wearing her clueless expression.

"Are you trying to get fresh with me?"

He grunted and patted his lap. "Come here, woman."

"Oh, alright." She huffed but complied like his well-mannered girl, smiling as she came around the table to settle sideways on his lap. Her ass was pure perfection, and he gripped the top of her thigh where the sleep shorts rested on her leg. "I don't have time for funny business, Diamond. My first appointment with the realtor is at nine."

"I want you to do two things."

She bounced both eyebrows high. "Are they sex things?"

"Woman," he chuckled, "you're a sex maniac." Luckily, their libidos were a perfect match.

"I know." She whimpered, putting her head on his shoulder. "It's all your fault. I didn't know you'd be a god in bed. You've ruined me for all men."

He'd tackle that later because there would be no other men. Ruin wasn't the only one capable of going on a killing spree; Diamond could, too.

"What are these two things?"

"First, give me a kiss and then to listen."

It was scorching and speedy, and it lessened Diamond's irritation. She tasted of sweetness, mint, and everything that made him addicted to Joelle.

"Right, listen up. You're not moving out. We already live together. Here, or wherever, if you need a bigger house. But I'm not living in a mausoleum, Joelle. We're only gonna be three people; that's too much. And I don't want staff around either. That's our home. What if we walk around naked, or I wanna fuck you up against the fridge after baking your treats? Can't do that if we have a chef chopping carrots. I'll compromise on anything you want. Just pick a house with four or five bedrooms. And I pay."

While he'd laid out his intentions, Joelle had stared at him, her eyes growing wider, then slitting to narrow lines. Now she was slack-jawed, and he kissed the tip of her nose.

"Don't tell me I finally rendered you speechless."

Since she was probably lost in thought, he planted kisses on her neck. He only looked at her when she pushed him away.

"You seriously decided for me?"

Unrepentant, Diamond responded, "Yes." And then added. "You want to live with me, Bluebell. You know you do."

She didn't deny it. "You could have asked me, you know, the polite thing! You could have said it through a decision we made together."

If she were itching for a fight, she wouldn't get it now.

For the past couple of weeks, the pregnancy had been rough on her. He found pleasure in soothing her sore body parts during sleepless nights. And suddenly, certain foods and scents became unpleasant to her. He switched soap because it made her feel sick.

And her distaste for red meat meant he only ate steaks at the clubhouse now.

"Sweetheart, will you live with me?"

"No." she lamented.

Diamond grinned and pressed his lips to her cheek. "My colorful Bluebell, I don't know if you've noticed yet, but you thrive in my hands and care when I make the decisions."

If she got any cuter with her clueless expression, as she bit her bottom lip, Diamond would lose his composure and maul her.

"The day of the explosion, you came home with me without a fight. You settled in like we'd always lived together."

"But that was extenuating circumstances."

"It was because you were where you were meant to be. With me. You could have insisted I take you to a hotel, baby." He reminded her, and she frowned again. He kissed the lines on her forehead. "Every day since then, I've taken shit off your hands, and you come alive like you do when you're wearing all the rainbow. Colors heighten your mood, baby. But so do I."

"Diamond." She breathed, clasping both sides of his face, looking him square in the eyes until realization settled home. Then she repeated his name.

"I'm right here, baby."

He shielded her from the press by managing her locations. He lessened her stress by ensuring her parents only saw her at their townhouse, never at Diamond's, because her father wasn't pleased about a Diablo biker being the baby's father. Diamond wanted her to have a safe space to relax. And he was the man looking into finding the creepy texter. He took her to her appointments and was there for the spikes and dips in her hormones. There was nothing he wouldn't do for Joelle's happiness.

"Tell me this. Do you wanna live in a huge, impersonal mansion that has none of your colorful flare?"

"No," she answered. "But I wasn't going to look at large properties even before I stayed here."

"Before you moved in here." He amended.

"Tomato, lettuce." She rolled her pretty eyes at him.

"Then we downsize or upscale from this place, and you get to decorate it any color you want."

"You're trying to bribe me, aren't you?" she half-smiled.

"Whatever works."

"Do you want us to live together?"

"Baby, we *are* living together. You're the only one who doesn't realize it."

"I like it here," she sighed. "It feels..."

"Feels what?"

"Cozy. Like an actual home. I've never had that, Diamond."

"So why are you bitching at me about this, Joelle? You thrive under my decision making."

"The ego on you." She laughed and nuzzled her face into his neck. "Okay, I'll stop house hunting for now. Until the baby is born."

"Then we find somewhere together."

"This is fast, Diamond."

"But it feels right, yeah?"

She took a second, but nodded against his neck. "It feels right. You won't always get your way, you know?"

He smirked. Diamond looked forward to every challenge they faced together.

It took them two weeks to furnish the spare bedroom into a nursery.

Spending every spare moment at home with Joelle felt like a slice of paradise neither of them knew they needed.

Keeping his woman happy was a vocation he had exceeded in.

Like a daddy biker, Diamond christened the baby's room by sitting Joelle in the new rocking chair, getting on his knees, and making her come with his mouth.

If sexual coercion was a thing, he was going to become an expert because his woman was magnificent under his hands.

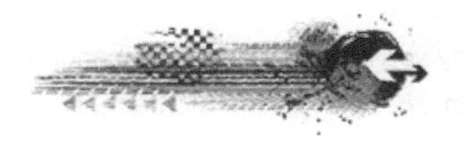

It wasn't every day Diamond arrived home from the club to hear Joelle on the phone, refusing a date with another man.

She was a terrible cook. Like she could burn water without trying. Diamond walked into the kitchen to smell the burning. Sure enough, the white chicken chili inside one of his expensive pots looked charred. He switched off the stove and pushed the pot to the back.

It was then he heard. "No, sorry, Trent, I can't."

Trent? The pompous tie-wearing dickfuck was calling her, and she was talking to him like old pals?

Not the fuck on his watch.

Without ditching his cut or kicking off his boots, Diamond came up behind her and stroked a hand on her rounded belly. She had one month before the baby arrived, and his kid was kicking up a storm today. He'd talk to the bubba soon, as he did every night after rubbing Joelle's sore feet, but first.

His lips touched her face, and she turned her dazzling smile on him.

She looked like a bag of skittles. Red leggings, yellow socks, and a green and blue tank t-shirt. Her purple hair was tied high in a ponytail, giving him access to her nape. That's where he landed his lips next.

He'd had plans to eat her up when he walked through the door. It had been all he'd thought about since she'd texted him that dinner was cooking. He'd known he'd have to order takeout first to replace her culinary effort.

"Tell the pussy you're carrying my baby and to fuck off."

She gave him an elbow to the stomach. Diamond caught the arm and pinned it to her side.

"I'm not available for a date, Trent. No, not next week, either."

"Tell him now, Joelle." He warned low and pressed himself to her back. His woman, sassy as ever, dared to turn around and motion for him to quiet before giving him her back again.

That was not happening unless she wanted him to snap that guy's neck in ten places.

Diamond skimmed a hand around her stomach and went down until he was inside her leggings. He felt her jolt, and she fired him a *what are you doing* stare over her shoulder while she appeased the intellectually challenged idiot on the phone.

"My father had no right telling you to call me, Trent. We've been over for a long time. I won't have this conversation again. No, Trent, there are no second chances for us."

He'd heard enough, and he fed two fingers into her panties and found wet heat along her tight slit.

His proper girl wouldn't react even if the house burned around them.

She had better manners than that. Better manners than a biker fingering his girl.

But Diamond wasn't above playing dirty to make her realize who she belonged to.

He wasn't touching to tease her, he had a point to make.

He started with a fast strum and didn't let up. Not even when her ass shuddered against his crotch, with his mouth on the shell of her ear, he groaned. "Tell that dead man walking who your forever man is. How deep and for how long I satisfy this insane body, Joelle. Tell him my fingers are gonna fuck your tight cunt until you gush down my hand and drip onto the floor." He went from her clit down to her soaked hole, and Diamond angled two long fingers into his woman. No pussy had ever welcomed him like hers did, and he grunted against her warm skin. "Get him off the phone, Joelle, before I break all of his fucking bones."

"Oh, my days." She wheezed and latched her free hand onto his wrist, but she wasn't pulling him free. She was actively driving her pussy into his fingers, arching her ass until he was humping her from that end, too. "No, Trent. I don't want to date you. Why? Because I'm having a baby, that's why! I'm involved with someone, and he'll likely cut you up if you dare call me again. Yes, you heard me. Now, excuse me, I'm about to have sex on the kitchen floor." She pressed to end the call and then moaned so languidly he felt it in his bones.

"I hope he fucking heard that," Diamond said, finger-fucking Joelle against the counter. He pinned her in place, forcing her to take his ownership.

*His woman.*

The roar to mark her all over was real. He'd force her fingers around his cock next to work him over until he splattered his pleasure all over her pale skin. *Mine.*

"You're so dirty. Oh... my... god, Diamond, I'm going to come." She moaned and came into his hand with a great shudder. "You are a bad boy." She scolded some minutes later, turning into his chest. Her arms latched onto his waist while Diamond licked his fingers clean.

"What the fuck was that jackass calling you for?"

"I honestly don't even know. Something about seeing my father at the country club, and he called me. It was quite pathetic, but I think he finally gets the message I'm a taken girl."

"Damn right you're taken. If he calls again, Joelle, I'm breaking his neck."

"You can't break everyone's neck." She said, cuddling deeper into him. She became a cuddler after sex, and he fucking loved it. They were wrapped around each other in the kitchen. He still sported an erection hard enough to hammer nails, but he was in no rush to fix that. Not when Joelle needed her after-sex cuddles.

"Watch me."

"I will watch you," she spoke, nuzzling his t-shirt. "Then we'll probably have sex afterward because everything you do turns me on. Even breaking necks."

Diamond burst out laughing.

She was too much. His sassy rainbow girl.

They were intricately intertwined.

But their lives were still kept separate. Only Chains, Axel, and Scarlett knew he was well and truly hooked up with a woman.

The threat of the Irish had dwindled. The insane woman's revenge streak, thankfully, hadn't come near Joelle. Though that threat was downgraded, and she'd been able to go off to her lavish events if she'd wanted to, they'd been joined at the hip most days.

He was selfish enough to need her in his world more prominently.

Right now, they were living between her lifestyle and his.

When she smiled dreamily, he saw something he'd been aching for in the eyes of his forever woman.

She loved him.

It was written all over her unguarded features, and Diamond felt every heavy thud of his heart.

She loved him.

That gave him the rights to own her.

His possessiveness bellowed like a physical sound inside his chest.

But if her shithead father thought he could play matchmaker and try to edge Diamond out, it was over his dead body.

"Bluebell, you burned the dinner again."

"It wasn't entirely my fault this time. Trent called and distracted me."

Diamond growled. "Don't answer him next time."

She sighed and squeezed him tighter, nuzzling his chest. "Are you mad about the dinner? I tried."

His jealousy turned to amusement, and he patted her ass. "Get off your feet, woman. I'll order dinner, and then I'll rub them."

He knew that would get a reaction out of her. Joelle was a fiend for a foot rub. If not for being swollen and pregnant, he'd assume it was her fetish.

His intentions were entirely deviant, though.

Once he got his hands on her, they'd fuck. And there was nothing better than being connected to her while she called out his name.

"You are a saint! You're a king! A god!"

"Am I your saint? Your king? Your god?"

Her face filled with color, and she nodded shyly. "Yes. Order a mushroom pizza, please. I'll get my toes comfortable."

Damn, she was cute. His eyes ate her up as she sashayed into the living room.

"River! I can't hear you talking to the pizza place." She called out.

"Woman, you have no patience." He smiled, grabbing the menus.

He wanted her to be impatient for everything. Voicing her needs because she trusted him to deliver.

Ravenous.

Grabby.
Demanding.
And all his.

## Diamond

"This is the only time I'll warn you, Snow, your daughter belongs to me."

The old man's craggy features twisted in contempt. "Don't be so disgusting."

He'd crashed into his office and now faced the man sitting at his wealthy desk like he was Don Corleone.

"She's having my baby. We live together."

"That was an interim to ensure her safety." He snapped. "We've asked her several times to move into the townhouse."

"And she's said no. Because she's happier with me, where she doesn't get dragged into your crazy mobster bitch bullshit."

Snow's scowl softened a bit when the truth hit, but he still couldn't keep his mouth shut.

"You're no better than I am. You're beneath my daughter, and she deserves someone of a higher class, not a biker who tramples through the dirt. You forget, I know your MC is far from squeaky clean."

"No, I'm not better," Diamond answered evenly. "But I'd throw myself on top of Joelle to protect her and our baby when her fucking house blows up. Can you say the same? Joelle is my priority, Snow. And I get the impression she's never been that to anyone. Least of all her family."

He turned red, face muscles twitching with restrained anger. "That's not true. I love my daughter."

"Pity you don't show it." Diamond slid both hands down into the front pockets of his jeans. "I'm not here to barter for her. Joelle is mine and staying mine. I'm here to tell you to back the fuck off from trying to get that weasel Trent back in her life. She ended that relationship for a reason. If you were any decent father, you'd know that reason. If he calls her again on your say-so, I'll be the one to step in. And it won't only be Trent, I deal with."

"That sounds like a threat." Snow narrowed his eyes.

"Take it however you want to take it. You don't like me or my club, Snow, though you've paid us enough over the years. I don't like you, either. We have Joelle in common, and whether you approve is here nor there, your grandchild is due soon. How you proceed from here determines if I let you see my kid."

Snow could take that as a threat, too.

Snow's pale pallor and tense jaw made the warning resonate deeply.

"I expected nothing less than a threat from someone like you."

"I'm glad you recognize who I am exactly." Smirked Diamond. "It's the difference between you and me, Snow. I protect what's mine. I bust my balls to make them happy. Whether you're in Joelle and my kid's life means jackshit to me. But it does to her. She's chosen me, so this is your only chance to do better. I won't allow you to treat her indifferently anymore. Just give me a reason to cut her ties with you, and I'd fucking love it."

On that note, he turned on his heavy biker boots, trekked across the carpet, and exited the office, giving the worried secretary a wink to show he was harmless.

There was tension when he entered the clubhouse doors.

Diamond couldn't see anything immediately that was wrong, but something was up for sure. He jutted his chin at the newest prospect, and the guy sauntered over.

"Who does the new bike outside belong to?" he asked Price.

"Dunno, boss. Some big dude. Had a face like the iceberg from that movie that sank a ship." Then Price lowered his voice and indicated to Scarlett, Kylie, and Nina, sitting with a younger girl he didn't recognize. "And he came in holding that chick's hand. He told her to wait. Then he went into the office with the Prez and VP."

Diamond nodded. "Get back to work, probie. The garage needs cleaning top to bottom."

The other man groaned but slunk off to do his grunt work.

If Axel needed him, someone would come for Diamond, so he helped himself to a coffee and then parked his ass at the bar. The old ladies were chatting as usual. The new girl was mid-twenties, maybe, and appeared nervous.

When Splice came in from the workshop, he grabbed a can of soda from behind the bar and sat next to Diamond.

"Did you see who turned up earlier?"

"No, who?"

"Atom. No word of warning. Just blazed through the gates while I was working on a sweet as fuck Bentley. He had a chick riding backpack, too. Didn't even stop to chew the fat. He got in a huddle with the Prez and VP, and then they went into Axel's office. They've been there ever since."

"For real? Shit must be happening."

"I agree." He turned around on the stool and smirked. "Look at the tiny thing he brought. I wonder if she's a gift. Isn't she cute?"

Diamond snorted. "If the girl came in with Atom, he's likely to rip your eyes out for looking at her like you are, my brother."

Splice chuckled and rubbed his mouth with the back of his hand, eating the girl up. It was his funeral. "No harm in looking. I'm off sex, anyway."

Diamond nearly choked.

Out of all the crap Splice could have declared, that was the most strange. He did all his flirting with his junk out and claimed he'd never met a woman he didn't want to sleep with. From way back, he's been proudly owning the title of loveable manwhore and swears he won't change.

"Sure, my Pinocchio brother. Can I interest you in buying some flying pigs?"

Splice only rolled a shoulder, gave a crooked smile, and rose off the stool. "I gotta get back to the Bentley. A classy cougar has paid for a rush job."

The pair brushed knuckles, and Diamond watched him leaving.

After over an hour, Atom and the rest exited the back office. Axel didn't look happy. Neither did Chains. The girl rushed to her feet and didn't stop moving until she was standing in front of Atom, immediately grabbing hold of his cut. They looked comical. Atom was six feet six, and the girl had to be five feet tall.

Diamond didn't know the Nomad all that well. He'd been a wanderer even before Diamond joined the club and only rolled into Laketon several times a year. He was mainly on the road, doing recon missions for the MC. No one had seen him in a while.

He still had a face set like frigid thunder, like he was permanently pissed off at the world and didn't mind letting people know about it.

The woman's sudden outburst made Diamond stop beside Chains and Axel.

"No! You promised. You promised, and now you're fucking lying! I can't stay here, I won't!"

He cocked an eyebrow at Chains, who mouthed. "Trouble."

*Oh, fuck.*

Diamond folded his arms and watched the conversation between Atom and his woman. Was she his woman? Diamond couldn't remember Atom ever having a girlfriend or anyone special. People thought he was gay because he never gave in to the flirty advances from the sweet bottoms.

With their height difference, Atom bent his neck. "I told you I'd sort it, didn't I? Listen to me, Brogan, this is happening, so get the fuck on board and stop pouting like a little girl, or I'll give you something to pout about."

*Shit.* That was a threat to kill her, or it was some weird foreplay.

Axel gestured for Scarlett to come to him. The club queen left her seat, skirted around the arguing couple, and nestled into the Prez's arms, where he bent his head, speaking only for her.

Atom sighed a few times, scraping ring-covered fingers through his hair, and then their heads angled in together. Some of the conversation was too low to overhear.

It was weird that they hadn't caught wind of Atom getting involved. The gossip network within the Diablos was legendary.

But then, Diamond thought, only three people knew about his Joelle.

Something he had to rectify because he didn't like the secret shit.

He knew he'd get some pushback from certain brothers, who wouldn't trust a member of the Snow family to be among them and not try to weed out Diablos' secrets.

But Joelle was not like that, far from it.

"I don't want to be here without you," the woman said, her lower lip wobbling. Atom caught hold of her chin, tipping her head back.

"But you're gonna do it without complaining, aren't you?"

She took a while, but she nodded. Then she rushed into Atom's chest and bawled her eyes out. If they were together, Atom's body language was odd when he awkwardly patted the woman's back like he wasn't used to touching her.

"You'll come back for me, won't you?"

Atom only grunted. And with little fanfare, with the girl trailing behind him, he exited like an apparition, climbing onto his bike. Once he left, Scarlett took over with Brogan, leading her to the back rooms.

Diamond was still confused as hell.

The details Diamond found out later in an emergency church meeting blew everyone's minds and put every brother on high alert. It was suggested that they didn't even mention Atom had been in town. As far as anyone could know, the last time they'd seen their brother was a couple of years ago.

Well-meaning questions like, "Is it safe to bring my old lady here now?" were asked and answered. For such a big decision, they had to take a vote.

It wasn't unanimous. But the Ayes had enough.

This meant that, for the foreseeable future, Brogan Morales would live at the clubhouse under the Diablos' protection. No one was to talk about her to anyone.

Climbing into bed that night next to Joelle, he pressed his chest against her back, curling an arm around her sleeping form. Worry clung to his mind. In Atom's position, he knew he would do the same thing for Joelle.

There wasn't anything he wouldn't do for her or to protect her.

They were about to become a little family of three.

His world had changed the moment he stepped into hers.

He'd always be a biker, but he was something more now. A different man with stronger connections and priorities.

He was Joelle Snow's man. And soon to be a daddy. Diamond didn't deserve a woman like her or to have a baby with her. He hadn't seen it coming, but someone was handing him paradise. He wouldn't question a good thing. She was a treasure he would cherish and adore for the rest of his life.

And if he died first, he'd haunt any motherfucker who tried to sniff around his rainbow woman. He wasn't above doing poltergeist shit, either.

She murmured in her sleep, turning toward him, and he captured her lips softly.

"River?"

"Yeah, it's me. Go back to sleep."

She was already nestling in, sticking her cold feet between his calves. "Love you," she muttered, dropping back into sleep.

Leaving Diamond wrecked from the inside with euphoria.

She loved him.

*Fuck him.* How could he find sleep now while he was longing to push his grateful cock inside his heaven and have her warming his shaft all night?

Grunting, Diamond buried his face in Joelle's neck.

"I love you more, Bluebell."

Never had something been so undeniably true.

## Diamond

**M**oving inside of Joelle was the perfect way to start his day.

She had a body that made a man go to war.

And a sexual appetite he was addicted to.

Her cries made the world drift away, focusing solely on his vibrant woman.

"Harder, River. *Please*." Sweetly begging, she dug her nails into his forearm.

He gripped her thigh and brought it over the back of his, opening her up for a deeper slam as requested. His little savage needed his dick like he needed air, and he was here to provide.

"My Bluebell is taking it so good. Is the tightness hurting?"

"Yes." She hissed in pleasure, "Don't stop."

The more time together that passed, the hungrier he became for her. He was at a feral level to pleasure her.

"Ohh, River, your dick is magic." She whined, exploding his ego. Diamond chuckled into her neck. "Thank you, baby."

"It's sorcery, the things it makes me feel."

He smirked into her neck. "I love it when I turn you dirty."

"Will you do that thing I like?" she panted.

Diamond thrust and tweaked one of her nipples to make her howl with pleasure. "What thing?"

"Where you talk like a club-carrying Neanderthal."

In the early sunrise, shadows cast around their bedroom, Diamond smirked, knowing what she wanted. He kissed the lobe of her ear and started pistoning his hips when her pussy became tighter around his cock. He loved taking her from behind. She was close. And he was about to throw her over the cliff edge.

"This pussy is all mine, Bluebell. It's the most gorgeous thing I've ever seen and tasted. I like my tongue fucked so deep in this pussy until you drown me, don't I? But nothing feels as good as it does right now. Being buried in you, baby, is a fucking paradise I don't deserve." He rolled his fingers over her clit and felt how much harder she clenched him.

His Joelle got off on his dirty talk.

Such a good, well-brought-up girl, liking it indecently.

She was exactly what he needed.

"You're drenched and soaking the sheets." He rolled his stomach against her soft ass. It wasn't a hard fuck, not how they fucked like feral animals months ago. She was too delicate for that, but Diamond kept a steady rhythm, knowing how to move Joelle to get her there.

"Please make me come, River. I need it. I need *you*."

Hearing her say that last part unhinged him.

When he felt her ready to detonate, he increased his speed on her clit, and his rhythm went deep to pound her g-spot. He nearly went blind with bliss as she came with a husky cry, and he followed right after, his veins burning up with flames.

"Such a greedy pussy my Bluebell has. You squeezed every drop out of me," he grunted against the side of her neck. She let off a tinkling, pleased laugh, scraping her nails down his inner wrist.

"Well, if you push that big thing into me before I'm awake..."

"You were seducing me in your sleep." He groaned. "Rubbing this sweet ass back on me. I had no choice. You needed my fuck, and I was happy to service."

"How about a special back massage if we shower together?" she suggested, and his buried cock perked at the idea.

"Is that good girl speak for screwing you again?" He hoped.

Joelle laughed and elbowed him. "No, it means you soap me up and rub your very pregnant girlfriend's lower back."

"Are you aching?"

"All over."

They hopped in the shower, and he massaged Joelle's lower back, where she'd been sore for days.

Diamond was not ready for the liquid to splash on his feet while he was drying her with a towel.

They both looked at each other. *Stunned.*

Then she started laughing.

Panic came a few minutes later when they realized what was to come.

"River, you need to calm down," she told him repeatedly in the following hours.

She looked like a serene goddess even though the labor pains had started.

"I'll calm down when I have you strapped to a hospital bed."

"They don't strap me down." She giggled, looking lovelier than ever. Her eyes were sparkling. Her skin was glowing.

And he was losing his shit.

He hadn't prepared.

Why the fuck didn't he put it together that being pregnant meant his woman had to go through labor, too?

Thank fuck she was the smart one in their relationship, because not ten hours later, Diamond was holding a slimy bundle in his arms while his son blistered the air with his tiny screams.

"If I ever complain about a headache again, remind me of what you did today, baby." He said in awe. Leaning over the bed, he pressed his lips to Joelle's warm forehead and then down to kiss her lips. "You are a fucking warrior." He rasped. "I love you, Bluebell. I'm so goddamn in love with you."

"I love you, too." She said with tears leaking out the corners of her eyes. She was exhausted yet still beaming a smile.

Nothing would ever be the same again.

It was like all of Diamond's organs rearranged themselves the moment his son was pushed into the world.

His Bluebell and his son. His entire world.

He was the luckiest biker on earth.

The rest of forever started now.

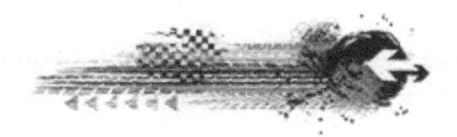

"You have to go," Joelle said from the rocking chair in Abraham's nursery. If it was possible to fall deeper in love and worship with his woman, he did each time he watched her nursing their son. Abraham's greediness matched Diamond's feelings for her. Wearing only a ratty pair of jeans, he trekked barefoot into the room and placed a glass of lemonade beside her. Then, he leaned down, and they met in the middle for a kiss. "Bash wants you there, Diamond."

"I'm not going until you come with me."

It wasn't anything he hadn't said in the last three weeks since they'd brought Abraham home from the hospital. They'd lived in a bubble. An idyllic bubble, and he was reluctant to leave them. Only when Joelle was sleeping did he ever slip out for work, but he soon got his ass back home.

Becoming a dad had tested his limits.

While it was the best thing he could have ever imagined, he was also the most tired a person had ever felt before. The kid was up at all hours, screaming and flailing his skinny arms and legs. He would only sleep when swaddled like a burrito and cradled in someone's arms. Clever little shit always sensed when they attempted to put him down.

He didn't want to go to a club party tonight and leave Joelle to look after him alone.

"I already told you that once he settles down, I'll happily meet everyone at the clubhouse."

"You better, or I'm throwing you over my shoulder, woman." He made it sound like a warning, but she only smiled. Even his threats didn't work. He was so in love with this woman. It was driving him mad.

"Please go. We're fine, I promise."

Bash had met the love of his life a year ago, a nurse at the hospital. He'd pursued her like a missile, and finally, she'd fallen for him only recently. Tonight, Bash was giving her his *Property Of* patch and wanted the brotherhood in attendance. Knowing it was important, Diamond hesitated to leave her, even for an hour.

She finally got him out of the house. But he wasn't happy about it.

He loved the MC and would always be a Diablo, but the need to be home with his family was greater.

Once there, Diamond toasted the happy couple and talked to a few of his brothers after texting to check on Joelle.

She hadn't answered, but that wasn't unusual, not when she liked to cat nap while Abraham slept his average of twenty minutes.

He was antsy and couldn't stop the gut feeling that something was wrong.

Diamond was addicted. That was true.

He only felt peace these days when he was close to Joelle.

Although he was happy for Bash and his brothers finding their old ladies, he felt a weight in his gut knowing that hardly anyone knew he had found one, too. As Bash fell in love in the open, Diamond's relationship was being kept under wraps.

Charlotte sat with Bash, proudly wearing her *Property Of Bash* cut.

He knew he wanted to have his property patch on Joelle's back.

He'd solidify that decision when he went home.

When was too soon to leave a party?

Deciding to give it another twenty minutes, the name Snow on the TV caught his attention. Expecting another ego-bloating feature on the Judge, his heart nearly flatlined seeing amateur footage of his woman being arrested!

"What the fuck?" he spat out.

Was he so sleep-drunk that he was seeing shit?

It had to be a dead ringer for Joelle or some gag piece because she was at home with Abraham. She would've let him know if she had plans to go out.

His girl was not a troublemaker. Why the fuck was some bozo cop putting cuffs on her and manhandling her into the squad car?

A cold rush went through his blood. Abraham! Where the fuck was his son?

Immediately, he reached for his phone, but she didn't pick up.

They kept mentioning her connection to Judge Snow. Diamond felt like he'd been shot. A bystander recorded it and sent it to the news station.

His fists clenched, his jaw felt like it was ready to crack.

Diamond knew Joelle inside and out. She was the least trouble-causing person there was, and she hated conflict.

Every moment with her was etched in his memory, and what he was looking at was his scared, frantic woman.

He shot forward in the chair. Fire coursed through his veins. His brain was about to explode, with many unanswered questions piling up.

This shit was not happening.

His girl was not a troublemaker, not by a longshot.

Either they got the wrong person, or the fucking cops were just flexing their muscles.

"Fucking hell, Joelle. What have you done?"

Not for a second did he think she had broken the law. Diamond would gladly clean up after her if his good girl enjoyed causing chaos. Crimes didn't faze him at all. Her sudden departure left him perplexed.

The worry clawed his throat raw; all he could think about was getting to her and Abraham.

Everyone was staring at him, but he didn't give a damn about explaining.

As the news bulletin finished, he rushed to his feet, grabbing the leather jacket. He was already marching off as he swung into it. "Where the fuck is my son, Joelle?"

He'd snap necks if anyone had put their hands on his child.

He all but steam-rolled Axel down in the entryway.

"Whoa. What's the rush, Diamond?"

"Joelle was on the news, getting fucking *arrested*. I don't know who the fuck has my son!"

"*Shit*. Let's go." Axel whistled to Chains across the forecourt and pointed to the bikes. He was already calling their new lawyer to meet them at the sheriff's department.

Diamond was breaking all the speed limits to get there in no time. Chains and Axel stuck with him the whole time.

As a trio, they stalked into the cop department. Their informant, Officer Sofia Fielding, was in the entryway, having been warned they were coming.

She pierced them with a stare, her voice hushed. "Do not start any shit here. She's fine. Your lawyer is already with her."

"She's fucking fine?" he gritted through his teeth. He could murder every person in the building and not give a shit. "What the fuck is she even doing here, Fielding?"

Maybe later, he could also thank Axel for contacting her, but he had no composure. Not when he was frayed at the edges and holding onto his sanity.

"Keep it together, D." Chains said, touching his shoulder. "What can you tell us, Fielding?"

"She hit a cop."

"*Bullshit*." Diamond spat.

"She was in an altercation with an unknown civilian, and when the officers turned up, she swung at him. That's all I currently know."

He was not buying that crap. If they were trying to pin a trumped-up charge on her because of her surname, he'd shoot the fucking lot of them.

"I wanna see her now! And who the fuck has my son?"

Diamond was seething from the inside out.

Holding on to what little saneness he had left.

He wanted to take the building apart brick by brick until he got his eyes on Joelle.

Axel and Chains were there as his calm wall, doing the talking when his rage became too big.

It felt like endless hours he waited until a door opened, and a guy in a cashmere sweater and pressed pants, carrying a briefcase, ushered Joelle out in front of him.

Diamond stopped pacing, and the moment she saw him, it was like she sprouted wings to get to him, throwing herself into his chest, weeping.

"Where's Abraham, Joelle?"

"Mom has him," she cried, clinging to him as tightly as Diamond held her.

He finally felt the relief a man on death row would feel when granted a reprieve.

Behind him, he caught the lawyer explaining to Axel that there would be no charges, but all Diamond concentrated on was the love of his existence, sobbing in his arms.

"I got you, Bluebell." He reassured her and himself.

Joelle fit against him like she'd been designed solely for him.

He was still feeling untamed and feral, but as her arms banded around his waist, her warmth coated his soul.

"Can we get out of here? I need out of this place, Diamond."

Once outside, he saw his truck. A prospect had dropped it off thanks to Axel's instructions.

"There were only the formalities to go through once I arrived," the club lawyer explained. "Judge Snow had already called the chief of police."

"We need to get that video taken down from every outlet," Diamond told him gravely, and Joelle gasped. "There's footage?"

"Already working on it, brother." Chains said. And the lawyer chimed in with the same. He would use his legal language to have it removed from news websites.

Cupping her face, he brushed away the streaks of tears with his thumbs. "Tell me what happened. You didn't let me know you were going out."

She hiccupped. He could only imagine how frightened she'd been. "Mom wanted to see Abraham. You know how she gets. It was easier to go to her, and I wanted some fresh air, anyway. I didn't even get inside their townhouse when Trent came bounding out of his car."

"Trent?" Diamond hissed, feeling the return of his rage. "This is because of that cocksucking Trent?"

"It was him, Diamond. All those weird texts, for all these months, it's been him sending them." She paused with a stuttering inhale. "I was blindsided. He called me pretty. The texts always called me pretty. He was stoned and just wouldn't stop going on about how we were supposed to be together and how I messed it all up by having a kid with someone else. He was unhinged, Diamond. I didn't know what to do."

"None of this is your fault, baby." He put his lips to her temple. Diamond locked eyes with Axel and mouthed. "Find him." The prez nodded, and he and Chains quickly climbed on their bikes and shot off.

"He wouldn't stop pulling my arm. All I wanted was to go inside with Abraham."

"Did that motherfucker get arrested and put in cuffs, too?" he snarled at the lawyer.

"No, he fled the scene, but I'm informed an arrest warrant has been issued for harassment and attempted kidnapping. We will press charges."

Diamond would break his fucking neck when he caught up with him.

"I've never seen him like that before, Diamond." She whimpered against his chest. "But I had to do something when he tried to pull at the baby carrier. Someone must have seen me hit him and called the police. I didn't mean to hit the officer. It was all just a blur; he must have come up behind me as I tried to reach the townhouse steps, and I thought it was Trent following me."

"Baby, none of this shit is your fault." Then he turned to the lawyer. "None of this bullshit sticks to her, got it?"

"It won't. Joelle was a mother under duress and was fearful for her safety. I'll be pursuing a reprimand for the over-zealous arresting officer who ignored her distress and the obvious attempt to kidnap her and the child."

With one arm around Joelle, he shook the guy's hand. "Thanks for getting here so quickly. Sorry, we're meeting like this. I'm Diamond."

The lawyer grinned and flashed two dimples. "Good to meet you, Diamond. I'm James. I'm sure we'll talk again. Try to have a better night, Miss Snow." He sauntered off to his Beemer.

Diamond helped Joelle into the truck, buckled her up, and hopped into the driver's seat. He immediately reached for her thigh.

"Why does your mom have Abraham?"

"She must have heard the disturbance. I screamed for her to take him before they could drag me away. It all happened so fast. She called my father. I guess it's fortunate to have contacts like the chief of police." She sighed, looking so pale. "I was scared. I can't believe Trent would act that way. He wanted to separate me from Abraham; I don't think he cared how he did it."

Diamond had countless evil thoughts about his actions when he found him.

But his priority was getting Joelle to Abraham. Her relief became a shallow cry when her mom met them at the door, holding him.

While Joelle fussed over Abraham, and her mother fussed over her, Diamond stood centurion in the hallway, seething underneath his skin, waiting for the second he could go hunting.

The Judge arrived home with Reeves in tow as they were about to leave.

Diamond didn't know who appeared more shocked by the affection when Snow hugged Joelle. But he got it. They were all fucked up because of Joelle's arrest. Even Reeves toned down his usual teasing and was nice to her.

Diamond's nerve endings were still buzzing with rage.

Snow was all worked up, holding a scotch and discussing throwing the book at Trent. Diamond didn't bother chiming in because he had a more direct approach to doling out the punishment.

It would be swift.

And harsh.

And he'd make that motherfucker suffer for every second he'd terrorized Diamond's woman.

## Joelle

Regardless of how ridiculously in love with Diamond she was, it meant nothing when Joelle wanted to choke him for not giving her a heads-up.

"Baby, they're gonna love you."

"You haven't even prepared me, River!" she scowled, looking at him and then at the large brick building through the truck window.

He'd brought her to the Diablos HQ.

She'd thought they were going out to lunch. The first date since Abraham came along.

Their first date *ever*.

And this is what he sprang on her!

"You promised me a date."

He chuckled and reached for her hand, bringing it to his mouth. "I promise we'll go on so many dates, especially now your mom is crazy for Abraham, and we'll have a babysitter anytime."

Joelle was not ready to leave the baby with anyone. It was lovely to witness her mom's affection for her one-month-old grandson. Even her father monopolized Abraham when she took him for a visit.

She stared at the intimidating building again. His found family was in there. Joelle felt she knew them all because of how Diamond talked about them, but she was also worried about how they might react when they learned her surname.

Despite Diamond's reassurance, Joelle remained nervous.

She wanted his family to approve of her.

But what if she didn't like them?

How would their life together be if she couldn't be around his people?

She watched Diamond round the hood to open her door. He leaned in and tapped a kiss on the tip of her nose. The adorable big bear. He never stopped making her fall in love with him.

Just this morning, when she'd been covered in spit-up and dealing with a fussy Abraham, he'd made a stack of pancakes and then taken the baby to wander around the yard so she could eat and shower.

So many trivial things made her love her man.

The most significant factor was the way he stared at her.

He gazed at her as if she was the center of his universe.

Joelle waited for Diamond to assist her in getting down from the high truck, yet she remained near the door, clinging to his long fingers.

"Do I look okay?"

Fortunately, she wore a fashionable patterned maxi dress with chunky sandals instead of staying in her stay-at-home-mom leggings. She had even taken the time to wash and style her hair in anticipation of their date. It had been quite the moment.

She was presentable for the firing squad, at least.

"You look fuckable, baby."

Her cheeks flamed.

"Don't flirt right now. I'm still deciding if I'm mad at you."

He grinned mischievously and brought their foreheads close together. His hand slid around the back of her neck.

"They're excited to meet you."

"Really?"

He assured her so.

"Do I get to meet your blood family one day?"

"Sure, if that's what you want."

She tested that by asking. "What if I never want to meet them?"

"Then you don't."

She blinked up at him. "You don't care?"

"Bluebell, you've spent a lifetime doing shit to appease others. I'm not gonna force you into something you're not comfortable with. Do I want you to meet them? Fuck yeah, I want them to see the woman I'm crazy about, who I'm gonna be with for the rest of my life. That means something to me. But not above how you feel."

"Big bear, don't make me cry before I face all your biker family." She laughed a little. He was absolutely perfect. "I want to meet them, by the way."

"Good, 'cause I already booked plane tickets." He flashed her the most boyish grin.

"You," she grumbled playfully. "What am I going to do with you, hm?"

"Keep me."

"Well, yeah. You're hard to get rid of, so I better keep you."

Joelle saw his head descend and tilted hers up to receive his soft kiss.

He kissed her gently, taking his time, tasting her fully, making her whimper.

Diamond drew back, and she forced her heavy eyelids open.

Both of them locked eyes, and a change happened. The air stirring had nothing to do with the gentle breeze and everything to do with their relationship, knitting together tightly, a permanent bond forming.

With a kernel of desire budding in her stomach, suddenly, she was no longer afraid of anything in front of her.

She could do anything, be anything, with Diamond at her side.

The man had been her rock for so long. Her protection and stability.

Life could throw a mountain of surprises their way, and she knew they'd cope just fine.

Without conscious effort, Joelle had drawn the line between her old life and the new one she would work hard to keep.

Just yesterday, her father called to tell her that Trent was found dead in his car and not to talk to any reporters if they called. Just let her lawyer deal with it. It was blasted all over the news. An apparent suicide inside his garage. The grave-faced reporter discussed the charges Trent had been facing against her and then revealed that it was discovered he had been defrauding his law firm. The reason for his suicide. She'd instantly looked at Diamond, who'd been listening to the speakerphone conversation, and her first thought had been, *did he do this*?

Her second thought was, if he had done it, it was to protect his family. Their family. She'd never ask him the question because she didn't need the answer.

She'd known then the line was drawn. She was on the side of Diamond, the man she loved. *Always*.

She loved him endlessly, with a force she didn't know she could feel.

"You don't have to deal with things alone anymore, Joelle. I'm right here." He told her. "If people in there have preconceived notions about who you are, that shit is on them. But they'll soon learn you're fucking incredible, with a soft, giving heart. You let me into it, didn't you?" he smirked. "We didn't mean to fall in love, but I'll kill anyone to keep it."

"River," she breathed, seeing his sincerity and hearing it in his deep voice.

Her stomach fluttered with butterflies, a sign of her infatuation with him. She would have never expected that her perfect match in everything would be a biker who spoke freely and used foul language as much as he did. But like Diamond declared, there was no limit on what she'd do to keep him and their happiness.

His presence alone brought a lightness to her heart. A refreshing new chapter in her life.

All this time, Diamond had been objectively good to her.

He gave her space when she needed to regroup her thoughts, but reassured her that in a heartbeat, she could click her fingers, and he'd be there.

He protected her ruthlessly. He provided for their family.

There was nothing she couldn't ask for, knowing he'd get it for her.

And with compromise, they'd each stepped into the middle to merge their different lifestyles, making something uniquely theirs.

The chemistry between them was undeniable. It shimmered like a new rainbow in every longing look, in the way he held her hand and laughed against the skin of her neck.

Abraham whimpered in the backseat, reminding his parents who the main character was.

"You love me?" He asked.

"More than ever."

He smiled. "Then it's you and me against the world, hm? Nothing can touch us, Joelle. You'll be my bad girl, old lady, when we're here, and I'll be your hot piece of ass in a tuxedo when you need me to go to one of those ridiculous posh galas."

She chuckled and couldn't wait to see that hot ass filling out a tuxedo.

Neither of them had to worry about money. But they were richer with love.

They were more fortunate than most.

Finding him in an unlikely situation was a blessing for her.

His teeth nipped her lower lip, patiently coaxing. That was her Diamond. Joelle reached up to curl a hand around his neck, aching for his mouth.

"Are you two making out all day, or you gonna come in so we can meet your girl and son?" boomed a voice, and Joelle turned to see a mountain of a man filling the doorway with his formidable size and grin.

"Be right there, Tomb." Shouted back Diamond. "That's Tomb. You remember he's married to Nina?"

She nodded distractedly. "Are all your MC brothers as big as him?"

With a playful growl, Diamond teasingly nipped at Joelle's chin, reminding her where her focus should be.

"If you're gonna be drooling over everyone, I'll take you home right now."

She laughed and poked his hard belly. "Let's go in, big bear. Suddenly, I don't feel so nervous anymore."

She loved teasing him.

With her hand tucked firmly into his, Diamond carried Abraham in the car seat and walked them inside.

The second they were in the clubhouse, an eruption of "SURPRISE!" assaulted her ears, and she looked around at the gathering sea of men and women.

"What's this?" asked Diamond.

Sweet angels above. Joelle was not without sin by noticing how handsome all the bikers were. Her friends would die a thousand deaths just to be ogling them. She'd need to take covert photos for Sadie and Molly.

A towering blond man came forward, and Diamond told her it was Denver.

"It was the old ladies' scheme."

"It's called an idea, baby." Interjected a stunning woman, who she assumed was Casey, his wife.

"Yeah, that's what I said. The old ladies wanted to throw you a post-baby shower slash welcome to the family party. It's good to meet you, Joelle."

Oh.

Then she noticed all the smiling faces, especially from the women.

Joelle squeezed Diamond's hand and smiled back.

"This is lovely. Thank you."

It was a whirlwind of introductions after that.

Over the years, she'd met poets, artists, dignitaries, and Broadway stars, but nothing came close to being star-struck when she met the pop star Rory Kidd!

The only woman she felt a colder vibe from was Kelly. While she said hi to Joelle and fawned over Abraham, Kelly didn't seem as welcoming, and she kept a close eye on Joelle more than anyone else that day. It was early days, and Joelle figured she didn't have to be friends with everyone. That wasn't how life worked.

Hours seemed to go by in minutes.

"He is perfection, and I could eat him up." Monroe gushed, holding Joelle's son.

The women had gathered on the couches while the guys stood at the bar. Every time she looked over, Diamond looked back, smiling, ensuring she was okay. Her big protective bear.

"Hey, don't hog the adorable baby. I need a turn, too." Scarlett grumbled.

"You've already had a turn!" Kylie said, sipping champagne. Joelle's drink was non-alcoholic because she was nursing.

"I need the practice." Announced Scarlett. She smiled widely, stunning the others into silence.

It was Nina who asked. "Girlie, are you pregnant?"

"Yep," beamed the red-headed pixie, holding up her champagne glass. "I've been drinking the non-alcoholic stuff for weeks now."

"I thought you and Axel weren't doing kids?"

"Well," she chuckled. "When you have a husband as hot as mine, who loves to have sex as much as we do, oopsies happen. But we're completely thrilled about it. I can't wait to see him holding a baby. It will explode my ovaries."

Congratulatory hugs were exchanged.

"Well, I don't want to steal your thunder, but..." Monroe said minutes later, wearing the same radiant smile.

"Holy crap, you too?" Casey laughed. "What's in the water fountain around here?"

"We found out last week."

"Birthing twins!" announced Scarlett.

"We need to add Joelle to the gang group chat. We'll need pregnancy advice."

"Absolutely." Replied Scarlett, who was already pulling out her phone to do that. "I need to know if my vagina will recover. Axel is huge. This baby is going to tear me open."

"Ice-pack panties," Joelle interjected, capturing everyone's attention.

"Say what now?"

"For your vagina," she chuckled. "They're a lifesaver. You slide ice-packs into your underwear to help the pain and swelling."

Casey, who had twin girls, nodded in agreement. "Absolute lifesaver."

"Thank the weeping angels I'm never having kids," Nina pulled a face but nuzzled Abraham's rosy cheek. "I like my vagina straddling Tomb's face, not an iceberg."

Just then, a dark-haired woman dressed in hospital scrubs rushed over.

"Hi, sorry, I'm late. Bash got frisky when he picked me up from work. Oh, a baby! Is this little Abraham? Oh, my god, I'm next to hold him. Hi, I'm Lottie. Welcome to the circus, Joelle. I'm brand new around here, too. What are we talking about?"

"Vagina's the size of the grand canyon and ice cubes." Chuckled Nina. Everyone started a ripple of laughter. "Oh, and these two have buns in the oven."

Diamond came to check on her not long later. Abraham was in his arms, making her man the sexiest creature on earth.

"Give me a kiss, Bluebell."

"Here?" she whispered. But no one was watching them, so she stood on her tiptoes to plant a kiss on him. But what do you know? A rumbling of cheers went up as her lips met his, and she turned her blushing face into Diamond's arm.

"That means they like you, baby." He pulled her in closer. "I love you, you know that?"

"I love you back."

And it was the truth.

Colors had been Joelle's mood stabilizer for a long time. They brought happiness to her daily life.

But now, so did Diamond and Abraham.

She could not have predicted a year ago that she'd be happy in a relationship with a biker and they'd have a son together.

Also, be deliriously happy, like pigs in the dirt happy.

She didn't know if she'd be an adequate biker's old lady.

Or if Diamond could fit in with her socialites.

But what she knew without question. They fit together somewhere in the middle.

They created their own world, making their own rules.

And she was thrilled to see what their future brought.

Being a biker's bad girl would be the most fun she'd ever had.

## Diamond
### CHRISTMAS - FIVE YEARS LATER

There were lots of traditions surrounding Christmas Eve.

Most of them included family.

For the entire month, Joelle had kept him busy attending fucking galas and friend parties. And then they hosted house parties. Raucous, unorganized, and fun. And not a fancy suit in sight.

He'd endured ten-course family meals at the Snow mansion. Judge Snow wasn't his favorite person; he tolerated the man for Joelle's sake but respected him for being a hands-on grandpa. Both sides of the family spoiled Abraham.

But this, right here, was Diamond and Joelle's Christmas Eve tradition.

It was still the early hours of the morning. He finished putting toys together and climbed into bed to wake his woman for festive love.

She panted, and he rolled his pelvis, embedding his cock in wet heaven.

All it had taken for them both to enjoy the season was being together. Now, his woman didn't want to speed through December like she once had, and he didn't mind doing anything that made her happy.

Nipping at the side of her neck, Diamond spoke low.

"You might not want to get my name inked on your creamy skin, but I've branded you here, haven't I, Bluebell? Your pussy knows the shape of my cock. Greedy thing, constantly sucking me in, trying to keep me there." Diamond shoved his hips forward, hitting that soft place to make her eyes roll back into her head. Yeah, he grinned as he relentlessly moved inside the most perfect pussy he'd ever been in. He'd marked his woman so fucking deep inside she'd never be able to get rid of him.

His refined biker old lady was the stuff dreams were made of.

At no point in history did men like him get the best offerings in life, but somehow, Diamond lucked out and has been happy ever since.

"Shut up and keep fucking me," she whined, leaving her marks along his forearms while he rammed her from behind. "I need you to fuck me harder than 2020 did."

In no hurry, as if he had all the time in the world, instead of being on a time crunch because family from both sides were descending on them in just a few hours, Diamond rolled Joelle over, notching in place as she spread her legs for him. His wife was so generous, and he smiled into her mouth, tasting her sleepy kisses.

He kissed her until she was feverishly undulating beneath him as he delivered hard stroke after hard stroke.

After five years of marriage, they were as wild for each other today as the first time. Any chance Diamond got to shove his wife into a closet and have his filthy way with her, he took it.

He loved scandalizing her pristine values.

Feeling the boil of lust turn his skin molten hot, he stroked her tongue, swallowing her cries of bliss, and it took next to no time for them to come together.

"We need to do this earlier next Christmas Eve, or we'll be like zombies serving the turkey." She stated dreamily, running her fingertips down his sides.

"Maybe we'll go away next year, just you, me, and Abe. My wife's greedy, demanding pussy is my priority. Let the family make their own fucking turkey and cranberry sauce."

She giggled, and he took that as an incentive to look into a villa in Snowmass, Colorado.

"That sounds wonderful. But you know you love showing off your baking delights."

"What I love is accosting my wife in the kitchen to grope her perfect ass and feed her little sugary treats."

Joelle purred. If she kept stroking him the way she was, he'd be ready for round two and screw getting any sleep to cope with the Christmas chaos later.

"You do it so well, River. Were you able to put Abe's robot together?"

"I had to call Tomb," she chuckled at his confession. "The thing needed a PhD to read the instructions, Joelle."

"I know, my clever man." She appeased and kissed his chin. She was growing sleepier, so he pulled out of her body, did the fast cleanup of them both, and then curled around her back. "Did you check on Abe?"

"Always do, baby." His son was sleeping like the dead, but sure as shit, the hellion would be wide awake and going at full speed around five a.m. He had the energy of ten kids and didn't possess an off switch. It amazed them they had survived the past five years with so little sleep. Diamond was contemplating building him a backyard treehouse to live in.

"Merry Christmas, River." She murmured before dropping into sleep.

Diamond threw his leg over Joelle in case his woman got the bright idea of leaving him. It hadn't happened yet, but a man had to have his wits about him with a goddess on his hands. He couldn't have her escaping now, not when he was so fucking obsessed with her.

"Love you, Bluebell. Merry Christmas."

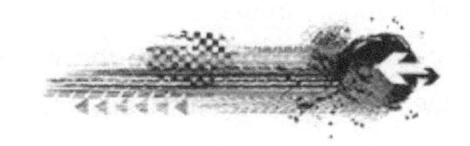

### CHRISTMAS – SIX YEARS LATER

Over the years, the old ladies influenced Joelle because their house became overstuffed with décor in every color each Christmas. A tree in every room, sometimes three fucking trees, and twinkle lights wherever the eye landed.

As Diamond trekked through his house, leaving his very sated wife in bed, he searched for a replenishing drink of water. She'd drained him dry. If the day came when Diamond complained after his wife woke him up by climbing on his cock, it would be the day to shoot him between the eyes.

He grinned, following the hallway of lights, scratching his bare torso over his Joelle tattoo.

Tomorrow night was Christmas Eve, and they'd be doing the usual family stuff. But tonight, they'd head into the clubhouse, where they held their annual Christmas meal. Just the patched brothers and their families. He could have only hoped Joelle would be as ingratiated into the club lifestyle as she'd become over the years. And while his pink-haired wife was still the most sophisticated, well-mannered woman he'd ever known, she was also his colorful rainbow who loved riding on the back of his bike, squealing in his ear to go faster. She was his avant-garde biker old lady who enjoyed helping Scarlett plan club parties.

As Diamond headed to the kitchen, he saw movement in the family room. The Christmas tree was the only source of light in the room.

"What are you doing out of bed so late, Abe?"

His son turned and climbed off his knees, standing with his hair in tufts all over his head, and flashed a grin. At nearly twelve, his son no longer believed in Santa Claus, much to Joelle's distress. Abe would be as tall as Diamond with a couple more growth spurts. He looked grown up in plaid PJs, but Diamond would always see his little boy.

"I wanted to stash mom's gift at the back of the tree so she didn't see."

Joelle was notorious for wanting to know about surprises in advance, though she denied it with her little nose pointed in the air like anyone would dare accuse her of such a crime. His adorable baby.

Abe had been doing odd jobs around the clubhouse for spare money all summer. He was proud that his son had taken it upon himself to buy stuff for Christmas. He wrapped his arm around Abe's skinny shoulder and ruffled his boy's hair.

"Daaaad." He complained, grinning.

"You want a snack while you're up?"

Stupid question. The boy was a bottomless trash can.

"Yeah! Are there any of those sugar cookies left?"

"Might be." Smiled Diamond.

And between them, they polished off a full plate of cookies.

"If your mom asks, Santa ate them."

"Got it." Abe nodded. "Can I hang out with Atlas and Levi in the morning? We wanna go sledding."

"If you get your chores done."

Abe was best friends with Axel's and Bash's sons. Diamond would lay money on them getting into more trouble than he and his brothers ever had in years to come.

God help them all when the legacy kids took over the running of the Diablos.

Once Abe was back in bed and Diamond locked the house securely, he climbed the stairs and slipped quietly into bed, spooning around a warm Joelle.

"How many cookies did you eat?" he heard, and he smiled in the darkness.

"Who, me?"

"Let me taste your lips."

"Baby, if you wanted to seduce me, you only had to say so. I'm an easy lay."

She snorted. "That much I know. I hope you left some cookies. You know they're my dad's favorite."

Diamond groaned, knowing he'd be baking at the butt crack of dawn to keep the peace with his now-retired father-in-law.

"It was Santa."

Joelle turned in his arms; her leg was over his, and her hand curled around his cheek. "You are so full of it, River Durand."

Diamond's desire-soaked groan rushed up his throat, taking hold of his soft-bodied wife. Her curves would forever turn him on.

"I'm not, but you're about to be full of me, wife."

He slipped inside of her easily.

And in the early morning, their loving was as effortless and consuming as it always had been.

Nothing would break his addiction to his colorful wife.

She brought peace.

She brought excitement.

She brought a love that filled their house.

She brought out an unhinged quality in him to protect what was his.

Years back, he'd even killed for her, to make sure Trent was unable to frighten his wife again.

Diamond would take on any battle for his Joelle.

Even a sugar cookie-addicted father-in-law.

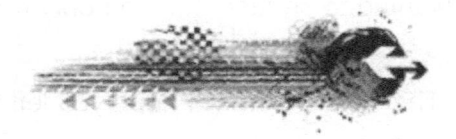

## Abraham Durand
### SOME YEARS LATER

The little maniac was in such trouble, and she didn't even know it.

Abe leaned against the side of the blacked-out SUV, his boots crossed at the ankles and arms folded against his chest until the leather of his jacket creaked.

Any onlookers would only see three men talking.

No one would suspect the devious shit going on in his head.

Stay out of his business. He'd been *clear*. And he'd given more than one chance, something he rarely did unless it was family.

No one could claim later that any of this was because it was *deranged*.

"I like a good stalking as well as the next psycho, but what are we doing here?" Asked Levi, with the same leaning stance.

The club nicknamed them the three wrecking balls.

Each of them had a particular skill set, but put them together, and they were indestructible.

They were also his best friends.

Alibi or help. It was all the same noise.

The other two turned up when one needed something, and no questions were asked.

Okay, they asked questions because they were fucking nosy.

As yet, Atlas hadn't chimed in.

But he would.

Abe hadn't drawn his eyes away from the building across the street. The neighborhood only went up ten years ago. The club invested and owned over eighty percent of the brownstone houses.

A bunch of wealthy folks owned most of them as vacation houses. Abe knew it all, so he could point out the empty brownstones where foreigners were laundering money.

Only one lit window interested him, though.

She'd be in there. The tiny maniac making a racket with her keyboard.

She was probably shaking with excitement at what she'd witnessed and couldn't wait to report on her little website.

What sort of man would he be if he let shit go, huh?

A weak man. A man to walk all over.

"Earth to Abe. Come in, Abe." Levi knocked his shoulder and turned a raised eyebrow at his friend and club brother.

"We're watching."

"Oh, good." He snarked. "I wanted to waste a night watching a building. Are we hoping it sprouts legs?"

"Text Foxie, for fuck's sake, you're not you when you're being a snarky little bitch." He advised. "Better still, go screw your sister and burn off the tension you've forced us all to endure forever."

Levi grunted but said nothing, as always, when it was about Foxie. She wasn't his sister exactly, but that was his story.

On the other side, Atlas snickered. "I put Lola off for this. It better be sinister enough to make it worthwhile."

Abe didn't give a shit about Atlas' sex life with a sweet bottom.

He rechecked his watch.

Two minutes to go.

He stood to his full height, cracking his neck from side to side, and as a trio, they set off across the street with heavy footsteps, waiting on the corner.

Right then, the one-way street was plunged into darkness.

He smirked as the second-floor window became dark.

Everyone would assume a power outage and wait for the power company to sort it out.

People were so gullible.

They wouldn't suspect it was nefarious. That Abe had paid for the power to be cut to the street.

She'd seen too much.

The time for threats was over.

Abe was all about the action. Putting his money where his mouth was.

He'd never issued a threat he didn't back up with action.

"Is this about the chick at the club last night?" Asked Atlas. "The one with the tight little ass and cute dimple. There are easier ways to get laid without creeping around. We see enough of that from Lev."

Abe threw his arm out and wrapped a hand around Atlas' throat without knowing he was doing it.

All in good fun, of course.

"Is that any way to talk about my future bride, Atlas?"

Abe didn't make a plan without thinking it forward and backward.

Atlas made a choking noise, and Abe remembered to loosen his grip. He earned a punch on the shoulder. "You fucking prick. What do you mean, your bride?"

"She saw me last night." He didn't have to say what he was doing. These two knew.

"So? Deal with it."

They weren't in the habit of offing women.

Abe loved women. All the soft bodies and pink lips wrapped around his dick.

But he didn't like nosy women.

Nosy women who saw too much, and now he had to ruin his night's plans and prepare his penthouse apartment for a future guest. A long-term one.

A guest against her will.

"She saw? *Shit*."

Yeah. Shit. It was a fucking problem.

How did he know it?

Because he was the Diablos' fucking Pope.

It was his job to know everything.

He was the information gatherer.

The hunter.

Having the monocle of the Pope didn't only mean father.

It encompassed so much.

He was trusted and relied on. He could do things others couldn't.

And sometimes that meant hog-tying a woman and saying his I Do's.

"Are you serious about this?"

Abe cast a glance toward Atlas and smirked. "Never more so. What's a bit of kidnapping and forced marriage to stop the little wifey from ever testifying against her husband?"

Was it deranged as fuck? All answers pointed to yes. Absolutely.

It might be his most diabolical plan to date.

There was one thing about Abe: he always ran toward what made his blood pump the hardest. And right now, his veins were on fucking fire.

He couldn't wait.

*Game on, little maniac.*

He hoped she was ready for her husband.

The next Diablo Disciples MC will be Splice!
Coming 2025

### Renegade Souls MC Series:
Dirty Salvation
Preacher Man
Tracking Luxe
Hades Novella
Filthy Love
Finally Winter
Mistletoe and Outlaws Novella
Resurfaced Passion
Intimately Faithful Novella
Indecent Lies
Law Maker Novella
Savage Outlaw
Renegade Souls MC Collection Boxset 1-3
Prince Charming
Forever Zara Novella
Veiled Amor
Renegade Souls MC Collection Boxset 4-6
Blazing Hope
Darling Psycho


### Taboo Love Duet:
It Was Love
It Was Always Love
Taboo Love Collection

Forever Love Companion

From Manhattan Series:
Manhattan Sugar
Manhattan Bet
Manhattan Storm
Manhattan Secret
Manhattan Heart
Manhattan Target
Manhattan Tormentor
Manhattan Muse
Manhattan Protector
Manhattan Memory

Naughty Irish Series:
Naughty Irish Liar

Diablo Disciples MC:

Chains

Reno

Axel

Ruin

Tomb

Bash

*Website*: www.VTheiaBooks.com
*Author Facebook*: www.facebook.com/VTheia
*Readers Group*: Vs Biker Babes


Be the first to know when V. Theia's next book is available. Follow her on Bookbub to get an alert whenever she has a new release.

Made in United States
Cleveland, OH
11 March 2025